AFTER THE MARRIAGE VOWS

As the carriage rolled away from the chapel, Cicely endeavored to set matters straight with the man who was now legally her lord and master.

"I am my own person, Ravenwood, and I should take a very dim view of it if you were to attempt to demand subservience from me. I will go my own way. As . . . as you will go yours, of course."

"Will I?" Ravenwood sounded surprised.

"I am more than seven, sir. I know how married men conduct their affairs," Cicely said. "I am quite prepared to accept an opera dancer or—or a ladybird or Cytherean, sir."

Ravenwood cocked his head a little to one side, but Cicely could not read his expression. "Am I . . . ah . . . to assume that I shall be expected to display equal tolerance toward similar pursuits on your part?"

"Of course," Cicely responded calmly, though she could not mask the blush rising to her cheeks at the very idea.

RAVENWOOD'S LADY

Dear Reader:

As you know, Signet is proud to keep bringing you the best in romance and now we're happy to announce that we are now presenting you with even more of what you love!

The Regency has long been one of the most popular settings for romances and it's easy to see why. It was an age of elegance and opulence, of wickedness and wit. It was also a time of tumultuous change, the beginning of the modern age and the end of illusion, when money began to mean as much as birth, but still an age when manners often meant more than morality.

Now Signet has commissioned some of its finest authors to write some bigger romances—longer, lusher, more exquisitely sensuous than ever before—wonderful love stories that encompass even more of the flavor of this glittering and flamboyant age. We are calling them "Super Regencies" because they have been liberated from category conventions and have the room to take the Regency novel even further—to the limits of the Regency itself.

Because we want to bring you only the very best, we are publishing these books only on an occasional basis, only when we feel that we can bring you something special. The first of the Super Regencies, *Love in Disguise* by Edith Layton, was published in August to rave reviews and has won two awards. It was followed by two other outstanding titles, *The Guarded Heart* by Barbara Hazard, published in October and *Indigo Moon* by Patricia Rice, published in February. Watch for future Signet Super Regencies in upcoming months in your favorite bookstore.

Sincerely,

Hilary Ross
Associate Executive Editor

RAVENWOOD'S LADY

by

Amanda Scott

A SIGNET BOOK

NEW AMERICAN LIBRARY

NAL BOOKS ARE AVAILABLE AT QUANTITY DISCOUNTS WHEN USED
TO PROMOTE PRODUCTS OR SERVICES. FOR INFORMATION PLEASE
WRITE TO PREMIUM MARKETING DIVISION, NEW AMERICAN LIBRARY,
1633 BROADWAY, NEW YORK, NEW YORK 10019.

SIGNET TRADEMARK REG. U.S. PAT. OFF. AND FOREIGN COUNTRIES
REGISTERED TRADEMARK—MARCA REGISTRADA
HECHO EN CHICAGO, U.S.A.

SIGNET, SIGNET CLASSIC, MENTOR, ONYX, PLUME, MERIDIAN
and NAL BOOKS are published by NAL PENGUIN INC.,
1633 Broadway, New York, New York 10019

First Printing, March, 1984

3 4 5 6 7 8 9 10 11

PRINTED IN THE UNITED STATES OF AMERICA

For Rick
a prince of thieftakers
and my good friend

1

Bright morning sunshine poured through the tall, narrow east windows of the breakfast parlor, giving promise of the fine spring day ahead. The occupants of the room were not, however, enjoying the sort of peaceful meal to which the adults of the household had accustomed themselves, for, in a manner completely at odds with an all-consuming anxiety to please her employers, Miss Fellows, their ladyships' governess, had taken to her bed with a putrid sore throat.

As a result of their mentor's indisposition, three bright-haired young ladies who would normally have broken their fast by the schoolroom fire had been allowed to join their parents and two older sisters in the breakfast parlor. Consequently, an unceasing cacophony of high-pitched feminine chatter mingled with the clatter of crockery and the clink of ornate silverware against fine Sèvres breakfast china, causing the Duke of Malmesbury's bushy grey eyebrows to draw together ominously above his long, narrow countenance. From time to time, he could clearly be seen to clench his jaw, and his eldest daughter, the Lady Cicely Leighton, watching him with some misgiving, was certain her father was grinding his teeth. If he was, however, the sound could not have been heard, not even by her youngest sister, the pixielike Lady Amalie, aged seven, who squirmed impatiently in the chair next to his.

Diverted momentarily by a stirring of her blue-sprigged muslin skirts, which was promptly followed by the touch of a cold, wet nose pressing against her silk-clad leg, Cicely slipped a smidgen of bacon from her plate and held it under the table, where it was promptly nipped from her fingers. She wiped them daintily on her serviette, then glanced warily at

7

her father to see if he had observed the gesture. His attention, however, was firmly rooted to his breakfast plate.

"Mama, shall Tani wear feathers and a hoop?" piped Amalie suddenly over the general din. Having intended her words to reach the plump, pink-cheeked, lace-capped lady at the foot of the table, she had pitched her voice quite loudly, startling the others. The ensuing silence and the sudden turning of six pairs of eyes toward her small self brought a rush of color to her freckle-dusted cheeks, but she tilted her chin bravely. "Well, shall she?"

"Of course she will, you little bagpipe," put in thirteen-year-old Lady Alicia, flipping a strand of long, wheat-colored hair over her shoulder. "What else, pray, does one wear when one is presented? I just hope the old Queen don't cock up her toes before it is my turn!"

The duke turned a disapproving eye toward his outspoken younger daughter, but it was fourteen-year-old Arabella who leaped into the breach, saying with quick firmness, "Lissa, apologize for that at once. You know Papa don't like it when you speak disrespectfully of the Royal Family."

"Well, I'm sorry, then," said Alicia before adding with her customary candor, "but 'twould be prodigious unfair for one to miss being presented merely because one had the misfortune to be a fourth-born child."

The duke had not yet returned his attention to his plate, so Cicely was not at all surprised to hear the Lady Brittany, closest of her four sisters to herself in age, speak up in her gentle voice. "I am afraid you are still being impertinent, Alicia. There is, in any case, no reason to fear you will not be presented. There is always the Princess Caroline, you know."

"Yes," Cicely put in, slipping another bit of bacon under the table, "if his highness ever allows her to return from her exile in Italy. But, Lissa, considering that Tani, thanks to Uncle Ashley's death, had to postpone her come-out for a whole year, and that I have been here rusticating for that same length of time when I might have been on the lookout for a husband, it is a bit much for you to be worrying about a presentation that is still some years off."

"Well, Tani is scarcely on the shelf," said Lady Alicia scornfully, "and you did have two full seasons in which to find a husband before Uncle Ashley died, and you know perfectly well that you sent scores of eligible suitors to the right-about. I certainly hope I shan't be so daft as that when my turn does come.''

''How shall Tani manage a hoop?'' asked Amalie, getting back to more important matters.

''Miss Fellows shall teach her, dear, just as she taught Cicely, though you won't remember so far back,'' responded the duchess vaguely, her mind clearly elsewhere.

''Mama, really,'' Cicely protested, laughing. '' 'So far back,' indeed! You make it sound like another century. It has been only three years.''

''Yes, dear. But you know, although I cannot commend her manner of speaking, Alicia is perfectly right. You were very difficult.''

''They called her the Ice Princess,'' Amalie chuckled. Then, encountering a strait look from her eldest sister, she insisted, ''They did! Lissa told me so.''

''Lissa had as little business saying such things to you as you have repeating them, my dear,'' reproved the duchess. ''Not that it isn't perfectly true,'' she added with a long-suffering sigh. ''You know it is, Cicely, and I cannot help but think it is going to make matters very difficult indeed when we go to London. If we could have given you a third Season last year, I'm sure I should have had no hesitation in putting off your sister's presentation, and no doubt matters would have arranged themselves perfectly well. But she is eighteen now and simply must make her come-out this year. And people will think it odd if she goes off before you, so if you mean to continue in the same finicking manner . . .'' Her voice trailed off, and she made a helpless little gesture with her hands. ''It really was a pity that your poor Uncle Ashley died when he did. I'm sure he didn't mean to cause any difficulties—''

''Ha!'' snorted Alicia. ''It was just the sort of disobliging thing he *would* do. And two days before *my* birthday, which spoilt it entirely, for what must we do but cancel all the invitations and sit about glooming at each other. Why, even Papa was used to say Uncle Ashley was as selfish as be da—''

''That will do!'' The duke's fork crashed onto his plate, and Cicely jumped, ignoring the impatient paw at her knee when his grace turned a withering glare and an accusing finger upon the erring Alicia. "You will leave this table at once, young lady, to seek your bedchamber, where you will contemplate your extreme lack of conduct until eleven o'clock, at which time you will present yourself to me in the bookroom, in order to discuss this matter further."

Lady Alicia stared at him in dismay, but even she was not outspoken enough to defy him. A footman stepped forward hastily to pull back her chair, and with a look of helpless reluctance, she stood up. Moving toward the door, she paused and glanced over her shoulder, but the looks of shock and sympathy still imprinted upon her sisters' countenances seemed to give little comfort, and her expression was dismal when she turned away again. While the footman was occupied with opening and shutting the door for her, the duke pushed his own chair back impatiently and got to his feet, transferring his glare to his unfortunate wife.

"I cannot conceive, madam," he growled harshly, "how it comes about that in thirteen years you have not yet managed to teach that chit some manners, but she is not to dine with the family again until she has acquired some!"

He turned toward the door, and at that ill-conceived moment a shrill, indignant yap was heard from under the table. The sound froze everyone in place, but the duke recovered quickly, turning without hesitation upon his eldest daughter.

"Cicely! What is that damned mongrel doing under my breakfast table again when I have expressly forbidden his presence at meals?"

She looked up guiltily. "I'm sorry, Papa. He must have been there when we came in."

"And you have been feeding him again, have you not?" Biting her lower lip, she nodded. Malmesbury gave an exasperated snort and barked an order at the interested footman to "remove that animal." It seemed for a moment that this would be an impossible task, for the animal in question objected at the top of his voice to such a procedure and dashed from one end of the space under the table to the other in his attempt to evade capture. Amalie laughed, ignoring Arabella's hushed attempts to silence her, and Brittany spoke coaxingly to the culprit while the poor footman did his possible but with no signal success.

The much-tried duke roared for silence, whereupon Cicely put her hand under the table and snapped her fingers. "Come,

Charlie.'' Her voice rang with authority, and a brief moment later a small King Charles spaniel, with eyes that glinted mischief, fell panting to his belly near her left foot. She scooped him up and handed him to the grateful footman. ''Take him into the garden, Paul.''

''At once, m'lady.'' He slipped quickly past the still-glaring duke.

''I am going to read the *Morning Post*,'' Malmesbury announced. ''But when you have quite finished your breakfast, Cicely, you will attend me in the bookroom, if you please.''

''Y-yes, Papa,'' she replied, her stomach tightening into a familiar knot, despite the fact that she had long since outgrown any real fear of him.

He turned back to his duchess, glaring down his long nose at her. ''You need not bother your head, madam. The problem you anticipate is well on its way to being solved.''

''G-goodness,'' Arabella breathed when the door had shut behind her. ''Whatever do you suppose he meant by that?''

''I don't know,'' Cicely replied. ''I confess to being a good deal more interested in why he wishes to speak with me.''

''P'raps he means to thrash you for feeding Charlie under the table,'' suggested Amalie helpfully.

''Don't be a goose, Amalie.'' Lady Brittany smiled, but her gaze was fixed encouragingly upon her elder sister. ''Papa wouldn't thrash any of us for such a small thing as that. Besides,'' she added on a wry note, ''I've no doubt he means to save his strength for Lissa.''

There being nothing to say to that, a small silence ensued, during which Cicely wondered if it might be simply a matter of a trimming for encouraging Charlie to beg at table. Then Arabella suggested that it would be just as well for both Cicely and Alicia if their father found nothing to annoy him in the political columns of his morning papers, and Cicely joined in the chuckles that met the sally. Only her grace seemed detached.

''I do wish he would be more precise,'' she complained. ''How on earth does he propose to solve the problem of establishing Cicely before Brittany's come-out?''

That she did not seem particularly distressed by the duke's burst of temper came as no surprise to any of her daughters. The duchess had long since become inured to such scenes, as well as to the fact that his grace generally seemed to lay the blame for any of their offspring's peccadilloes at her door. Lord Ashley Leighton, the duke's younger brother and erstwhile heir, had once said that Malmesbury had been a cantankerous old man since the day he came into the title; and despite the fact that the duke had scarcely passed his twenty-second birthday when that notable event took place, Cicely, for one, was quite certain her uncle had had the right of it.

She supposed she had once or twice seen her father smile, but she knew she would be hard pressed to name an occasion. He was not a genial man at the best of times. Nevertheless, his daughters had learned at a tender age that although he would have preferred sons, he meant his daughters no harm, and however much he blustered and scolded, he was rarely moved to sterner methods. She smiled a little to herself when it occurred to her that Alicia might presently choose to dispute that last notion.

Poor Alicia. She was at that awkward age when no one, least of all Alicia herself, knew what outrageous thing she would say or do next. As far as Cicely could remember, neither gentle Brittany nor practical Arabella had suffered through such a stage, but she remembered her own difficulties only too well. For what had seemed an incredibly long passage of time, beginning midway through her twelfth year and continuing well into her fourteenth, it had seemed to Cicely that she spent an inordinate amount of time on the carpet in the bookroom. And a good number of those scenes, besides being vocal, had been painful as well. She, probably more than Arabella or Brittany, could sympathize with Alicia's present predicament.

She glanced toward Amalie, wondering whether she would have a difficult time. She doubted it. Amalie, being so much younger than her sisters, might have been spoiled by them all had it not been for her innate sense of dignity. But she was very like Arabella, if a good deal more precocious, and possessed self-assurance beyond her years. She had a tendency to treat the duke much as she might a tame bear, with a certain wary but indulgent tolerance.

Cicely realized suddenly that the object of her thoughts was staring rather pointedly at her, and she glanced toward the others to see that they had all finished eating. When Amalie wriggled again, Cicely grinned at her and waved to the footman to clear her place.

"Please, ma'am," Amalie said promptly, "may I leave the table now?"

The duchess nodded, smiling, and the others soon followed the child's example. Brittany and Arabella announced that they meant to examine some drawings in the *Lady's Monthly Museum* to discover what accessories were deemed necessary for a young lady in her first Season, and the duchess said she would join them as soon as she had spoken with her housekeeper. Cicely only shook her head in response to Brittany's lifted eyebrow.

"Don't look for me," she said quietly. "I expect I'll exercise Connie after I've heard whatever it is Papa will say to me."

"Why the gloomy face? You don't truly think he will lose his temper, and only Bella quakes like a blanc mange when he summons her. You never do."

"It's not fear, just a presentiment of sorts." They had reached the stairway now, and she paused with her hand on the polished oak rail, smiling at her younger sister. "Don't fret, Tani. I'm certain poor Lissa merits your sympathy far more than I do."

Lady Brittany chuckled, and a glint of sunlight from the gallery window danced across her burnished gold tresses. Cicely quickly suppressed the familiar pang of envy. Next to her golden sister, she always felt pale and washed out. Always one to underrate her own beauty, she had once said that she had been sketched in charcoal, whereas Tani had been painted in vivid colors. Others stared to hear her say such things, however, so she had learned to keep her opinions in the matter to herself.

The two girls were at opposite ends of the palette that had colored the five Leighton sisters. Cicely, with her straight, flaxen hair, clear gray eyes, and pale complexion fit her London nickname of Ice Princess very well. But to call herself "washed out" was to carry things too far. Her eyes were large, and the long lashes that outlined them were startlingly black, as were the rims around her pupils. And her lips and cheekbones were tinted with the delicate blush of roses.

Brittany, by comparison, was taller and more buxom, with eyes of deep blue-violet, skin the color of ripe peaches, and that glorious mop of golden hair, piled artlessly at the moment atop her well-shaped head. She would, Cicely was sure, take London by storm, and no doubt would contract an eligible marriage in the twinkling of a bedpost. It occurred to her that the thought was scarcely a proper one, and she grinned, giving her sister a quick hug. "I'd better go before he sends for me."

As she descended the long, curving stairway she saw her youngest sister scamper across the great hall below. A red knitted cap had been jammed over her light-brown curls, and she was attempting to drag a disreputable duffle coat over her light woolen frock as she hastened toward the front door. A footman sprang to open it for her, and Amalie turned at the last moment to wave to Cicely before disappearing down the front steps. Cicely chuckled. Her little sister clearly meant to enjoy the brief reprieve from studies Miss Fellows's illness had occasioned. No doubt she was on her way to the stables, a visit that would not have been allowed had their governess been on her feet, for normally the three youngest girls would have spent the morning at their studies.

The door to the bookroom was closed, but the same footman saw her approaching and stepped quickly to open it for her. Cicely smiled her thanks and his eyes warmed in response. The gentlemen in London might have dubbed her chilly, but they would have been hard pressed to find a servant, either at Malmesbury Park or at the huge ducal manse occupying a full city block in Mayfair, who would have agreed with them.

The footman did not announce her, of course, and for a brief moment Cicely thought her father, seated at the huge library table, surrounded by newspapers, was unaware of her presence. But when she drew breath to speak, he stopped her with a small gesture. There was another moment's silence before he put down his paper and peered at her through his quizzing glass. She straightened her shoulders.

"Papa, I'm sorry about Charlie."

"Never mind that," he said brusquely, waving toward a chair opposite himself at the huge table. "Sit down, Cicely." She obeyed, not taking her eyes from him. He clearly didn't intend to scold her for anything, but he looked like a man determined to take the bull by the horns, and she was very curious. "Your mother is right," he said suddenly.

"She is?"

"Don't be impertinent, my girl. She very often is, as I've

discovered over the years. But this time I fancy I've got the jump on her.'' Did Cicely imagine it, or was there a glint of satisfaction in his eye?

"H-have you, sir?'' Her breath seemed to catch in her throat as she executed a rapid mental review of the conversation in the breakfast parlor. She could imagine only one solution to the problem outlined by her mother—short of her own early demise, at any rate.

"Damned right I have,'' he growled now. "M' duchess wants you married before she fires that chit Brittany into the beau monde, so married you'll be, and there's an end to it. 'Tis all arranged.''

"Married! Arranged!'' Cicely stared at him, her senses all on end. "How?'' Astonishment vied with awakening excitement, but only a deepening of the roses in her cheeks betrayed her. The duke's eyes narrowed.

"Wouldn't it be more to the purpose to ask 'who'?''

Cicely took a deep breath and folded her hands more tightly in her lap. "Of course. I beg your pardon, Papa. 'Tis merely that this takes me by surprise. I daresay no one suspected—''

"No reason they should suspect a thing. I believe in playing my cards close to my chest. But it has been in the works for a good many years, and now's the time to bring matters to a head. And so I've done, and without your mother's advice, at that. But she'll be well enough pleased, I've no doubt.''

Cicely only nodded. She was completely confused now. She was also surprised to feel no anger, only shock and that rising sense of excitement. And why she should be excited there was no telling. For all she knew, her father meant to marry her off to some wealthy decrepit or even to one of the Royal Dukes. The fact that he'd been working at it for some time certainly made the latter a possibility. Both thoughts were equally distasteful. But for some reason she felt no fear, only anticipation. "Who is it, Papa? Do I know him?''

"Aye, you know him,'' he responded, regarding her enigmatically. "'Tis Ravenwood.''

The name fell between them. Cicely frowned, searching her memory. There was something familiar, something that nagged at her, but she couldn't pin it down. She tilted her head quizzically. "I'm sorry. You'll think me foolish, but—''

The duke snorted. "More like, I'll think ye daft, girl.

'Twould do you good to pay more heed to the family names. He's your cousin, Gilbert Leighton, now Viscount Ravenwood. More important than that, he's my heir.''

"Gilbert Leighton!" Her mind was suddenly possessed by the vision of a tall, thin boy of nearly twenty summers with overstarched shirt points and a wicked gleam of mischief in his eye.

The duke was still watching her, and his expression indicated momentary expectation of fireworks. Cicely remembered now that Gilbert's father, the duke's first cousin, had been called Ravenwood, but from the circumstance of her never having laid eyes upon him, it was no wonder to her that the fact had slipped her mind. She had, however, laid eyes upon Gilbert Leighton. Those same grey eyes narrowed now at the memory.

"It has been some six years since the occasion of his visit to us," the duke said now, "but you do remember him, do you not?"

"Oh, I remember him," she said musingly. "A skinny fop who took his pleasure from teasing children."

"No doubt you will find him changed somewhat with the passage of time," said the duke acidly. "He strikes me as a man of sense and one who is well able to fill my shoes."

"You have seen him?"

"Not for four years. He has been dancing attendance on Wellington, you know. One of Sir Charles Stuart's lads. But when I first broached the subject of a match between you, I expected him to snap at it."

"And did he not?" Cicely was astonished by a surge of indignation. Could it be that he hadn't wanted her? After her experiences of two London Seasons, such a thing seemed quite absurdly impossible. She was, after all, the duke's eldest daughter and would bring to her marriage a portion of approximately ten thousand pounds per annum.

Her father's eyes gleamed in response to her tone. "Thought you wouldn't like this match above half yourself, girl. And don't tell me you formed a passion for the lad at the tender age of fourteen, for I don't recall it that way myself."

She flushed under his gaze as his words brought back the final day of Gilbert Leighton's one and only visit to Malmesbury. It was not a memory she cherished. "Of course I did no such thing. It would merely surprise me to learn that he had refused such an offer. I cannot think of another gentleman of my acquaintance who would do that.'' The chilly glaze that had iced her expression throughout two Seasons descended now as she remembered various incidents arising from the greed her suitors, to a man, had seemed to possess.

"Well, Ravenwood—or Leighton, as he was then—certainly did. Said he'd never seen the slightest indication that you held him in affection, and that he wouldn't consider the match until you'd had at least one Season and an opportunity to meet other eligible young men. Thought him daft myself, but there was no persuading him to any other course.''

"Perhaps he thought he could do better for himself. He is heir to a dukedom, after all.''

Malmesbury shook his head. "Can't see that m'self. Name's never been linked with any particular female, though considering the life he's led on the Continent, I can't say it would have surprised me. Quite a social set, the Stuart contingent was.'' He grimaced slightly. "Besides, he ought to want the money.''

Cicely remembered such details as a clouded cane and a handkerchief that wafted sweet scent as its owner made airy, affected gestures. She smiled wryly. "Perhaps he preferred the gentlemen of Sir Charles's party to the ladies,'' she murmured unthinkingly.

There was silence. Glancing up to find the duke's expression dark with anger, Cicely swallowed carefully but didn't look away.

"I trust you will keep such opinions under your tongue, miss,'' he said grimly.

"Yes, Papa. I beg your pardon.''

He grunted. "I trust as well that you've no intention of making difficulties over this business. You have not, as it happens, formed an attachment for any of the gentlemen you met in London, despite the fact that I—most reluctantly, I might add—gave several of them leave to address you.''

"None of them was the least interested in me, Papa.''

"Nonsense. They were all sufficiently interested to approach me for permission to court you.''

"Not one of them saw beyond my rank and fortune, sir. It was daunting, to say the least, but I promise you, I would prefer a man who disapproved of everything I said and did over one who would be hard pressed to repeat a single opinion of my giving. They never listened. They were interested only in agreeing with everything I said, no matter how outrageous, just to show how they cherished me. It was humiliating, sir.''

"Drivel," retorted his grace. "No female's got two thoughts worth rubbing together, let alone listening to. You should be grateful instead that so many paid heed to you. There are dozens of young women out there who'd give all they possess to be in your shoes. Not," he added more blandly, "that I'm not pleased you didn't form an attachment. I've a mind to see my own grandson sporting the ducal strawberry leaves.''

"Well, you'll scarcely see that, sir," Cicely responded more sharply than might ordinarily have been consistent with wisdom. "You'll be six feet under long before that event should come to pass. Before your grandson may inherit, not only must you die, but Ravenwood as well. Assuming I do marry him, of course, and assuming we do have a son," she added thoughtfully.

"Well, you're going to marry him," the duke said firmly. "He's agreed to it, and he's coming down from London to discuss settlements and to sign the marriage contracts. As for sons, I'll leave that to him. Your comments notwithstanding, I daresay he will know precisely how to go about it.'' He paused, shooting her a penetrating look. "I hadn't meant to discuss this with you so soon. It was my intention to await his arrival in hopes that you might find him to your liking. But I cannot have your mother in a twit. And once I'd decided to impart my plan to her, it became necessary to explain it to you, lest she spill the gaff in her usual fashion.''

Cicely nodded. It was an accepted fact that the duchess was constitutionally incapable of keeping a still tongue in her head. Therefore, they had all learned to tell her nothing that was not meant for the public domain.

Cicely took a deep breath. "You said you hoped it would be to my liking, sir. What if it is not?''

His features hardened. " 'Tis of no account. You have been indulged beyond permission as it is, and for that you may thank that popinjay Napoleon for keeping Ravenwood occupied, thus permitting you an extra Season. But the time has certainly come to be getting on with the matter at hand. 'Tis my duty as your father to provide you with a suitable husband, and 'twill be Ravenwood's to secure the succession.

I prefer that it be secured in the direct line, if at all possible. 'Tis a shame your mother found it impossible to beget healthy sons. Still, 'tis folly to rail against fate, and far wiser to hedge one's bets. You will obey me, Cicely.''

His gaze was direct, his voice harsh. She sighed. ''Yes, Papa.'' There was nothing else to be said. It was her duty to obey him, and there could be nothing but unhappiness to be gained by defiance. If her spirit rebelled against so casual a disposal of her future, then that same spirit gave her the strength to conceal the fact. She needed time to think, time to digest this sudden turn of events. She had often wondered, during her two unsuccessful Seasons, at her father's uncharacteristic display of patience. One might have expected to be summarily ordered to wed the most eligible applicant for her hand. Instead, although her mother had indulged in occasional fits of pique over what she'd termed ''Cicely's stubborness,'' his grace had seemingly ignored it. Not that he had never scolded her, of course. That would have been a great deal too much to expect. But he had reserved his temper and his lectures for those occasions—and there had, unfortunately, been several—when she had gone beyond the line of what was pleasing. A stolen visit to the Haymarket in order to see for oneself what ''Haymarketware'' looked like, a costume ball with a too-forward escort resulting in rescue by a stalwart hackney coachman, a tipsy venture into the forbidden realms of Dionysus—each had resulted in a prodigiously uncomfortable interview with the duke. But not one word had he said against her continued indifference toward a veritable army of eligible suitors. Now she knew why.

Her thoughts were interrupted at this point by the opening of the bookroom door. She looked over her shoulder to see the footman in the act of closing that same door behind a rather pale-faced Lady Alicia.

''I-I beg pardon, Papa, if I am intruding, but you said I was to come to you at eleven o'clock, and 'tis a few minutes past that hour now.'' Her chin was up and her hands were firmly at her sides. After that first hesitation she had taken control of herself, and now faced the duke bravely.

''You may be excused, Cicely.'' She got quickly to her feet. ''I trust,'' he added pointedly, ''that you will not disappoint me.''

''No, sir,'' she replied, carefully calm. ''I know my duty.''

"Very well." His gaze dismissed her, then shifted to her sister. His voice sharpened noticeably. "Now then, Alicia, I shall be most interested to hear how you mean to defend your despicable conduct at breakfast this morning. Pray step forward, miss."

Cicely fled.

2

With the exception of a housemaid polishing candle sconces and the footman seated in the high-backed porter's chair, the great hall was empty when Cicely emerged from the bookroom. Her slippered feet made no sound as she hurried across the stone floor to the swooping marble stairway. From the carpeted gallery above, she passed through a suite of elegant saloons to an antechamber with a staircase that led to the upper reaches of the huge ducal mansion.

Amazingly, she managed to reach the sanctuary of her own bedchamber without encountering any of her sisters or her mother. Miss Fellows, of course, was safely laid down upon her own bed. Cicely was grateful to find the bedchamber empty. Her abigail, Meg Hardy, had threatened a general turnout of her wardrobe in order to make a final inventory in preparation for the upcoming London Season, but she had either finished or not yet begun, for the room was as neat as a pin.

The sunlight streaming through the high arched windows set sparkling dust motes dancing and touched the heavy blue velvet bed hangings with glints of silver gilt. A crimson-and-indigo Turkey carpet covered most of the floor, and several petit-point cushions, created by skillful hands to reflect variations of the carpet pattern, were scattered about on the bed and on the simple Adam settee between the two windows.

The duchess had several times suggested redoing the bedchamber in colors more suited to Cicely's pale complexion and silvery hair, but her daughter had firmly resisted all such attempts. The vivid colors did not seem at all overpowering to her, whereas the pink and silver suggested by her grace was certain to be of an insipidness past all bearing.

Her spirits lifted now as they always did when she entered the cheerful room, but she knew she could not remain there. It had been an instinctive thing to seek out the one place she could truly call her own. But either Brittany would come to find her or Meg Hardy would bustle in to get to her task. And although Brittany might easily be sent away again, Meg Hardy was a more formidable opponent. Having been raised at Malmesbury and begun service there as a between maid before being trained first as chambermaid and later as Cicely's dresser, she had the familiar manners of a longtime servant and would not hesitate to set her mistress to work counting lace collars and net mittens or trying on dresses, for that matter. Cicely shuddered.

Suddenly she needed space and freedom. The papered walls with their wide-spaced red pinstripes seemed to hover about her, making her feel suddenly small and helpless, a pawn on a giant chessboard about to be captured by the opposition. She wanted to throw something or, better yet, shoot something . . . or someone.

On the thought, she hurried to the wardrobe and snatched out a light-grey velvet riding habit trimmed with emerald-green braid. Discarding her morning frock and tossing it haphazardly on the bed, she stepped quickly into the velvet skirt, fastened it, and drew on the matching spencer directly over her lacy shift. It occurred to her as she unearthed her shiny black leather boots that she ought to don knit stockings in place of the silk ones she was wearing, but she was in too much of a hurry for such details. Nonetheless, she could not go out with her flaxen tresses streaming down her back as they were. That would be to invite the sort of comment that most distressed the duchess. Accordingly, she searched out a green net snood and stuffed the long, straight hair inside before binding it at the nape of her neck with an emerald ribbon. A jaunty little grey felt hat was soon pinned into place atop her smooth head, and picking up her whip and black kid gloves, she hastened back downstairs and out to the stables.

Connie, her dappled gelding, was soon saddled, and Cicely accepted a leg up from her groom before curtly ordering him to remain where he was.

"Beggin' yer pardon, m'lady, but ye know full well 'is

grace said I was t' go wi' ye when ye ride. 'Twill be 'avin' me 'ead on a platter, 'e will.''

"Not today, Toby. I want to be alone. If his grace comes down heavy, I'll stand the nonsense, I promise. But today I want to be by myself. I need to think.''

'' 'Tisn't fittin', m'lady,'' the thin, grizzled little man pointed out stubbornly, pushing his well-worn cap farther back on his head. ''Even if ye stay t' the woods, there be the danger o' poachers.''

"Nonsense, Toby,'' she chuckled. ''No self-respecting poacher would so demean his calling as to enter Papa's woods in broad daylight. Mr. Kennedy and his muscle-bound sons would dispatch such a fool right quickly, and well you know it. Besides,'' she added hastily, in an attempt to forestall further opposition, ''I've got my pistol in the saddle holster. You know I do, for you put it there yourself as you always do.''

"And a right daft thing, too,'' he muttered with the irascible irreverence of a servant who has known one since one sat one's first pony. ''A female wi' a barker. What'll they be up to next, I'm wonderin'.''

"I'm a better shot than most men, Toby Wilder, and well do you know it. So we'll have no more of your impertinence, if you please. You will stay here as you are bid. I want to hear no more about it.''

"Aye,'' he responded promptly, ''I've no doubt o' that. No more doubt than I've got that we'll the both o' us be hearin' more on't ere the day is out. Thanks be, 'is grace be a fair man. Me ears may ring a bit, but I doubt I'll be losin' m' place over it.''

Cicely chuckled again. ''You are a foolish old man, Toby Wilder. But I mustn't stay to chat.'' Just as she moved to turn the gelding she thought of something else. ''Did the Lady Amalie come down here?''

"Oh, aye.'' His eyes twinkled. ''Like a wee chick escapin' the coop, she was. She be long gone toward the river. Not to worry, though. Dickon went with 'er. She at least knows better than t' flout 'is grace's orders,'' he added with an air of trying for the last word.

"As well she should.'' Cicely acknowledged, grinning. ''She knows what to expect should she disobey him. But I am a good deal older, Toby, and his grace'll not beat me for an hour's stolen privacy. Nor will he chastise you for allowing it.''

''Whist, m'lady,'' the old man scoffed, his eyes still atwinkle, ''as though I thought 'e might. Get along wi' ye, then.''

Still smiling, she wheeled the gelding toward the main carriage drive and soon gave him his head. Connie willingly broke into an easy lope, and Cicely held her face up to the breeze's easy caress as she relaxed in the saddle. The carriage-way was flat and hard, as was the road it intersected a mile or so from the house. Cicely crossed the road and followed a pathway into the woods opposite the tall iron gates flanking the entrance to Malmesbury Park. She knew she should proba-bly have taken a route that would keep her inside the park itself, where there were numerous bridle paths alongside the lake and throughout the huge home wood and deer park. But this was her father's land, too, and since she liked the wilder-ness flavor of these woods better, she had headed for them without thinking. Here the underbrush was thicker, more tangled, for there was no army of keepers to keep it cleared away. Only the meandering dirt path was clear, and even so, one had to watch for low-hanging branches. Ordinarily she would follow the path until it came out again onto the main road and then would follow the road back to the main gate of the park. But today, groomless, she realized it would be wiser to follow the woods path back again once she neared the road. It would not do to meet anyone.

There were wild flowers here and a sense of peace that was lacking in the home wood, where one might come upon one of the keepers at any time. Her father might not approve, but if he found out about it, it would mean he had already discovered that she'd left without Toby. Since he would scold her for the one, he might just as well scold her for the other while he was about it. A momentary vision intruded of her sister Alicia standing pale-faced just inside the bookroom door. She had no doubt of Alicia's fate, but she was shrewd enough to realize that Malmesbury would tend to be lenient in her own case. He might bellow at her, but unless she defied him in the more important matter of her proposed marriage, she did not think she need fear any harsher treatment. It had been years since he had used her so, and now that she came to think of it, Gilbert Leighton, the man she was expected to marry, had been responsible for that incident.

No longer could she avoid thinking about the marriage. It was not, of course, the notion of the marriage itself that distressed her, for she had been raised to expect that one would eventually be arranged for her. It had been far more surprising to discover that her parents had been willing to indulge her fancies in the matter. Even now, she realized, she had no reason to doubt that his grace would have indulged her whims entirely, had she chanced to form a grand passion for one of her myriad suitors. After all, the duke still had Brittany or even Arabella to offer to Ravenwood as alternatives. Cicely could scarcely imagine herself ill-used. She had been given plenty of opportunity to go her own way.

Slashing rays of sunlight made golden puddles on the pathway ahead. Birds chirped merrily, and leaves rustled gently in the slight, March-crisp breeze. Cicely knew she had reacted emotionally, that she had felt momentarily trapped by her heritage.

Remembering the onset of her first Season in London, she knew she had approached it with eager anticipation and romantic dreams of meeting a perfect mate and tumbling into love like the best of storybook heroines, to live happily ever after. Those naive hopes had been dashed by the time of her second visit to Almack's famous assembly rooms. Two full weeks of being introduced to ogling young men who fairly drooled over her—and whose questions about her home, family, and fortune at best bordered upon rudeness and at worst were blatantly impertinent—were quite enough for Cicely. Realizing how naive she had been, she had determined to set matters right, and although she enjoyed the parties and entertainments, and was unfailingly polite to everyone, she began to guard herself against any emotional entanglements. She had learned to trust no one. Even if a gentleman pretended to like her for herself, she knew perfectly well that behind his charming façade, he was mentally counting the coins in her coffer.

At least, once she was safely married, that would no longer present a problem. If a gentleman asked her to dance then, she would know it was merely because he wished to dance with her.

She turned this tasty thought over once or twice in her

mind. Marriage *per se* might have certain advantages. After all, hers would simply be a marriage of convenience, and in this day and age, even partners in a love match did not live in one another's pockets. Married ladies had a good deal more freedom than their unmarried sisters. Surely Ravenwood would allow her a cicisbeo or two and would not expect her to be constantly at his beck and call. As a matter of fact, he would very likely have his own diversions, most probably, of course, amongst the muslin company. How would she like that?

As she ducked to avoid a sprawling oak branch, she dismissed the notion that such diversions might annoy her. Every man had them. She would not interfere with Ravenwood any more than he would interfere with her. A chuckle escaped her when she tried to conjure up a vision of that thin youth of six years ago enjoying sport with a Cytherean. Try as she might, all she could manage was the gracefully bowing image of a bean-pole dandy who waggled a quizzing glass in one hand while languidly drifting a scent-laden handkerchief under a twitching nose with the other. Impossible to imagine such a creature interfering with one. By now, in fact, if he had gone on as he'd begun, he must be so taken up with his wardrobe as to have little time for anything else. The thought of six years spent in Wellington's company occurred to her, only to be dismissed with a nearly contemptuous smile. He had been with Sir Charles Stuart, after all, more a diplomatic post than a military one. Just the sort of position for a fop. Lots of balls and parties, if all she'd heard was correct, including a ball at the Duchess of Richmond's town house in Brussels the very night before Waterloo. It was all of a piece!

Connie sidestepped nervously, and Cicely recollected herself to call him to order. She realized she must be nearing the road again, for in the distance, drawing nearer, came the clatter and rattle of a swiftly moving vehicle. Suddenly there was a stamp of impatient hooves nearer at hand, followed by a shout and the thunder of hoofbeats on the hard road. Then, startling her, came the unmistakable bark of a pistol. The oncoming vehicle slowed, and there was more hoarse shouting.

Unhesitantly Cicely snatched the pistol from her saddle holster and dug her heel into the gelding's side. Connie responded instantly, and within seconds they had emerged onto the roadway to be greeted by the sight of a duffel-coated ruffian looking down the barrel of a wicked horse pistol into the interior of an elegant, crested carriage. Cicely paused only long enough to take in the sight of a restless, steaming team of matched greys and the two men frozen in place on the box before she leveled her own weapon, sighted carefully over the gelding's ears, and fired.

Connie's ears scarcely twitched at the echoing blast, but, to her astonishment, the highwayman slumped in his saddle, hovered momentarily in what seemed, considering the force of gravity, to be an impossible position, then slid to the ground with a sickening thump. Connie had slowed his pace of his own accord and now drew to a halt some feet from the body.

"Merciful heavens!" Cicely breathed. "He cannot be dead."

"I sincerely trust he *is* dead," drawled a lazy, masculine voice from the recesses of the carriage. Dark-gloved fingers curled on the upper portion of the low door, the door opened, and one elegantly clad leg stretched gracefully forth. A shining top boot with a gleaming white upper touched the dusty road with gentle disdain, and soon its mate appeared beside it as the proprietor of that low, somehow stirring drawl extricated himself from the carriage. Cicely found herself staring at a debonair, dark-haired, well-tanned gentleman dressed in the height of fashion in buff breeches and a perfectly tailored coat of Weston's famous *bleu céleste*. " 'Twould be a monstrous shame," he added as he stretched to his full, not insignificant, height, directing a pair of deep blue eyes up at her, "if after expending the price of a bullet on the villain, it should yet become necessary to put this county to the expense of a rope."

"But I can't have shot him!" Cicely cried. "I aimed well above his head, I assure you, and though this pistol does have a tendency to throw left, it never shoots low. Oh, sir, do please examine him. Perhaps he has only fainted."

A sardonic lift of an eyebrow was quickly controlled when she turned her beseeching gaze upon him. Almost apologetically, he lifted his right hand, thus bringing to view a small, silver-mounted pistol. "He has not fainted, ma'am. We must have fired simultaneously, and I regret to confess that I did not aim high. Not knowing," he added politely and with a small bow, "that there were ladies present."

Her eyes flashed. "I should hope that had little to do with it, sir. I meant only to frighten him away myself, but I quite see that that might not have answered the purpose at all, for he would very likely have shot you once he'd realized I had only the one piece." She gazed down at the victim. "What is to be done now?"

A flicker of respect glinted in the blue eyes before his lids drooped lazily. "Done? Why, I shall continue my journey, ma'am, and you shall return to your home. What more?"

"Well, we certainly cannot leave him lying in the road like this!"

"Why not?"

Cicely glared at him. Really, his attitude was most annoying. "Why not! He is a *human being*, sir!"

"Debatable." But he glanced vaguely toward the two men on the box. Neither had moved from his place, but the younger regarded his master warily, his face nearly colorless. "Ah, True, be so good as to remove this corpse. The sight of it offends my sweet rescuer. Moreover, it clutters the road."

"Aye, m'lord," the man muttered as he jumped to the road. "Uh . . ." He paused, looking upward. "What d'ye want I should do with him, sir?"

"Do with him? Why, just drag him off the road, of course."

"We cannot leave him here at all," Cicely stated flatly.

The elegant gentleman lifted his quizzing glass at that and regarded her as though she were a rare discovery. Cicely squirmed a bit in her saddle under that lazy, somewhat amused gaze. "What would you, my lady? I confess an aversion to sharing my carriage with him."

Cicely choked back an unexpected gurgle of laughter and forced herself to speak sternly. "Of course you should do no such thing, sir, but it seems to me it would be a simple matter to heave the fellow over his own saddle. Then your man there could lead the horse to the village and turn him over to the constable."

The gentleman appeared to give serious consideration to her words before awarding the notion a sad shake of his head. "If you say it would be simple, I daresay you're in the right of it, ma'am, but the thing is I shouldn't know how to go about it. Tom there"—he indicated his coachman—"has got a troublesome back, and although True is a stout lad, in my experience, corpses are infernally uncooperative. He'd most likely drop the fellow several times before he'd succeed in slinging him aboard that saddle."

"You could help him," she pointed out.

"I?" He thought about it, bringing the quizzing glass into play again as he surveyed first the rather bloody corpse and then, measuringly, the distance from the ground to the man's saddle. "I think not. Such exertion would no doubt prove to be both messy and exhausting. You cannot have noticed the state of the fellow's coat, or I'm sure you'd not have suggested such a course."

Cicely's lips twitched again, but she spoke sharply. "You cannot simply order your man to drag him from the road and thus be done with the matter. Why, a *child* might discover him!"

"My experience with the unceasingly ghoulish nature of children leads me to suspect that such a discovery would vastly improve the lucky urchin's status amongst his peers," the gentleman drawled, incorrigibly unperturbed. But he watched her from under those lazy lids as he spoke, and when her color heightened with real anger, he continued pacifically. "Very well, ma'am. After he removes the body from our sight, True shall take one of the carriage horses and ride for the constable." He allowed himself a long-suffering sigh. "I shall even engage to await that worthy myself in order to explain what took place here."

"An excellent notion, sir," she approved, "but there is no cause for your man to go. I can easily fetch the constable myself."

With a grace that belied the speed of his action, the gentleman moved a hand to Connie's bridle. "Unnecessary, ma'am. True wishes to go, and I think you should remain here with me so I don't become bored in the interim. Conversation with my coachman is hardly like to entertain me." Then, without so much as a by-your-leave, his hands were at her waist, and Cicely found herself lifted to stand beside him on the ground.

Breathless, she peered up at him. His hands, still firm at her waist, seemed to send rays of warmth through her body despite his gloves and her own thick velvet habit, making her intensely aware of his masculinity. Suddenly aware that her mouth was agape, she snapped it shut and tried, self-consciously, to step away from him. She had no business to be standing in the road with him like this. If anyone saw her, the duke would be the first to hear of it, and there would be no escaping the scene that would follow with a whole skin.

But his hands, instead of releasing her, seemed momentarily to tighten.

"Please, sir," she muttered hoarsely, looking down at her boots. "This is not seemly. I—I must go."

Patently reluctant, he released her. But when she turned back toward Connie, a gentle hand at her elbow stopped her. She trembled at even this light touch. "Do not go yet," he said softly. "It will be some time before True returns with your blasted constable, and I'd as lief not be left to kick my heels without company until then."

For a moment the drawl had disappeared, and he sounded almost boyish. She glanced quickly up at him as a memory chord was plucked. But it couldn't be. This gentleman, though certainly a dandy of the first stare—if one was to judge by those clinging buff breeches and that excellently cut coat, not to mention the fabulous flower-decked silk waistcoat and intricately tied neckcloth—was entirely too broad across the shoulders and too muscular of calf and thigh even to be related to the youth she remembered. And there was no softness in the chiseled planes of that handsome, tanned face. There was perhaps a faint resemblance, actually, but that was all. She dismissed the uncomfortable notion that had nipped at her mind and, drawing a deep breath, allowed him to guide her a short distance from the carriage.

The coachman had descended from his perch while True dealt with the corpse and was engaged in detaching one of the magnificent greys from its teammates. Cicely watched the process idly, then said impulsively, "I suppose your man could take Connie, sir. He would be a deal easier to manage than a horse unused to riders."

"True will cope," the gentleman smiled. "I daresay he would object to a sidesaddle, you know." Then, before she could point out that the sidesaddle could be removed, he frowned musingly. "Connie does not seem to be an apt name for that splendid-looking creature. I trust it is short for Constantine or even Conrad. Some such, at any rate."

"Not Conrad." She laughed, watching True climb aboard the skittish mount chosen by the coachman. "I've a cousin by that name, and I wouldn't name a favorite horse after him. 'Tis short for Conabos, one of the four horses of Ares, the Greek god of war."

He nodded. "I remember. Conabos stood for tumult, did

he not?'' She smiled, following his ironic gaze to the placidly grazing gelding.

"As a colt he was very wild," she explained. "I tamed him first, then broke him to saddle and bridle. I wanted to breed him," she added with a touch of sadness, "but my father ordered it otherwise."

"And quite right, too," stated her companion firmly. "A spirited stallion is no proper mount for a gently bred female." She glared at him, but he only responded with that lazy smile. "Don't snap my head off, ma'am. I'm not casting aspersions on your horsemanship, I assure you. Could tell at a glance from your excellent seat that you must be a bruising rider. Nevertheless, there would be moments when he might well fail his training, and you'd be no match for him in strength."

It was a reasonable point but one she had bitterly resented when it had been raised by her father. Somehow the same words coming from this amiable stranger standing so near as to send prickles dancing up and down her skin stirred no resentment at all. She nodded slowly in vague agreement but was far more conscious of his size and presence than of his words. "I suppose you're right," she said, feeling she ought to say something. Conversation with him was a good deal less unnerving than his silence.

"Oh, I'm right," he said with a teasing smile, "and I daresay your father said much the same thing." She blinked at him, and the smile grew broader, making her look away again. Silence fell once more. When she dared to glance up at him, it was to find that his eyes had narrowed speculatively. The humor that seemed generally to lighten them was gone. "Where is your groom, my lady? Surely a parent who insists upon a safe mount would also insist upon an escort."

Cicely flushed, uncomfortable under his suddenly direct gaze. "I—I decided to ride alone today, sir." Hearing herself, she gathered her wits and squared her shoulders, meeting that gaze unblinkingly. "My father tends to be a trifle overprotective, but I assure you I am perfectly accustomed to looking out for myself."

"Of course you are," he said with exaggerated kindness. "You would no doubt know precisely what to do in any given circumstance. For example," he drawled, placing a hand on her shoulder, "if you were to find yourself quite

alone with a gentleman who wished to kiss you, I've no
doubt at all you would know exactly how to cope with the
situation.''

Cicely stared at him. A twinkle lurked in the deep blue,
hooded eyes, and she felt no fear, though she felt a good
many other things. She looked down again quickly. His hand
on her shoulder seemed unnaturally heavy. His waistcoat was
very near, and she was astonishingly well aware of the rise
and fall of the broad chest underneath it. Was it imagination,
or did the pace of his breathing increase under her very eye?

Slowly she let her gaze drift upward to the lace-edged
neckcloth—such an affectation—then to that firm chin. Almost
reluctantly and with a slight, jerky motion, she brought her
gaze to linger on his lips, soft now and slightly parted,
revealing just a hint of even white teeth behind. She forced
herself to look into his eyes again, only to see the twinkle
darken to something warmer. Mesmerized now, she watched
as his eyes came nearer. The hand on her shoulder moved to
the small of her waist, drawing her to him, while his other
hand gently curved under her chin, tilting her face up to let
his lips meet hers. Cicely was aware of the smooth leather
glove against her soft skin, aware of the warm scent of the
leather itself, but the sensation was brief, for suddenly every
sense was focused upon the kiss itself.

She had often imagined what it would be like to be kissed
by a man, but her imagination seemed to have fallen far short
of the reality. His lips felt incredibly soft against hers, yet the
sensations that spread through her whole body belied such
softness. Her knees felt weak, and without his hand securely
against her back, she must surely have crumpled at his feet.
And the tingling! It didn't start where his lips touched hers
but a good deal lower, nearer to the center of her body. And
from there it spread to her toes and fingertips, numbing her
and at the same time stimulating every nerve.

When he set her back on her heels again, she continued to
gaze up at him, swaying slightly, astonished that she could
even stand upright unaided. But when the lazy smile dawned
again, she remembered his taunting words and came sharply
to her senses. Color suffused her cheeks as anger claimed
her, and she drew herself up haughtily.

''I had thought myself in the company of a gentleman, sir,
but since I find I much mistook your status, I assure you I

know precisely how to deal with the matter.'' And with that, she snatched her skirts out of the way and delivered a swift kick to his left kneecap with all the force of her small body behind it.

The gentleman yelped with pain and automatically bent to grasp his injured knee, whereupon Cicely doubled up her fist and dealt him a stunning roundhouse blow to the chin. He staggered sideways, caught completely off guard, and disdainfully she turned her back on him and stepped with angry pride toward the patient Connie. But her opponent's recovery was quicker than she had any reason to expect, and without warning, she suddenly found herself scooped off her feet and into his arms.

''You little vixen,'' he muttered wrathfully, ''you deserve to have your backside soundly smacked for that little trick. Don't worry,'' he added with grim restraint when she gasped indignantly, ''I shan't do anything so 'ungentlemanly' this time. I know I provoked it.'' He strode with her in his arms, not so much as a slight limp betraying any pain he might have felt, until he came to her horse. Then, lifting her easily, he plumped her down on her saddle with enough force to make her teeth snap together. Gathering her reins, he handed them up to her, but when she would have wheeled the gelding away, she found to her chagrin that he still held Connie's bridle.

''One moment, my lady,'' he said evenly. ''You deserve that I should keep you here until that constable arrives and then leave you to explain to your father how it comes about that you were involved in such an incident as this.'' Cicely caught her breath. She had quite forgotten the awkwardness of her position, but his words brought it back to her with a vengeance. She saw that he was watching her closely, and once again, there was nothing lazy about the look. Her sudden stillness and loss of color seemed to satisfy him, however, for he stepped away, loosing her bridle. His voice was gentle. ''I shall not mention your presence, ma'am, but you must give me your word that you will go straight home.''

She could not seem to speak, so she merely nodded. Her gaze seemed somehow locked with his. The twinkle returned to the aquamarine depths.

''Good girl,'' he approved. ''Now get along with you and stay off the road.'' Slowly she turned the dappled gelding toward the woods path. A sudden chuckle from behind made her straighten her shoulders and wrap herself in dignity. "Chilly," he said softly.

She snapped her head around to stare at him over her shoulder.

"I still have your letter," he grinned.

3

Although her sisters all had nicknames, only one person had ever called Cicely Cilly. Heat rushed to her face, and with a small cry much like that of an angry kitten, she jammed her heel into Connie's flank and leaned low over his neck as he charged with startled haste into the woods. She kept up the mad pace until she was halfway home. But then common sense reasserted itself, and she reined the gelding to a walk. It would not be wise to return him to his stable with his sides heaving and his coat lathered.

She touched her hat and was amazed to find it still in place—probably the only thing about her that Ravenwood had not disturbed. She knew now that the elegant gentleman was none other than her cousin Gilbert Leighton, Viscount Ravenwood. Indeed, though she had stubbornly suppressed the notion, she had suspected it from the outset. But this Ravenwood was too unlike her image of the ineffectual fop for comfort. Therefore, she had wished the suspicion away. But it had been useless, merely wishful thinking. It was he. None other. And he still had her letter. That dreadful, humiliating letter.

Her youngest sister was in the stableyard overseeing the grooming of her bay pony when Cicely rode in. Amalie waved.

"Is it not a splendid day?"

"Indeed it is," Cicely smiled, allowing one of the undergrooms to assist her to the ground. She was perfectly capable of springing down unaided, but she knew they felt privileged to help her. Also, she thought, inwardly grimacing, she was expected to act in a manner befitting a duke's daughter. Only a hoyden or other such underbred creature, according to her mother, leaped to her horse's back without making use of the mounting block or slid gracelessly down again when the ride was over.

"Are you coming up now?" Amalie asked anxiously, pulling the red knitted cap from her glossy curls. "Cook said she would make gingerbread, and I mean to see if she's finished it yet."

Cicely chuckled and put an arm around her little sister, her good humor restored. "To be sure I'll come." She followed the skipping child to the house, where she allowed herself to be tempted into a generous slice of fresh-baked gingerbread, still warm from the great oven, before going up to change her dress. Lady Brittany intercepted her in the corridor, her violet eyes alight with curiosity.

"You have been an age, Cicely, and I wish to know what Papa wanted with you in the bookroom."

"Come with me, then," Cicely said. There was no one in the long corridor, but she had long since learned to be careful. Servants always seemed to know one's business better than one did oneself, but there was no sense to making them a gift of one's private affairs. She led the way to her bedchamber, and once inside, Brittany shut the door and folded her hands expectantly at her breast.

"Well?"

Cicely could see no reason to prolong the matter. "He wants me to marry Viscount Ravenwood." Brittany looked perplexed. The name was clearly no better known to her than it had been to Cicely. "Our cousin—actually, our second cousin," she corrected. "Gilbert Leighton. Surely you remember."

"That awful popinjay who folded my bedsheet and put Bella up in the great oak? The one you—" She broke off, staring guiltily at Cicely.

Cicely grimaced. "The very same. He's even still got that awful letter Papa made me write. But I don't think he's precisely a popinjay anymore."

"How on earth can you know that when you've not clapped eyes on the man in five—no, it's six years, isn't it? You surely don't take Papa's word in such a case."

Cicely felt the warmth rushing to her cheeks and turned quickly away, but Brittany, although far from being the most intelligent of the five sisters, was easily the most sensitive to the others' moods. She moved quickly now, laying a gentle hand on Cicely's arm. Cicely turned back, a rueful smile tugging at her lips.

"You must say nothing, but I've seen him."

"Where?"

"On the road. Just now. He's coming here, I expect. Papa said he would come."

"But how did you know it was he? Does he look the same? How close were you?"

"He called me Cilly. But I didn't recognize him at first. He's changed, Tani. He's changed a great deal."

"How?"

"Oh, bigger. Not taller, for he was always tall, but heavier, more solid. And he no longer looks like a boy playing dress-up. He's . . . he's elegant. Very handsome." She remembered his touch, his dark blue eyes staring deep into her own, his kiss. Blushing a fiery red, she turned away again.

"But how came he to speak to you?"

Patiently Cicely managed to sketch the scene without going into great detail. She made no mention of her own part in the action except as a bystander, saying simply that a highwayman had been killed and that in the course of determining the proper procedure to be followed, she had come to recognize Ravenwood.

"Well, I think it sounds most romantic," Brittany said when she had finished. "Nothing so exciting ever happens to me. Though I daresay," she added with frowning honesty, "that if someone were to shoot off a pistol anywhere near me, I should in all likelihood faint dead away and miss all the fun. Is he really handsome?"

Cicely qualified the word this time, saying merely that she supposed he was well enough. "Very tanned and masculine, you know. And though he still smiles a good deal and affects a rather easy manner, I think he likes to get his own way about things."

"Well, what man does not?" Brittany asked practically. "But it sounds as though the match might do very well. At least Papa's not proposing to sell you off to settle his gaming debts like that poor girl we heard about last Season."

Cicely chuckled and began searching out something to wear, but she could not rid herself of the notion that her marriage might not be quite so convenient as she had previously thought.

"At least now Mama will not continually be harping upon the problem of your disposal," Brittany said musingly, "and will be able to concentrate upon me completely. That has never previously been the case, you know."

Cicely's attention came back to her sister at once. She, who had had a good deal of her parents' attention by virtue of being the eldest child, as well as having required at least a modicum of notice throughout her two Seasons, suddenly realized that her sisters had spent much more time with their nannies and governesses than with either the duke or his duchess.

"Do you feel that you have been neglected in the past, Tani?"

"Oh, no," she responded with her gentle smile. "How could I be so ungrateful as to feel neglected when I have been continually surrounded by people who love me? 'Tis merely that to spend so much time in Mama's company—indeed, even so much as I've spent in the last month—is a new experience for me." Her eyes twinkled. "Did you fear I had been pining away in the schoolroom? I promise it was no such thing. I had my music, and though Miss Fellows quite despairs of ever teaching me to speak Italian properly, I have much enjoyed her company and her efforts on my behalf."

"I should have joined you at your Italian lessons." Cicely's voice was muffled, for, having discarded the velvet habit, she had flung a cream-colored muslin gown over her head. After a moment's wriggling, her head emerged once more and the gown slid into place. She moved toward Brittany and turned her back. Obligingly the younger girl began to do up the many tiny, satin-covered buttons on the pleated, high-necked bodice. "I might have done so, had I wished to remain indoors," she added, "but I prefer to be with my horses. Indeed, I felt restricted enough this past year just being in mourning dress and having to stay at home."

"You could have gone visiting with Mama to the cousins and to Grandmama Satterthwaite's," Brittany pointed out.

Cicely responded with an expressive grimace, then, realizing her sister couldn't see her face, said brusquely, "I'd rather have died, thank you. All that gloom and gossip is not for me."

"Well, I think I should have enjoyed it. There!" She finished the last button with a satisfied smile. "Which sash will you wear?"

"The lavender satin, I think." Cicely found it in her sash drawer and discovered two narrower, matching ribbons folded with it. "These Meg usually twists through my hair. Where is she, do you suppose? I had expected to find her here tossing things about and making lists. She's the only one who can do my hair so that it doesn't all fall down again."

Brittany laughed and nodded pointedly at the bell rope near the bed. "I daresay she hasn't forgotten how to come when you call, dearest. Or shall I pull the bell for you?"

Cicely wrinkled her nose. "Wretch. I'll do it myself." While Brittany went on idly outlining plans for the future, Cicely suddenly found herself wondering if the constable had arrived yet and what tale he had been told. She remembered the sight of True perched uneasily on the broad bare back of the splendid carriage horse, the reins of a utilitarian spare bridle in his hand, and hoped he had run into no difficulty. She doubted his master would be patient with delay. True had looked a trifle worried about a possible reprimand anyway, no doubt because he had failed to scotch the highwayman's attack himself. But since he had clearly been unarmed, Cicely was certain he need not have worried. His master would be fair.

Now, why on earth, she asked herself, did she believe that? For all she knew, Ravenwood might be entirely capricious, the sort who would look for a scapegoat whenever anything unpleasant occurred. Why, then, was she so instinctively sure he was not anything of the sort? She smiled. Undoubtedly it was because he seemed too sleepy ever to deliver a proper rebuke to an underling. But then she remembered his quick action after she had struck him, those harsh words snapped into her ear as he carried her to her horse and sent her on her way. Definitely there was more to Ravenwood than mere laziness and sartorial splendor.

Brittany's accusation that she was not attending interrupted her train of thought, but Meg Hardy's bustling entrance at the same moment spared Cicely from having to respond. Meg, a plump, mouse-haired, wholesome-looking young woman, had a sharp tongue that was quickly put to use while she surveyed the scene before her.

"And just what have you been about, Miss Cicely, not to have sent for me the moment you returned from your ride, I should like to know? Not but what that dress will do, I suppose, if you haven't wrinkled it past decency with your usual wriggling and yanking. But your hair is a proper disaster, m'lady, and no mistake. And what with a gentleman in the house which is hopeful to see you again after six long years, 'tis time and more we set you to rights. Not," she added with a wry twist of her mouth, "that there's need to rush, for the top-lofty gent what says he's his lordship's valet only just arrived, though his master's been here nigh onto half an hour already, little though he appears to be the sort who would hurry himself. Still, it'll be an hour and more, no doubt, before his lordship'll be fit for viewin'. I know his sort well enough."

As she delivered these strictures she fairly pushed her mistress across the room and into the dressing chair, waving comb and brush to punctuate her words. Brittany moved toward the window seat, clearly intending to be entertained. It was not to be, however.

"Just what might you be doing, miss?" Meg demanded tartly. "You're to dine in company tonight, you are, and that good-for-naught, Sarah Basehart, needs a precious good bit of time if she's to turn you out in style, though it's as well she'll be getting some practice, I'm thinking. I don't mind telling you," she stated unnecessarily, "I doubt she's up to snuff yet for the rigors of a London Season. But we'll manage, never you fret. Just you run along now and let her try her hand at getting you ready for dinner with his lordship."

Brittany was no match for her and fled without protest, leaving Cicely to grin into the mirror at her tirewoman, who was frowning thoughtfully as she drew the silvery tresses through her fingers. Cicely chuckled. "You are a wicked fraud, Meg Hardy," she said with mock sternness. "You know perfectly well that Tani's Sarah was with Lady Colton before she accepted Mama's offer. Her references are impeccable, and Mama has been prodigiously pleased with her."

"Be that as it may, miss," Met uttered righteously, "we all of us have room to improve ourselves, particularly those of us who forget our place and think to come it over our betters."

"Ah," said Cicely, understanding the matter more clearly. "So Sarah has attempted to snub you. Without success, I'd wager."

"Wager, would you? I'll have you know, Miss Cicely, that I'll thank you to do no such godless thing on my account. Nor be it necessary. That baggage knows her place well enough, though she be a hoity-toity bit of goods at best. Saying she was accustomed to being called Miss Basehart, if you please. Just puffing off her consequence, of course, not but what the servants at Colton Hall, not knowing better, might have been bullied into calling her so. I'm not one to doubt another's word. But it'll do her no good to be putting on airs in this establishment, for we do know the proper way of things, and so Miss Fortescue told her."

Cicely could well believe it, for the duchess's formidable dresser was a good deal higher in the instep than the duchess herself. If Fortescue had seen fit to deliver a setdown, Cicely would not have been surprised to hear that Miss Sarah Basehart had withered into oblivion as a result of it. In that ducal household only one tirewoman could be honored with the title "Miss." And it would not be the wench who served the household's second daughter, no matter who her previous mistress might have been. Not that a baron's wife would cut much ice with the Malmesbury servants. The most Sarah could aspire to, as long as she remained in this household, at least, was to be called Basehart by the others. It had not been until Cicely's come-out, in fact, that Meg had achieved sufficient status to be called by her full name.

Cicely repressed a grin as she realized that Meg Hardy ought to welcome her forthcoming marriage with enthusiasm, since, in the nature of things, she might expect to reach the heady title "Miss Hardy" before Fortescue had entirely departed the scene. She would even, as the dresser of a reigning duchess, take precedence in the servants' hall over the dowager duchess's tirewoman. Oh yes, Meg Hardy would surely cheer the duke's arrangements!

When she entered the main saloon an hour later, Cicely looked serene and beautiful. Meg Hardy had combed her hair smoothly away from an arrow-straight center part into two plaits that began just behind her ears and then twisted intricately into each other at the nape of her neck. Then the two narrow lavender ribbons had been braided right along with her hair and tied in tiny bows just behind her ears. The style was simple, yet very effective. The gentleman lounging at his leisure in a Kent wing chair near the cheerfully crackling fire looked up, then lifted his gold-rimmed quizzing glass to peer at her with undisguised admiration.

"Dear me," he drawled, getting gracefully to his feet and executing an exaggerated bow, "it is the famous Ice Princess in the flesh. Your servant, ma'am." Except for the telltale bruise on the left side of his firm chin, he looked perfectly splendid himself, she noted. It had surely taken at least two men to get him into the form-fitting dark blue coat that he wore over tight cream-colored knee breeches. His exquisite, rose-colored, watered-silk waistcoat sported a watch chain with numerous gold fobs and seals, and his neckcloth— trimmed, like his shirt cuffs, with expensive Brussels lace— was tied in an intricate knot, with a large, dark sapphire sparkling from its folds. He wore no other jewelry, however, except for the large gold signet ring on the third finger of his right hand.

"Do behave yourself, Ravenwood," she said, her air of cool serenity firmly in place, despite the fact that her gaze, seemingly of its own accord, kept drifting to that bruise. "I did not think you would be down yet, or I'd have sought out my mother and sister before coming into this room."

"I protest, my lady. 'Twould have been a crime to delay this meeting. But why so certain I'd be elsewhere?"

She hesitated only briefly before deciding to tell him. "Because my abigail said your valet was delayed, and I couldn't imagine how you might achieve that"—her gesture took in his splendid appearance—"without him."

"Good God!" he exclaimed, looking down at himself in astonishment. "I say, I am seriously affronted, ma'am. Can it possibly be that you credit this splendor to the unworthy Pavenham?" He shook his dark head, though gently, so as not to disarrange the carefully windswept hair. "No, no, you could not be so insensitive to the labors I expend toward sartorial perfection."

Cicely regarded him narrowly. His indignation certainly seemed to be perfectly sincere. For a moment she hovered on the brink of an apology, before she noted that lurking twinkle.

"You're bamming me, sir. Just as I expect you were this afternoon when you insisted upon leaving the highwayman in the dust. You cannot think your appearance so important as all that.''

''On the contrary, ma'am,'' he corrected blandly. ''One's appearance is of the utmost importance. Sets the whole tone of one's personality, don't you know.''

''No, I *don't* know!'' she snapped, her serenity all but forgotten. ''The only time one's appearance is of any import is the moment one is deciding what dress to wear or what to do with one's hair. After that it must be of no consequence, or one will be taken for a conceited popinjay.'' She glared at him, wondering how he would respond to direct attack.

''You know,'' he drawled musingly as he withdrew a lace-trimmed handkerchief from his waistcoat pocket and dabbed gently at his lips, ''I cannot but think you had those very words from George Brummell. No doubt he crossed your path once ot twice before his fall from grace.''

''I knew Mr. Brummell,'' she retorted. ''I did not approve of his manners, but he dressed like a sensible man.''

''No flair,'' pronounced his lordship with a headshake, thus in two simple words dismissing the reputation of the famous beau who had ruled fashionable London for so many years before an accumulation of unpaid gaming debts had forced his retirement, in disgrace, to the Continent. ''Dull waistcoats, a sad lack of variety in his choice of colors, and nothing to set his taste apart from his fellows' except his infernal sameness. But don't be so fusty about his manners, my girl. I'd wager he said nothing more than what you'd have loved to have the courage to say yourself. A girl who uses words like 'bamming' is not entirely nice in her ways, I'm afraid. Coming it too strong, Cilly.''

Her hands clenched, and her precarious hold upon her temper snapped. ''Don't call me that, you ass-earred ape! You've not the slightest right to—''

''Cicely! Dearest, you mustn't speak so to his lordship. Apologize at once. Such language!'' The duchess swept in, trailing apricot chiffon skirts and a lacy shawl, and holding her cut-crystal vinaigrette poised for immediate use. Acknowledging Ravenwood's bow with a small nod, she turned back to her crimson-faced daughter. ''Cicely?''

Cicely was still recovering from the shock of her mother's interruption and congratulating herself that it had not been the duke instead. The very thought brought with it a clear vision

of the incidents just prior to her cousin's departure the last
time he had visited Malmesbury. Ravenwood had always
managed, with seemingly no effort, to goad her to extremes.
She would have to watch herself. Taking firm control, she
turned to face the duchess, dropping a small, contrite curtsy.

"I beg your pardon, Mama. I should not have spoken so to
his lordship."

"You must tell him, my dear, not me."

Gritting her teeth, Cicely turned to face him. His features
were as controlled as her own, but she could not fail to note
the damned twinkle in those hooded eyes. Ravenwood was
enjoying himself.

"Forgive me, my lord," she grated. As an apology it was
insufficient to meet the duchess's standard, but Cicely knew
she could manage no more. She could but pray that her grace
would reserve further reproval for the privacy of her boudoir.

After a brief silence, however, help came from an unexpected source when Ravenwood said smoothly, "Not at all,
my lady. There is nothing to forgive. Truly, your grace," he
added, turning back to the duchess with a charming smile, "it
is I who should beg pardon, for I confess I reverted almost on
the instant of renewing acquaintance with the Lady Cicely to
my old habit of provoking her."

" 'Tis kind of you to share the blame, Ravenwood," the
duchess said with a doubtful look at her daughter, who was
striving now to conceal astonishment. Never before had he
apologized for leading her into the briars. "Nevertheless,"
her grace continued, recalling her daughter's attention, " 'tis
most unseemly for a young lady of quality to speak in such
vulgar terms."

"Yes, Mama, you're perfectly right," Cicely said hastily.
"I shan't do so again, I assure you."

"Very well, my dear, then we shall say no more about it.
Won't you sit down, Ravenwood?"

"With pleasure, ma'am." He waited, however, until she
had made herself comfortable on a green velvet lion's-paw
settee, and when Cicely chanced to look at him, it was only
to find his eyes dancing with a spark of unholy mischief that
quickly led her to think he hadn't finished with her, but
meant to prove she couldn't hold her tongue when he was
about. Well, she would show him. Two Seasons of practicing

icy control ought to be worth something, she told herself firmly.

A welcome diversion occurred a few moments later with the entrance of the duke and Lady Brittany. The duke wore his customary dark coat, neatly tied neckcloth, and knee breeches. But it was not the sight of the duke that lifted Ravenwood to his feet with a nearly awestricken look. He rose, Cicely thought with wry amusement, a good deal more rapidly than he had done upon her entrance, though she could scarcely blame him. Brittany looked wonderful.

She wore a pale yellow muslin gown, nipped in just below her full breasts with a sapphire silk sash, and knots of matching ribbon decked the gown's scalloped hemline. Her golden curls had been confined artfully atop her head with a bandeau of the same blue silk, though one slim curl had been allowed to droop enticingly in front of her right ear. Her darker brows and lashes and the vivid coloring in her lips and cheeks owed nothing to artifice, and Brittany's nearly violet eyes sparkled with enthusiasm. It occurred to Cicely, watching her fondly, that the same London wags who had nicknamed her the Ice Princess might well dub her sister the Golden Goddess. It also occurred to her that if the men in London reacted to Brittany in the same fashion as Ravenwood was reacting, it was as well that she, Cicely, would be safely married and not in competition with her on the Marriage Mart.

Ravenwood let his quizzing glass fall at last. " 'Tis an honor to greet you, Lady Brittany. May I take the liberty of saying that you will take London by storm. Indeed, you will take the beau monde's collective breath away. Why, I can scarcely credit you to be the same chit whose plaits I pulled, whose ribs I tickled till she screamed for mercy, and—"

"And whose bed you sabotaged," Cicely put in tartly without thinking. She had meant only to bring the long encomium to an end, but her father's outraged exclamation and the viscount's expression of amused reproach brought her quickly to her senses. She turned toward the duke, hoping to explain, but once again it was Ravenwood who smoothed things over.

" 'Twas not the dastardly deed she makes it sound, your grace, I promise you. I did but turn the Lady Brittany's bedsheet back upon itself. A trick I scarcely need confess I learned at Eton. Reprehensible, perhaps, but not unforgivable, I believe.''

"No, of course not," grumbled the duke. "I should have remembered your taste for a joke, sir." He glanced up to find his butler at the door. "Dinner, Pinchbeck?"

"Dinner is served, your grace."

4

It was still light outside, but even in the country the duke preferred to dine by candlelight, so the heavy crimson velvet curtains had been drawn, and candles glowed in the massive chandelier suspended low over the dark walnut table. Their glow was softly reflected in the highly polished wood because her grace had long since introduced the Regent's fashion of dining off the wood, although upon occasion she still brought forth the elegant damask and linen tablecloths of yore.

The atmosphere was intimate, for all the leaves had been removed so that the diners need not sit at any great distance from one another. Also, the huge silver epergne that customarily formed the centerpiece for large dinners had been relegated to the sideboard, and a low, cheerful arrangement of early spring flowers had been set in its place.

Malmesbury took his place at the head of the table, where he was flanked by his two daughters, and Ravenwood sat to the right of the duchess, next to Cicely. She was grateful not to have to sit across from him, where she would have been forced to meet that mischievous gaze from time to time, but she was physically much more conscious of his nearness than she might have been, had he been seated next to Brittany instead. The small group made it possible for general conversation, so she was not expected to keep him entertained, as she would be if the occasion were more formal. And thankfully the telltale bruise was on the opposite side, which meant not only that she herself need not bear with its constant reminder of her earlier behavior, but also that the duke would not notice it and ask whence it had come.

In her opinion Ravenwood behaved very nearly like a sensible man throughout the meal. By the introduction of the second course, she was able to concentrate on her dressed crab with no fear that he might suddenly introduce an embarrassing topic of conversation. Since he had recently been in London, he was able to respond to her grace's request for the latest information regarding her cronies of the beau monde.

"'Tis very thin of company in Town these days," he said, politely dismissing a footman's attempt to serve him some fresh asparagus. "Prinny is still at Brighton, of course, and will no doubt remain there until just before the wedding. They say he is suffering as usual from the gout, but I have it on excellent authority that he has recently ridden his horse." His eyes twinkled. "In order to get him *on* the horse, they say it was necessary to construct an inclined plane. Then his royal highness was pushed in a chair on rollers up to a platform, which was then raised by some means or other so the horse could stand beneath. His royal highness was then let gently down into the saddle and thus allowed to receive the benefit of gentle exercise in good fresh air."

When the laughter that greeted this tale had died away, Brittany asked if the Princess Charlotte was still at Windsor.

"Yes, indeed, my lady. The Queen is choosing her trousseau, you know, and the princess is still in such alt over her forthcoming nuptials that she is behaving herself for once. In the meantime, her handsome Prince Leopold is displaying the tact for which he is justly famous by staying in Brighton until his future father-in-law shall have recovered the use of his legs."

"It is indeed kind of him," agreed the duchess. "I must say, the Season is going to open in fine style, what with the wedding one day and the opening of Almack's the next, not to mention our own ball, which is planned for the week following."

"What's going on in the House these days?" demanded his grace. "From what I read in the papers, it seems as if young Henry Grey Bennet's stirring up a hornet's nest. Daresay you'll have taken your seat by now."

"Mr. Bennet has organized a select committee to look into the possibility of reforming the London police system. There have been an extraordinary number of robberies this year, and the authorities are worried that it will get worse when everyone comes back to Town." He smiled ruefully. "I'm afraid, however, sir, that I have not yet taken my seat. Not quite my line of country.''

'' 'Tis your duty, sir,'' replied his grace sternly. ''You young folks take duty much too lightly these days.''

''Papa,'' Brittany put in, speaking in mild protest, ''Lord Ravenwood was at Waterloo, was he not?''

''He was,'' the duke agreed gruffly, '' and I am sure we are all very grateful for his efforts there and grateful as well that he was spared to us when so many were taken.'' He paused, frowning as though he had somehow lost himself.

Ravenwood smiled at Brittany. ''The one fact scarcely affects the other, my lady. I fear your respected father is in the right of things, as it is his usual habit to be. Military life provided much in the way of entertainment and excitement for those of us who followed Wellington across the Peninsula. We scarcely ever thought of it as duty, I'm afraid.''

''But so many were killed or crippled!'' Cicely protested.

He turned toward her, and in the candlelight there seemed to be a strange glitter in his eyes that she could not interpret. ''An unanswerable point, ma'am, but I fear 'tis one that we rarely allowed to distress us. Nearly all was fun and gig, I assure you.''

''But battle must have been terrifying!'' she exclaimed.

''I daresay one's first battle must always be a trifle unnerving,'' he responded, his drawl more pronounced than ever, ''but one grew accustomed, don't you know. One does not expect the gentle sex to comprehend such masculine idiosyncrasies, of course, and I fear the subject is not a suitable one for lengthy discourse at her grace's dining table. Suppose we agree to disagree, for the moment, at least.''

He smiled blandly at her, and Cicely found herself staring blankly back. It was with profound relief, therefore, that she heard the duchess, who had little interest in matters either parliamentary or military, state that she certainly hoped the good weather would hold for the duration of Ravenwood's visit.

''I daresay you might even have a day of hunting, provided the ground don't harden again,'' she said wisely.

Ravenwood responded suitably, and Cicely took advantage of what immediately became generalized conversation again to sit silently while she attempted to take his measure.

That he had changed a good deal in six years' time was

obvious. At times he still seemed affected to the point of foppishness, and much as she was beginning to suspect an overactive sense of humor, there could be no denying that he still cared a great deal for his appearance. He treated her parents with a marked degree of deference, yet there was none of the near obsequiousness she had seen displayed by other fops she had met. Or indeed by many others who seemed to greet her parents' rank with a respect bordering upon awe. Ravenwood did not. His was much more the attitude shown by a well-bred young man toward his elders. Now, though his tone was lazy and his eyelids half shut, he still managed to direct the conversation so that everyone took part. It was he who consistently encouraged comments from Brittany, who otherwise would undoubtedly have held her tongue. No doubt it was his diplomatic training that stood him in such good stead, but whatever it was, she could not fault his manners.

"And you, Lady Cicely, what do you think of these changing styles?" he inquired amiably.

Cicely felt the color rush to her cheeks. "Forgive me, sir," she said, forcing calm. "I fear I was not attending."

"Ravenwood was merely asking your opinion of the newer fashions, my dear," said the duchess. "Really, Cicely, where have your manners gone begging?"

"Sorry, Mama, I'm afraid I was in a brown study. The fashions, Ravenwood? I think you must be a far superior judge of such things than I. I merely wear the stuff, and mostly Mama or my dressmaker determines whether something is suitable, while 'tis the gentlemen who declare whether 'tis becoming or not."

Brittany giggled. "You should have been attending, Cicely. We were discussing *masculine* fashions—those outrageous Cossack trousers, to be precise."

The warmth in Cicely's cheeks deepened, but her eyes frosted glacially. "I daresay 'tis all of a piece," she said to Ravenwood. "I cannot even pretend to be interested in such idiocy. That is far more to your taste than it could ever be to that of any female of sense."

"Cicely!"

"That will do, daughter." The duke's stern tones overrode the shriller notes of his wife's exclamation.

Cicely faced each of them in turn, knowing she had once

more let her temper carry her beyond what was pleasing. Something about Ravenwood set her off. Even now, as she apologized for her hasty words, he merely watched her lazily from under those drooping lids. The twinkle was back, but he showed no inclination to excuse her thoughtlessness.

It was Brittany who came to the rescue. "I think there must always be outrageous fashions," she said gently. "People—some people—seem to enjoy making spectacles of themselves. Just think of that dreadful Oldenburgh poke bonnet two years ago! All because the Grand Duchess Oldenburgh wore such a thing when she visited Oxford."

"Very true, dear," smiled the duchess. "And why on earth anyone wanted to make a pattern card of that dreadful woman, I shall never understand, for a more underbred, bumptious female I'm sure none of us ever had the misfortune to meet."

Harsh words from a strait-laced lady, but Cicely, who had been privileged to meet the grand duchess upon several occasions during that lady's sojourn in London, could well understand the Duchess of Malmesbury's strictures. Many said the woman had been involved in some sort of secret negotiations for her brother, the Czar Alexander. Others said she was simply a spy, perhaps even for Napoleon himself. Others thought she was on the catch for a royal husband. And still others, like Brittany, only remembered the bonnet with the huge, upthrusting poke front that had caused such a sensation. Whatever the reason for the grand duchess's visit, she had caused quite a stir wherever she went.

Conversation passed easily enough to other topics, and in what seemed to be a short time, the duchess signaled to her daughters that they should leave the two gentlemen to their port. In the drawing room the duchess glanced once or twice at her eldest daughter, but if she had planned to say anything, she evidently thought better of it and requested the Lady Brittany to ring for a footman instead, giving orders upon his appearance to inform the younger ladies that their presence would be acceptable. Miss Fellows having insisted, upon notice of Ravenwood's arrival, that she had entirely recovered her health, they had taken their dinner, as usual, by the schoolroom fire.

Their entrance coincided with that of the duke. He greeted Miss Fellows almost cordially, told Amalie that she might remain no longer than half an hour before taking herself off to bed like a good girl, scowled at Alicia, and suggested that Arabella might entertain them with her latest effort on the pianoforte. These amenities over, he turned to his eldest daughter.

"Ravenwood wishes to speak with you in my bookroom."

Arabella, crossing the room to her instrument, paused and turned to stare at her sister. Amalie's blue eyes widened, and even Alicia seemed to forget her own woes at these interesting words.

Cicely had stood up when he entered, of course, and now faced him uncertainly. "I am to see him alone, sir?"

"Yes, yes," he muttered, irritated. "No harm in that. The man's a gentleman, after all. Just run along, girl, and see you don't disgrace me."

"Yes, Papa." But her feet seemed leaden as she went down the grand stair to the ground floor. The hall was empty for the moment, but darkness was rapidly spreading itself across the landscape outside, and the candles in the wall sconces, though not the ones in the huge, hanging chandelier, had already been lit. Slowly she crossed the stone floor to the heavy oaken door of the bookroom, which had been left slightly ajar. She pushed it open.

A fire crackled cheerfully in the small Adam fireplace. She could faintly smell woodsmoke. At first she didn't see him, for the curtains had been drawn and the room was not well lit. But then a movement caught her eye. He was standing in the east window. One hand was hooked in his waistcoat pocket; the other held the heavy curtain back just a trifle. He turned his head as she shut the door softly behind her.

"The moon is coming up with a lovely orange glow. I believe it thinks it has tumbled into autumn. Come and see."

The last thing she wanted to do was to stand near him gazing at a misplaced harvest moon. She cleared her throat briskly. "My father said you wish to speak with me, Ravenwood. Perhaps it would be best if you did so at once."

He let the curtain fall back into place and turned to face her, frowning slightly. "The Ice Princess again. I thought I had successfully sped her on her way."

"You talk in riddles, my lord."

"Don't freeze me, Cilly. I—"

"I wish you will not call me by that ridiculous, childish

nickname, sir. My name is Cicely. Not," she added haughtily, "that I can remember having given you leave to use it."

He bowed, then stepped a pace or two forward. She could not read his expression, but the drawling tone seemed more exaggerated than ever when next he spoke. "I protest, my lady, I meant no offense. I shall endeavor to be more circumspect. But perhaps you might find it in your heart to forgive a man overwhelmed by the emotions of the occasion. When I tell you—nay, when I fling myself upon my knees to kiss the hem of your elegant gown, to beg that you might find it in your heart to do me the honor—"

"Cut line, Ravenwood," she demanded, regarding him suspiciously. "Farce does not become you. Moreover, my father has already explained his arrangement with you. How long before we must be wed?"

His eyes opened at that, but his expression was more quizzical than shocked. It occurred to her that it would not be unnatural for a man to become angry at such a brusque response to a marriage proposal. But Ravenwood was not angry. Indeed, it seemed that she must have stirred his ready sense of the ridiculous, for the damned twinkle was back in his eye. She gritted her teeth, irritated with herself for allowing such a small thing to annoy her.

"Forgive me, my lady," he said with a slight bow. "I should never have been so foolish as to think you would prefer the business done up with a romantic ribbon. I should have remembered your dislike of theatrics. Do you mind telling me precisely how his grace explained the matter to you?"

"Not at all, sir," she replied, confident of her continued serenity despite the disturbing fact that he had taken a step nearer even as he spoke. "My father simply made it clear that he wishes, through us, to secure the succession in the direct line. I have always assumed that my marriage would be arranged by my parents, and I suppose you will do well enough as a husband." Just put that in your pipe, she thought, giving him an icy look down her nose.

He frowned. "I see. A marriage of convenience."

"Is that not how you see it yourself, sir? My portion, after all, is undoubtedly what enticed you to accept my father's arrangement."

"Your portion?" He looked puzzled for a moment but

recovered himself rapidly—no doubt, she thought sardonically, because he realized she was not such a cawker as to think he didn't know to the penny the amount of her marriage portion. After all, it would very likely be years before the duke died and Ravenwood would have access to the extensive rents and other income from the vast ducal estates. He brought his gaze back to her, letting it move from point to point on her body. "Your father," he said in measured tones, "is sometimes a trifle too busy, I think. I daresay he was largely responsible for that very affecting letter I received from you some six years ago."

She could not understand the sudden change of subject, but she nodded. "The words were mine, sir, but the sentiment, I fear, was his."

"I never imagined for a moment that the sentiment was sincere, my dear. 'Tis as well for you, I think, that he does not know what occurred between us today."

Her gaze flew to the bruise on his chin, visible even in the dim light, before she looked away again. "I—I was not nearly so violent the last time, my lord." She looked back at him, unable to disguise a sudden flash of amusement. "And you provoked that incident as well, sir. A nasty toad in my sash drawer, culminating a fortnight of such pranks."

"I disremember that bit, though I've no doubt you are correct," he admitted with a teasing smile. "Nonetheless, though your attack then might not have been so violent as your action today, you will concede that it has been a good deal easier to avoid mention of a sore knee and chin than it was to conceal the evidence of an entire bottle of claret emptied over my head."

A small choke of laughter escaped her. "It was a very good year for claret, my lord."

"A fact that I doubt did a thing to mitigate his grace's displeasure. As I recall, my last view of you that day was of an angry young miss striding off the field of battle in disgrace. But you left me to the fate of having a peal rung over my head before I was so much as allowed to change my clothes."

"I hope you do not expect sympathy, my lord. The fact that you suffered a well-deserved rebuke for your ungentlemanly behavior scarcely atones for the thrashing I received shortly after your departure."

"That, no doubt, had nothing to do with me," he responded virtuously. "More likely, it was in honor of having broached a claret of such excellent vintage to no good purpose. The letter, in fact, was your punishment for the rudeness of the act itself."

"It was certainly a far worse punishment," she agreed. "I squirmed through every word of apology, I assure you."

"I daresay." He took another step toward her. "You have grown very beautiful, Cilly." He seemed to have forgotten their conversation, and his gaze very nearly caressed her. Cicely suddenly felt an odd weakness creeping over her limbs. She wished he would speak further. Even more, she wished she could move away. But she seemed stuck to the floor. Her body seemed totally disconnected from her mind. She realized he had spoken, but she had no notion what it was he had said.

"I beg your pardon, sir," she said haltingly. "You said . . ."

"I said, my dear, that I shall do my possible to see that you do not regret your so generous decision." He stepped even nearer. Something was wrong with her skin, as if things were moving about upon it. It was a prickling sensation. No, she amended to herself, "prickly" denoted something unpleasant. This sensation was not at all unpleasant, merely disturbing. She remembered a similar feeling. It had occurred during the afternoon, when he kissed her. No doubt it was merely a sort of sixth sense that was warning her now that he meant to kiss her again.

He took another step. Her eyes widened. He was very close to her now, almost near enough to touch. But not that near. Not yet. She could not doubt his intent. But he was still too far away to touch her. So why on earth did she feel as if he were touching her already? She could surely feel his hands on her shoulders, feel his body against hers. Her soft curves seemed to submit to those hard muscles even as he watched her through lazy, drifting eyes. The languorous gaze drifted from her face downward, intensifying the sense that he was caressing her. Her breasts seemed to swell under that phantom touch, swelling until their tips pressed tautly against the material of her gown.

"Come here, Cicely."

His voice was low. It was gentle. But there was a hint of command there, and despite the emotional chaos within, she remembered that he had been a military officer for nearly six years. He was, that note reminded her, a man accustomed to obedience from those he commanded. She glanced at him uncertainly, aware with every fiber of her being of the size and strength of his body. She caught the scent of Imperial Water mixed with that of the woodsmoke she had smelled earlier. He did not repeat his command. He merely waited, but it seemed as though he drew her nearer whether she would go to him or not.

He did not move until she stood directly before him. Then, gently, he placed two fingers under her pointed little chin and tilted her face upward. She complied unresistingly. For the moment all her resistance, indeed most of her conscious thought, seemed to have suspended itself. She was aware only of his touch, his gaze, his presence.

"Wet your lips, little one," he said softly.

She obeyed, scarcely aware of his words, knowing only that time would be suspended until he ordered it otherwise. Ravenwood made no attempt to resist the invitation of those moist, softly parted lips. His initial touch was gentle, but as they met, there seemed to be a spark between them and with a sound very like a groan, he took her in his arms, crushing her body against his as he thrust his tongue between those yielding, velvety lips.

The invasion was a welcome one. Cicely felt him searching out hidden places, exploring the mysteries of her mouth, and she felt again that delicious tingling sensation emanating from the core of her body, perhaps from her very soul. As the tingling spread to the rest of her it seemed to intensify. Suddenly it was as though she could focus on a dozen things at once. She was aware for a brief moment that it was difficult to breathe. Then his arms relaxed, and his hands began to move over her body much as they had done earlier in her imagination. But as his fingertips moved lightly across her nipples he seemed suddenly to recollect himself.

His kiss became gentler, no longer exploratory. He kissed her cheek, then nibbled lightly at her ear before murmuring, "I hope you do not mean to teach me another lesson in the proper methods of feminine self-preservation."

Cicely relaxed, then looked up at him, her expression completely candid, though he would never know the effort it cost her to suppress a sudden, unexpected twinge of shyness.

" 'Tis perfectly proper for you to kiss me now, my lord.

My father and mother would never have allowed us such privacy were that not the case.''

If he was disappointed by so casual a response, he did not allow it to show. In fact, all she could read in his expression as he gazed down at her, his hands now lightly upon her shoulders, was that ubiquitous spark of amusement.

''Confess, Cilly, you enjoyed that.''

She paused, pretending to consider the matter, then, summoning up her coolest manner, she said, ''It was a new experience, sir, and not unpleasant. I daresay that in time I shall come to like it well enough.''

''Methinks the lady doth underrate herself,'' Ravenwood mused gently to the ambient air. Then he looked at Cicely. ''I daresay, my dear, that you are going to require delicate handling. But you may have every confidence in me. I shall not fail you. Now,'' he added, seeming not to notice her quizzical stare, ''shall we join the others in the drawing room?''

Numbly Cicely let him draw her hand into the crook of his arm. She was scarcely aware of anything beyond the light scent of him as he guided her from the room, his own composure completely unscathed.

5

For the next few days, although he was exceedingly polite to her, she found that she did not know what to expect from Ravenwood from one moment to the next. Though she might suddenly encounter that caressing gaze, he made no effort to kiss her again. Nor did he make the mistake of whispering sweet nothings into her ear, and for that much she was grateful, particularly after that one brief moment when she had feared he meant to insult her intelligence by pretending to carry a tenderness for her. She was certain the look in his eye that she found so disturbing was calculated on his part to do exactly that—to tease her—and so she made a studied effort of her own to pretend it did not affect her in the slightest. It would nearly always be replaced, as soon as she'd taken note of it, by that glint of lazy amusement, and if the latter expression was also disturbing to her emotions, it was nonetheless more easily dealt with. She would simply tilt her chin a trifle higher and pretend to ignore it.

The second day of his visit, the two of them went riding together, choosing a path that led along the lakeshore and through the Home Wood. On the way back, Cicely suddenly leaned over Connie's neck and gave spur, then shouted a challenge to her surprised escort. But Ravenwood hesitated barely a moment before setting off in pursuit of her, his own mount straining to catch the flying Conabos.

Cicely heard the thunder of hooves behind her on the lake trail, but she held her lead until they neared the stableyard, when automatically she began to rein the gelding to a slower pace. At that moment Ravenwood seemed to spur his mount to greater effort, thus passing through the gates and into the yard ahead of her.

"That was unfair," she said when they had dismounted.

"I don't like to lose," he replied. "And you set the pace, after all."

"But I slowed down, and you did not, so if the stablemaster tells Papa that we thundered into the yard like a pair of heathens—which is just the way he would tell it—I hope you will be gentleman enough to shoulder the responsibility, sir."

"Afraid we shall be sent to bed without our supper, Princess?" he teased.

She looked up at him again, the amusement in his eyes now reflected in her own. "A shabby thrust, my lord, though I suppose I should have guessed you'd find a way of throwing that business up to me again. How unhandsome of you! Moreover, if I recall that incident properly, only I was sent to bed. You dined in splendor."

He chuckled again, clearly pleased that she remembered the incident. "Where was it that we went that day?"

"Squire Treedle's," she replied promptly. "And then the long way home through the Deer Park to find Papa pacing back and forth in the yard, muttering to himself about what he would do to us if we ever returned. We were dreadfully late."

"A minor detail, as I remember it," he pointed out, "since we had roused the squire to fury by racing our horses directly across his seedling cornfield. Your challenge, of course."

"I thought 'twas merely a field of weeds," she reflected ruefully.

"It *was* mostly weeds. A worse-kept field I hope never to see again. I'd have a few choice things to say to someone if any of my fields ever looked like that one did. However, the duke cared less for that, as I recall it, than he did for his neighbor's good will. And lest you still think you bore the brunt of that business, my girl, let me take this opportunity to set the record straight. I may have got my supper, but I suffered through a right rare trimming for the privilege." The expression in his eyes warmed suddenly, and Cicely turned her attention toward the walkway, lengthening her stride.

"You were a good deal older than I and richly deserved a trimming, sir," she muttered. "I only wish I might have been privileged to hear it."

"My dear child," he murmured dulcetly, "I should have been more than happy to have *shared* it with you."

She laughed at that, turning her merry eyes up to his again, finding gratefully that the odd look that had so disturbed her had disappeared.

Three days later, when Ravenwood announced that he must leave in order to clear some trifling matters of business before the wedding, set for a date three weeks distant, Cicely felt that she still knew very little about the man. He was still a prankster of sorts and a tease. And he was at least dandified, if not entirely foppish. But she had caught an occasional glimpse of unsuspected strength of character as well. He was gentle with Brittany, entered into amusements with Amalie as though he were still a boy, talked sensibly with Arabella about her music, and let Alicia pit her skills in the French language against his own. He also exerted himself to be charming to the duchess and never failed to speak a kind word to Miss Fellows.

The thing that impressed Cicely from the outset, however, was his ability to understand Alicia's quicksilver nature. He seemed to have a gift for diverting her whenever she was about to make one of her inimitable faux pas, and when he failed in that, he generally managed to catch her before she was entirely in the briars.

On the last evening of Ravenwood's visit the duke agreed that she might join the family for dinner, and Alicia entered the saloon where the others had gathered, looking as self-conscious as though she was certain everyone must be thinking of her recent disgrace. Cicely, stepping forward quickly, did what she could to make Alicia forget about herself, but it was Ravenwood, coming to stand at her side, who successfully drew the younger girl into conversation.

"*Bon soir, mademoiselle,*" he said with a formal, elaborate bow.

Alicia, chuckling, replied in kind, and the two quickly launched into Gallic babbling. Cicely waited until she had twice seen the duke glance their way before intervening with a grin. "Not tonight, you two. None of us here wishes to stretch the mind to follow your so excellent French. Speak English, or don't speak at all."

Ravenwood grinned back at her, stirring that sudden tingling sensation that seemed to come when she least expected it. "Don't interrupt, my girl," he drawled. "The Lady Alicia has a knack for the *bon mot*. I find her conversation in either language extremely stimulating.''

Alicia blushed, but Cicely noticed that the glance the younger girl shot at the viscount was filled with warm gratitude. Moments later, however, when she showed a wish to continue their French conversation, Ravenwood deftly steered her back into English and thence into the general conversation around them. He did it so adroitly that Cicely was nearly certain her sister was unaware of being maneuvered, and by the time they went into dinner Alicia was her normal, buoyant self. Cicely realized that part of Ravenwood's success lay in the fact that he treated Alicia as though she were an equal. There was no condescension in his manner toward her. Nor was there any sign of the indulgent tone he often used with Brittany.

He was seated next to Cicely at the table, as usual, and from time to time she sent him a slanting look as she tried to analyze him again. It occurred to her that that had become nearly a constant process with her. But he intrigued her. There seemed to be so many facets to the man. All in all, however, she decided he was an enigma.

Conversation drifted to plans for the wedding and then, quite naturally, to the journey to London.

''I daresay our Aunt Uffington will have managed to reach Town before us,'' commented Arabella with a smile. ''She nearly always does so, does she not?''

''Indeed,'' replied the duchess, a glint of humor in her eye. ''Sometimes I doubt my sister ever actually takes the knocker from her London door. It is a good thing that she keeps such an excellent bailiff in Dorset, else her property there must go to rack and ruin for all the mind she pays it.''

''Surely Sir Conrad must keep an eye out for her interests,'' put in Cicely.

''If my nephew has a thought to waste upon anything but himself, I've never noticed it,'' stated her grace with unusual tartness. ''It would do him good to think of his mother's interests, but I doubt he spares the time.''

''She probably wouldn't heed him anyway,'' Alicia commented thoughtfully. ''I heard her say once that what her dunderhead son knew about the property wasn't worth the bit of paper it would take to scribble the words upon.''

''A Tartar, is she?'' Ravenwood said quickly, glancing

directly at the duke, whose complexion had taken on a deeper color at Alicia's thoughtless words. "I've a maternal aunt very much like that myself. Wears lace caps and looks like anyone's favorite sweet old lady, but she's got a tongue that would make a sailor blush. Told me once I wasn't worth the bit of powder one of the damned poachers that plague her lands would use to blow me away."

Malmesbury's only reaction was a curt shrug and a sound that might have been a grunt. If Cicely was initially surprised by his lack of comment on the interchange, she quickly realized that although he might well have scolded Alicia for her breach of manners, he could not do so now without rebuking Ravenwood as well. And though he might have taken a twenty-year-old youth to task for such talk, he would not reprimand a twenty-six-year-old man who was, furthermore, his daughter's intended husband.

Alicia had giggled and looked as though she might expound more of her views upon the subject of maternal aunts, but a quelling look from under Ravenwood's brows silenced her effectively. Cicely saw the look and was amazed that Alicia responded so easily and without resentment. Then she looked at her father again, still a little surprised that he had remained silent. Malmesbury had returned his full attention to his dinner, however, and the conversation went on, albeit along more conventional lines.

The following morning Ravenwood took his leave of them, and Cicely was astonished by the sense of emptiness he left behind. Each of her sisters seemed to miss him, and if she were honest with herself, she had to admit that she, too, felt a void in his wake.

But the days flew quickly, what with all the plans and preparations that had to be made, and Cicely soon found herself too wrapped up in the business at hand to think much about Ravenwood. Indeed, she did not think of him above two or three times each day.

He did not write to her, although to have done so would have been perfectly proper. Nor did any other communication arrive from him; although, since the duke had called in workmen to refurbish the north wing for the newlyweds' immediate occupancy and had written Ravenwood to solicit his suggestions in such important matters as color and furniture style, some sort of reply might have been expected.

The big day arrived at last, however, and Cicely, surrounded by her excited sisters, spent the early part of the
morning preparing herself for the ceremony, which was to
take place in the duke's private chapel. She knew that
Ravenwood, safely in the north wing of the great house so as
to take no chance of his accidentally laying eyes upon the
bride before the ceremony, was likewise preparing himself.
She had met his mother at supper the previous night, and her
thoughts dwelt for a moment upon the dowager viscountess.

Lady Ravenwood had proved to be a quiet-spoken woman
of fragile appearance who seemed to regard her large son
with the same lazy amusement in her eyes that Cicely had
seen so often in his. Other than that, there seemed to be no
resemblance between the slight, well-preserved, white-haired
lady and her broad-shouldered, dark, and drawling son. Cicely had liked her well enough, but thought her reserved. She
herself had been cool and serene, but Ravenwood had re-
frained for once from baiting her.

Now she watched critically as Meg Hardy twitched the
ivory silk skirt of her slim, high-waisted gown into place.
Amalie handed her the pearls that had been a bride gift from
her husband-to-be. They were particularly beautiful, perfectly
matched, and the clasp of rubies and diamonds formed her
initials. She fastened them around her neck, then turned so
that Brittany could settle the flowered headpiece into place.
Cicely's fine, straight hair flowed down her back, nearly to
her waist, gleaming almost silvery against the simple gown.
The headdress was anchored tightly over a long, soft, lacy
scarf, the ends of which were then draped over her arms at
the elbow. Stepping into dainty satin slippers, Cicely took a
final look at herself in the long cheval glass, then glanced a
bit nervously at the others.

Until that moment she had not given any real thought to the
finality of the step she was about to take. Annulment or
divorce—the latter possible only by act of Parliament in
extreme cases, though not unheard of even in ducal circles—
were not remedies Cicely could contemplate for herself. She
would be married until death separated her from Ravenwood.

Just as the finality of marriage had been a long while
occurring to her, so, too, had it taken her till those few
moments before departing for the chapel to wonder what
might be his reaction to her determination to maintain a

certain distance between them. She thought of it now and, with the aid of his three weeks' absence, was easily able to persuade herself that he would throw no rub in the way if she decided to enjoy the Season in London as a modern married lady. Indeed, she told herself, by refusing to live in his pocket, she would be thought a model wife. A tiny tickle of doubt greeted this last notion, but she suppressed it. Surely Ravenwood understood how marriages were conducted in London these days and would expect his wife to understand it, too. There would certainly be no point to pretending theirs was a love match instead of the marriage of convenience that it was. No one would expect that. Why, love matches were still considered by a good many people to be offensive. Everyone, including Ravenwood, would expect her to follow her own course.

Of course it would still be nearly two weeks before the family went up to Town, she reminded herself as she and her sisters walked the long corridors leading to the chapel. That meant she still had some time, and on her own ground at that, to make her views on the subject clear to him. Just in case he hadn't previously thought the matter out for himself.

The spacious chapel was decked with spring flowers and filled with guests. For the comfort of the elderly and other less hardy folk amongst them, the fires had been ordered kept up for the past four days, so the chapel was warm and its stone walls perfectly dry. But Cicely, entering on her father's arm, was scarcely conscious of the warmth or of the multitude of guests. Indeed, she went through the ceremony itself in a near daze, stirring only at the touch of Ravenwood's hand when he slipped the wide, intricately twisted gold band onto the third finger of her left hand.

She was suddenly conscious that the tall, dark, near stranger looming over her, making her almost forget the presence of the rector himself, let alone that of the many guests, was establishing his rights over her very body by this ceremony. No longer would she be subject to her father's will. Now she must bow to Ravenwood. She looked up at him, her eyes widening at the thought. She could not think he would be a cruel husband, though there would be little to protect her ~~n~~ him should he prove to be so, but she had no substantial ~~to~~ expect him to be a kind one, either. It would be up ~~to her she dec~~ided, to establish the fact as quickly as possible that she was no milk-and-water miss to bow to his simplest wish or cringe at his slightest displeasure.

The ceremony ended rather abruptly with the rector presenting the Viscount and Viscountess Ravenwood. "May God speed them well," he added kindly.

"Amen," came the fervent reply from the assembly, and Cicely was a married lady. As they walked together out of the chapel and into the adjoining garden court, she was more aware than ever of her husband's presence at her side. A moment later she felt his light touch between her shoulder blades and glanced up, almost shyly, to find him smiling at her.

"Yes, my lord?"

"My name is Gilbert, Cilly," he said gently.

Without thinking, she opened her mouth to inform him once again that she had not made him free of her name, let alone that awful nickname, only to feel warmth invading her cheeks as she realized, before the words were out, that she could no longer say such things to him. When a mocking gleam in his eye told her he had interpreted her fleeting expressions accurately, she looked away, nibbling at her lower lip in frustration.

"That lady in the green gown over there is attempting to engage your attention, my dear," he said softly near her ear. Cicely turned in the direction he indicated and saw Lady Treedle approaching, her customary country stride not in the least hampered by sensibly flowing skirts.

"What good weather you've managed for this do," she said cheerfully, holding out a hand to Cicely. Instead of the normal, light, two-fingered touch, Cicely found her hand grasped solidly between the other lady's two. "A good match, my dear," said Lady Treedle comfortably. "You'll take good care of her, I know, my lord."

"Indeed, I shall, ma'am. You've no need to worry on that head."

"I know that. I like what I see. Mind you, the lass has an odd kick in her gallop from time to time, but I daresay you'll keep a firm hand on the rein, Ravenwood."

Cicely stiffened with indignation, causing both Lady Treedle and Ravenwood to chuckle companionably. "Gently, Princess," he murmured. "Your frost is showing." She shot him what she hoped was an icy glare and gathered her dignity, grateful when Lady Treedle soon gave way to another well-wisher. Others followed after that until Ravenwood took her arm firmly and announced his intention of repairing to the dining room to begin the wedding breakfast. "Though why they want to call it breakfast I've never understood," he added with a provocative grin. "'Tis served well after one o'clock and the menu will doubtless contain little of such stuff as graces one's breakfast table, so I ask you . . ." He paused hopefully, but Cicely had no intention of entering into a semantical debate with him. Not when she knew perfectly well that his sole purpose in the exercise was to bait her into abandoning her careful serenity.

It was a banquet befitting the rank of the host and hostess, and as course followed course, side dishes were removed and replaced with a speed that was nearly unnerving. Not one of the guests would go home complaining that there was nothing fit to eat, because the duke's chef had outdone himself, and the footmen and maidservants provided such excellent service that scarcely did a guest make a wish known before it was satisfied. There was much laughter and some ribaldry, although the latter, due to the duke's well-known views on the subject, was kept to a bare minimum and indeed did not rear its head until well into the third course, by which time many glasses of wine had been consumed.

There were the usual toasts to the couple's happiness and hoped-for fertility. There were others to the pleasures both would presumably be leaving behind as well as to those that lay ahead, and it was such toasts as these that led to what ribaldry the guests did permit themselves. Cicely found herself blushing upon more than one occasion. At last, however, the huge bride cake, or wedding cake, as many were beginning to call it, was brought in and paraded around the long table so that all might have a good look before it was sliced. It was a magnificent thing, covered with white icing and decorated to resemble the great ducal house itself. Its appearance was greeted with applause, and before long a thick slice was handed to Cicely, that she might present the first taste to her husband from her own hand and thus symbolize her submission to his will. Hoping he would realize the gesture was merely symbolic, she held the piece toward him, ignoring the dancing humor in his eyes.

Her expression must have given her away because the light

humor suddenly changed to a glint of mockery, and Ravenwood's big hand encircled her small wrist, trapping it in place as he slowly took his bite, never taking his gaze from hers. Angrily she tried to pull away, but the grip tightened bruisingly, making her gasp at the sudden pain of it. The small sound seemed to make Ravenwood aware of what he had done, and he released her, apologizing smoothly.

"I fear I don't know my own strength, Princess. My turn now." So saying, he took what was left of the piece of cake from her hand and offered it to her. Obediently she took a small bite, but she was wishing furiously that she had had the nerve, when she'd had the opportunity, to gag him with it. It was not until she noticed Ravenwood's mocking grin that she realized the others were staring at her and knew that once again he had stirred her into betraying her feelings. Her grey eyes were flashing sparks, and her jaw was clenched with anger. With a struggle she brought her emotions under control again and turned back to watch the servants pass out cake to the guests.

There were more toasts, and she was beginning to feel sleepy, despite the fact that it was not yet even late afternoon, when suddenly Ravenwood leaned toward her and whispered, "If you don't want to leave here in your wedding gown, I suggest you excuse yourself to change."

She turned sharply to face him, her astonishment clear. "Leave here! But nothing was said about leaving. I understood that our bride tour had been postponed until after the Season closes, that we were to stay here until it was time to leave for Town." She nearly shivered with mixed feelings of exhilaration and apprehension.

"Those were indeed the plans outlined by his grace," Ravenwood agreed, still in an undertone, "but I must confess I did not second them. It seemed simpler somehow to play my cards close to my chest, however, since I had no wish to engage in a debate with him that he must lose."

She stared at him, amazed that he could determine what seemed to be such a bold course in the face of what would undoubtedly be incredible opposition. "But how? Papa will be furious. He expects us to live here with him and to stay at Malmesbury House in London."

"I can see no reason for not spending a good deal of time here later on, while I learn about my inheritance," he said quietly, "but since I have a perfectly good house of my own in London, I can think of no good reason for us to impose upon your parents whilst we are there. Nor can I think of one for permitting your esteemed father to dictate my movements or those of my wife. If you are ready, just make your excuses briefly. As soon as she sees you depart, Tani will follow to give you any assistance you might need."

"Tani! So she knows of this already?" He nodded. "But my clothes! How will we travel? Where are we going?" It was all she could do to keep her voice down.

He smiled encouragingly. "Your clothes are packed and by now should be on their way to London with my valet and Meg Hardy. We will travel in my traveling coach, of course. And, no, I don't intend that we shall reach London tonight. A friend has offered us the use of his house just south of Newmarket, however, so we shall have all the privacy we require without having to put up with the noise and bustle of a posting house." She still stared at him, finding it difficult to take in his words. It had been all settled in her mind that, although she would be married to him, she would remain with her own family, and here he was, casually informing her that he was as good as abducting her. He noticed her hesitation and covered her hand with his own, giving it a gentle squeeze. "Go now, Princess. I'll take care of matters here and meet you in the great hall in twenty minutes."

"You can't do this," she muttered, glaring at him. "I won't go."

The expression in his eyes hardened briefly before being replaced by that glimmer of amusement that maddened her so. "I confess, my dear, I intend to leave you no choice in the matter. Have you not promised to obey me?"

"Papa won't like this, my lord."

"Gilbert," he corrected gently. "And Papa has nothing to say to it, I fear. You are no longer his concern, you see, but mine. Now, don't sit there arguing, Princess. I assure you 'tis a waste of time."

Short of creating a scene in front of the assembled guests, she could think of nothing to do but obey him. Of course she could wrap herself in icy dignity and sit there like a rock, but that would afford her little in the way of victory and, depending upon his reaction, might well lead to a certain amount of embarrassment later, when their guests departed. The thought that he might simply pick her up and carry her out to the waiting coach flitted through her mind, leaving a small thrill in its wake. Nonetheless, she discarded the notion. He was entirely too sedentary of habit to do anything so energetic. Instead he would no doubt simply wait until things were more private and then insist that she obey. And she realized he was quite right in saying that although the duke would surely be annoyed, he could do nothing to stop Ravenwood from taking her away.

Accordingly, she excused herself to the gentleman on her left and nodded to the footman behind her chair. A moment later she had gained the relative quiet of the main corridor and was hurrying toward the stairway to her own bedchamber. A voice from behind halted her progress, and she turned to find Brittany upon her heels.

6

"My goodness," Brittany said. "You look just like Papa when he is in a rage, as he will be, of course, but Mama says she will manage him. Do you not think this is exciting?"

"I think the whole thing is high-handed and typical of Ravenwood, to say the very least."

"Why, how can you call it typical when you are forever saying he looks much too lazy to do anything exciting?"

Cicely was unable to answer that, but she insisted again that it was high-handed. "And did I understand you to say that my own mother has abetted him in this enterprise?"

"To be sure. And managed to keep still about it, as well," Brittany laughed. "Meg Hardy knows, too. She was so excited, it was all I could do to see that she kept her tongue between her teeth. But of course it would not have done for anyone else to know, lest the news somehow get to Papa. He would not have ignored it, you know, and Ravenwood feared it would lead to an estrangement between them if the matter were not handled adroitly."

"Adroitly! What about me? If my mother and sister could be told of it beforehand, why was I not informed? It is my life, after all, which is being ordered about without so much as an opinion being asked of me."

Brittany looked a trifle conscious. "We knew you would not like it, dear," she said in her gentle way. "However, we could not but agree with Ravenwood when he said you might cause the very stir he wished to avoid."

"I beg your pardon!" Cicely grated angrily.

"Well, you cannot deny that you have been doing what you can to annoy him, Cicely, ever since Papa's plan was made known to you. If we had told you of Ravenwood's decision, we feared you would go straight to Papa, if for no other reason than to make matters difficult for Ravenwood.''

Cicely opened her mouth indignantly to deny it, but honesty stifled the words at birth. She sighed. Brittany was right. She would have fought him, just as she fought him over everything. And since Malmesbury had already got it into his head that the newlyweds would remain at the park, it would have been a simple matter to enlist his aid on her behalf, thus causing just the sort of scene Ravenwood had hoped to avoid. ''I expect you are right, Tani,'' she said then. ''There is something about him that makes me want to strew his path with brambles. It's that sleepy look, I daresay. Makes me want to wake him up.''

Brittany chuckled, stepping into Cicely's bedchamber. ''I wouldn't count on that laziness, my dear. It seems to me that he has planned this little *coup* of his with military precision. Every arrangement has been made. Poor Meg thought she would never have your clothes packed in time. He told her only yesterday, you know, though he did manage to seek her out not five minutes after his arrival. Nevertheless, she was hard pressed to think how she could accomplish the task, particularly when it had to be done secretly.''

''However did she manage it?'' Cicely's traveling dress was laid out neatly upon her bed, and she let Brittany help her out of her wedding gown as she talked.

''Well, it is just as well you did not decide to search for something in your cupboards last night,'' Brittany said, smiling, ''for Meg had turned them all out whilst we were at dinner, and carried everything to my room. We had to take Sarah into our confidence, of course, but what with Meg threatening to throttle her and my telling her I should be most displeased if she breathed a word, we knew we could trust her to keep a still tongue. Nonetheless, the three of us were up until the wee hours finishing the task. Your trunks were loaded this morning, and the coach carrying them—and Meg as well, of course—will meet you at Lynsted Manor, where you will stay tonight. Oh, Cicely,'' she said suddenly, her violet eyes welling with tears, ''I shall miss you!''

''Draw rein, Tani,'' Cicely returned, her own voice suspiciously gruff. '' 'Tis only a matter of days now before we shall all be together in London.''

''But Ravenwood said—''

"Oh, don't be gooseish, for heaven's sake," snapped Cicely, not knowing whether her temper flared at the thought that they would not be together or at Brittany's continued use of the viscount's name. "I know we shall be in our own houses," she went on more gently, sorry now for the hurt look in her sister's eye, "but we shall see each other nearly every day. Ravenwood shan't have me on a leash, after all, and if I wish to see my sisters, I suppose I shall see them. And you must come to visit me, too. All of you. Why, do you realize that I can act as your chaperone? 'Twill be prodigious fun."

"I doubt Mama will permit it." Brittany smiled through her tears.

"Nonsense. Why should she not? When she was indisposed during my second Season, she turned me over to Aunt Uffington without a qualm."

"What qualm could she have?" Brittany asked with a chuckle. "Aunt Uffington is a dragon of the highest order. You'd not have dared to step out of line."

"True," Cicely agreed ruefully, "and if our positions were reversed, I daresay Mama would never let you be responsible for me. You would be too gentle to make me behave if I got the bit between my teeth. But she knows full well that she may trust *you* implicitly, Tani dear, no matter what doubts she may have about me. So I'll wager she will let you come out with me upon occasion."

Brittany was still doubtful, but she pursued the subject no further while Cicely continued to change from her wedding gown into the sof' dusky-rose, high-waisted gown with its matching light woolen spencer. With her sister's help she managed to confine her hair in a twisted plait at the nape of her neck. Then, pinching more color into her cheeks, she drew on her gloves and stepped away from the dressing table.

She still wore her lovely pearls, and she fingered them idly while she took a long look around the spacious bedchamber. It was the last time she would stand here as the duke's eldest daughter, she thought. Her feelings were mixed. There was a sadness at the thought of parting from her family, even from her irascible father. But there was also a sense of excitement at the new road that lay ahead of her. That the excitement was tinged with some apprehension was a matter not to be thought of just now. She had never been one to fear the future. She would not begin now.

"I suppose I'm ready to go downstairs," she said slowly.

Brittany gave an encouraging smile. "Are you a little frightened?"

"Not frightened, exactly," Cicely answered after a thoughtful pause. "Just . . . well, just curious about what lies ahead, I suppose."

Brittany stepped quickly forward and kissed her cheek. "It will go well with you, my dear. I know it will."

At that moment the door opened and the duchess entered. "Are you prepared to leave, Cicely dear? Ravenwood has spoken with your father, and I must say he seems to have taken it a good deal better than anyone might have expected."

"You mean he is not livid, ma'am?" Cicely asked, eyes wide.

"Not a bit of it. Ravenwood seems to have known just how to manage him."

"Well, how on earth . . ." Cicely began, only to break off when her mother flushed suddenly and looked guiltily at Brittany. But there was no help to be had from that quarter, for Brittany looked quite as curious as Cicely did. "Mama," said the latter firmly, "precisely what ruse did Ravenwood employ to make Papa agree so easily to his plan?"

"Well, he said . . ." began the duchess, only to have her words fade away when her courage failed her.

"Mama." There was warning in Cicely's tone that her temper was rising. The duchess regarded her unhappily.

"You will not like it, dearest."

"Of course I shall not," Cicely agreed calmly. "Has he not already proved himself capable of anything? What did he say?"

"I am certain he only thinks it will be better if the two of you have some time alone, away from the rest of the family, so that you might learn to know each other better."

Cicely stared at her for a moment speculatively. Then she frowned. "I daresay that's very likely true," she said, "but I shouldn't think that would weigh very heavily with Papa when he has got it into his head for us to live here. Ravenwood said something more than that, did he not?"

The duchess looked increasingly uncomfortable.

"What else did he say, Mama? No, no, do not look to Tani for assistance. Pray, ma'am, I do not mean to be uncivil, but

I have a strong interest in knowing what Ravenwood said, after all.''

The duchess took a deep breath to steady her nerves, but although she attempted to meet her eldest daughter's purposeful gaze, she could not seem to do so. At last, staring at a bedpost, she practically blurted the information that Ravenwood meant to use their time together to teach Cicely who was master.

''What?''

''Ravenwood never said such a thing, Mama,'' Brittany laughed over Cicely's protest. ''You must be making that up.''

''Well, to be sure, I did not hear their conversation,'' the duchess admitted, gazing doubtfully from one to the other, ''but those were the words your papa used when he described it to me. Ravenwood seems to have told him that it will be far easier for him to deal with Cicely if she cannot run to her family every time they have a falling out. And I must say, my dears, that is quite true. It *will* be better for both of you to get to know each other quite privately, without any interference from us, however well meant it might be. Your papa seemed to see that, too, you know, although what he said was that it will give Ravenwood more scope to see that . . . that is, to—''

''To put me in my place!'' Cicely snapped. ''Well, Ravenwood will soon find he has much mistaken the matter if he thinks to rule the roast entirely. I can promise you that. I have already shown him once that I can take care of myself, and, if necessary, it will afford me vast pleasure to remind him of the fact.'' She paced angrily to the window, muttering, ''Master, indeed! As though I were a puppy or a slave girl. Well!'' She turned, glaring. ''I am neither, Mama, and so he shall learn before he is very much older!''

''Cicely! Dearest, only calm yourself, and think what you are saying. Ravenwood is your husband now. He must be obeyed.''

''Fiddlesticks! Ours will be a modern marriage, and so I shall tell him. He will no doubt expect to have his amusements, you know, and what's sauce for the goose—no, he's the gander, is he not?—well, 'tis of no importance. What *is* important is that I mean to enjoy myself, and I've got no intention of catering to the whims of that . . . that . . .''

"Cicely!" The duchess was shocked. "Surely you cannot mean that you will . . . that you expect to entertain . . . that . . . that—" She broke off helplessly, and Cicely grinned at her distress.

"No, no, Mama, that's too bad of you! How could you think a daughter of yours would play her husband false?"

"Well, of course," hedged the duchess, "I did not truly believe it, dearest, only you sounded so vehement, you know, so . . . so angry."

"I *am* angry," Cicely acknowledged, "but I've no intention of cuckolding Ravenwood." The thought sent a sudden, unexpected shiver down her spine, but she braced herself against the discomforting sensation and continued glibly. "I certainly know better than to break such a hard-and-fast rule as to do so before the succession is secured at any rate."

Brittany chuckled, but their mother was not amused. Before she could make further protests, however, Cicely insisted that it was past time for her to meet Ravenwood in the great hall. Gathering up her fur-lined cloak, she took a last look around her bedchamber. Then, with a sigh, she turned toward the door.

The three descended the stairs together to be met by the rest of the family and a number of the guests. Other guests could be heard outside on the drive. Ravenwood looked up with a smile and stepped forward to meet his bride. Cicely glared at him, but he seemed not to notice, merely drawing her arm through his.

She kissed her mother and each of her sisters, then turned to the duke. Surprisingly he put out a hand and, when she placed hers within it, gave it a squeeze and pulled her nearer, looking directly into her eyes. Ravenwood stepped back, giving them a moment's privacy.

"You have made me a proud man today, daughter," Malmesbury said gruffly.

"Th-thank you, Papa," she replied, much moved by the unexpected words of praise from him.

He patted her shoulder. "See that you behave yourself, now. We'll all see you in London."

"Yes, Papa." She leaned forward impulsively and kissed his cheek. The hand on her shoulder tightened briefly, and then he stepped back. "Good-bye, Papa." She gazed up at him.

"God be with you, child."

Sudden tears sprang to her eyes, and she turned away quickly, barely aware of Ravenwood's hand at her elbow until his grip tightened, slowing her pace as they emerged onto the broad veranda under the high, pedimented portico. The guests assembled below, along the steps and drive, cheered their appearance, waving and shouting as they proceeded down the broad stone steps to the waiting coach. There was a general surge toward them; then, moments later, everyone stood quickly aside as Tom Coachman whipped up the team of magnificent bays. No one was so crass as to throw old boots, although the custom was one rapidly gaining favor at less genteel weddings. Instead they were sped on their way by an even louder chorus of cheers and good wishes for their future happiness. There were also one or two bits of shouted advice to which Cicely wisely turned a deaf ear.

Once they reached the main road, their pace slackened, and with the tall iron gates behind them, Cicely leaned back against the plush crimson squabs and forced herself to relax. She was well aware that her husband, seated opposite with his back to the horses, was watching her lazily. He wore the same outfit he had worn for the wedding, and he looked very well in it. Dark pantaloons fit skin tight over bulging calf and thigh muscles. His jacket was dark, as well, and certainly had required the efforts of someone besides Pavenham to urge it over those broad shoulders. As usual, his waistcoat was a thing of glory. Today he had chosen a cream-colored silk creation, embroidered with pink and gold roses and twining green leaves. He wore it over a white silk shirt, and again, both shirt and intricate neckcloth bore touches of fine lace. His gold-tasseled Hessians gleamed in a shaft of sunlight that had strayed through the glass window of the coach, and as she looked up again a ray of the sun sparkled on his signet ring, reminding her of the symbol of his possession that weighted her own left hand.

Glancing up still farther, she saw that he still watched her. His gaze held hers for a brief moment, but then she looked away again when he did not speak. Thus, for a time, she continued to ignore him. She was still thinking about her mother's words, but she couldn't think of a way by which she might introduce the subject of his conversation with her father without making him think she had more than a casual interest in the subject. From time to time she glanced at him, only to encounter that lazy look, which made her glance away again. It occurred to her that this was the first time she had ever been alone with a man in an enclosed carriage. By rights she ought to have been nervous, but she was not. Inwardly seething, she decided it was her anger with him that kept her from behaving like a shy miss.

How dared he tell her father such a thing! How dared he even think she would submit to his domination? She was no weak kitten. She was the daughter of a duke, and she had never bowed meekly to anyone's word. Had she been the sort of female who would kowtow to a man, she would certainly long since have bowed to her father, but of all his daughters, she had always been the least subservient. Though there had been times in her life when her father's bellowing had tied her stomach in knots, she had always been able to fight him when she felt she had to do so. She had not always won those fights, by any means, but she had never simply given in. And if the duke, with his temper, had not succeeded in developing submissiveness in her, certainly no sleepy dandy was going to achieve it.

Why didn't he speak? The carriage rambled noisily along the road, but thanks to the glass windows, it was not so noisy as to make conversation impossible. And the roads were not so dusty as they would be in summer. Then dust often invaded one's carriage despite any windows, making conversation a choking, coughing business at best. Cicely cleared her throat, unconsciously twisting the strand of pearls with one hand. Her anger seemed to be under control for the moment. Perhaps she could simply ask him about his conversation with the duke. It would be only natural for her to be curious, after all, and he could not know that her mother had already described it to her.

"Still angry?"

The two words, spoken casually, startled her. She looked up sharply to find him smiling at her.

"I am not angry, my lord." She spoke stiffly, however, and realized suddenly that her emotions were unpredictable. She did feel something, had felt it the moment he spoke. But whether it was anger or something else entirely, she did not know. Whatever it was, however, it seemed to make it difficult to answer him calmly.

"You were angry," he said now, still watching her under half-shut eyelids. "Was it because I took you by surprise, or was it something altogether different?"

Her eyes widened. "Surely your high-handed behavior is sufficient reason for my irritation, my lord."

"Perhaps," he agreed. "Still, I wonder why you choose to evade the question, Princess."

Blinking, she fought down an impulse to tell him precisely what she thought of him. Such an outburst could do her no good. Besides, she thought she had his measure sufficiently now to know how to manage him. She smiled.

"I confess, sir, there is perhaps a bit more to it than that, although 'tis not anger but my wretched female curiosity. I cannot imagine how you convinced Papa to accept our departure so meekly."

"I see." There followed a silence during which she thought she noted a brief glint of mockery in the lazily hooded eyes. But it disappeared before she could be certain. "I had thought somehow, from the rather conscious look upon her grace's countenance as the three of you came down the stairs, that she might already have described that scene to you," he said placidly.

Cicely felt the telltale warmth in her cheeks, but she ignored it, giving him look for look. "Mama was not present, sir, as you well know, and I found it difficult to credit the little she said Papa confided to her."

"How so?"

Cicely swallowed carefully. Did she dare? Careful phrasing was certainly necessary, so she spoke slowly, marshaling her thoughts as she talked. "Papa seems to think that you wanted me . . . wanted us, that is, to have some time alone in order to . . . well, so that you might assert some sort of—" She broke off, glancing at him to see if he would help her out. He merely gazed back, his expression showing nothing more than mild curiosity. Cicely gathered her wits. She simply wasn't the sort to deal in obscure phrasing. "Mama said that Papa said you meant to use the time to teach me who is master," she said bluntly. There, it was out. She looked at him again.

His expression did not change. "Do you need a master, Cilly?"

"No!" She flushed a little at her own vehemence,

but she managed to face him squarely. "I am my own person, Ravenwood, and since ours is merely a marriage of convenience—and your convenience, at that—I should take a very dim view of it if you were to attempt to demand subservience from me."

"I can imagine little that would be less appealing in you, my dear," he replied gently.

Her expression brightened. "Then you do not mean to interfere with me?"

An eyebrow lifted. "Interfere? You make it sound a most exhausting business. What sort of activities do you propose that might warrant husbandly interference?"

"Well, none precisely. But after what Mama said, I feared you might not be willing to let me go my own way about things. As . . . as you will go yours, of course."

"Will I?" He sounded surprised.

"Well, naturally, Ravenwood. Do not forget I am more than seven, sir. Scarcely a fledgling to Town ways. I know a great deal about how married men conduct their affairs."

"Do you indeed?" he inquired, looking amused.

"Of course I do. One cannot experience two London Seasons without learning a great deal. I am quite prepared to accept an opera dancer or . . . or a ladybird or Cytherean, sir."

"Not all at once, surely."

"Well, as to that, I am sure I don't know what the fashion is, but I daresay that to keep more than one or perhaps two at the outside might prove to be a trifle expensive."

"You might well say so. Not to mention that it would be prodigiously wearing." He cocked his head a little to one side, but she could not read his expression. "Am I . . . ah . . . to assume from these assurances of tolerance that I shall be expected to display equal tolerance toward similar pursuits on your part? To put the matter as delicately as possible," he murmured.

"Of course," she responded calmly. "Although I doubt it will be *exactly* the same."

"You cannot know how relieved I am to hear that. I really don't believe I could find sufficient generosity within myself to agree to finance a male opera dancer—or two—for my wife, you know."

Cicely chuckled, glad he was taking the matter so well.

"*Are* there such things as male opera dancers?" He shook his head as he smiled. "Well, you needn't be so absurd anyway, sir. You know perfectly well I never meant any such thing. I merely wanted to be certain that your conversation with Papa had been misinterpreted. I expected that, considering the circumstances of our marriage, you would have your own amusements and would leave me to mine. I was quite certain you would not want a wife watching over you every moment, but Mama's description of your talk with Papa made me fear you might expect me to be at your beck and call when you wished it and to sit quietly at home when you didn't. That would not agree with me at all, sir."

He regarded her seriously for a moment or two, long enough to make her wonder if he were displeased. But then his expression lightened. "Whatever I said to his grace, Cilly, I said in order to make it as easy as possible for him to let us go to London without a fuss. I don't expect you to live in my pocket. However," he added matter-of-factly, "I feel it only fair to warn you that it *is* possible to push me too far. I do not wish to seem unreasonable, of course, but I should take a strong dislike to my wife making a figure of herself among the beau monde."

"Well, I certainly shan't do that, my lord. I shall do nothing to disgrace you, and I can easily promise to do nothing that is not commonly done by married ladies in our circle."

"Perhaps that is why this whole conversation frightens the liver and lights out of me, madam," he replied with a wry little smile.

7

Cicely stared at him, but his expression was still as bland as though he had simply made a commonplace remark. She had no wish to pursue the subject, and Ravenwood made no attempt to change it, so there was little conversation between them after that. Leaning against the corner of the coach, she found that the rhythm of hoofbeats and rattling wheels soon became lulling, hypnotic. The scenery rolling past the opposite window began to blur around the edges. She settled more comfortably against the plush squabs, idly watching and listening. The next thing she heard was Ravenwood's low voice.

"You must wake up now, my dear."

Cicely blinked, disoriented. It was dark except for the orange glow from the square coach lanterns, which outlined Ravenwood's shape as he leaned over her. Then the coach slowed its pace, and the hoofbeats and carriage wheels made new sounds, higher pitched, no longer the thud and rattle of a vehicle on a dirt and gravel road but the clank and clatter of flag- or cobblestones. Then there were more lights, this time the lights of a large residence. At first she could see just the soft glow of candlelight through windows, but then the front door opened wide, spilling light onto a broad veranda. There was a flurry of shadowy shapes, and then torchlight sprang up, lighting the columns that flanked the entry as well as the shallow stone steps sweeping down to the drive.

"We have arrived at Lynsted Manor," Ravenwood said quietly. "I trust you enjoyed your nap."

"Nap!" Rubbing sleep from her eyes, she chuckled low in her throat. "I must have slept for hours. What time is it?"

"Only about half past eight. We lit the lanterns just an

hour or so ago. I expected you to wake when we stopped, but you slept right on.''

Cicely sat up a little straighter and realized that he had covered her with a woolen carriage blanket. She pushed it to one side and lifted a hand to her head, feeling the loose wisps of hair that had escaped her once-neat coif. "I must look a fright," she said.

She heard him laugh quietly. "Is this the same girl who said one should consider one's appearance only when one is choosing one's dress or deciding how to style one's hair?''

"Don't be daft, Ravenwood! Of course I must think of it now. You cannot want me to meet your friends looking like something dragged out of a gorse bush!''

"Better that, my dear, than risk having them frozen in place by one icy stare.''

"I don't do that!'' she exclaimed indignantly, still trying to set her appearance to rights.

"You must forgive me, then," he murmured as the coach door opened and a lackey wearing the Lynsted livery stood ready to assist them. Ravenwood stepped leisurely from the coach, then, dismissing the servant, offered to help her himself. "I have only hearsay to guide me, Cilly,'' he said as she put her hand in his, "but I have it on good authority that the term 'Ice Princess' was meant to cover more than just appearances.''

His large hand felt very warm as it wrapped around her much smaller one, but, reading disapproval in his words, she felt a tiny chill. She could think of nothing to say to the purpose, however, since she had no doubt that he was right. Therefore, shaking out her skirts, she drew herself up to her full height beside him and looked toward the front door.

"Where *are* your friends, Ravenwood?''

"I presume Lynsted is in London, my dear.''

"But I thought—''

"I said only that he was making his home and servants available, not that he would entertain us. I'm afraid we shall be left to our own devices in that regard.''

A suggestive note in his voice made her look up at him sharply and thus nearly lose her footing on the steps. But he steadied her easily, and a moment later they were in the main hall, and a very stiff footman was removing Cicely's cloak under the basilisk glare of an elderly butler. Once his minion had disappeared through a side door, however, the white-haired man unbent sufficiently to bestow a smile upon the viscount.

"Good to see you again, my lord. And this must be Lady Ravenwood?"

"Indeed she is, Mawson. Unless, of course, she wishes to remain Lady Cicely Leighton." He glanced at her. "We haven't discussed that, but it would be perfectly proper, you know."

She smiled at him. " 'Tis not a matter which must be decided on the instant, my lord."

"Of course not, my lady," he responded with a slight emphasis on the last two words. Then, blandly, he turned back to the butler. "Mawson, we shall require dinner. I hope you are prepared to serve it quickly, too, else I warn you I shall very likely perish from starvation."

"Very good, my lord. In twenty minutes. Perhaps you and her ladyship would care to partake of some light refreshment in the library whilst you wait. Madeira?"

"To be sure. Come along, Cicely. The library here is wonderful."

"I should be grateful for a small glass of wine, sir, but first, I beg of you, allow me a few moments to find Meg and repair my appearance."

He chuckled. "Take her upstairs, Mawson, and turn her over to her abigail. But mind, Princess, not above ten minutes. I truly do want to show you the library."

Cicely hurried up a wide, spiral staircase in the butler's wake and soon found herself in a splendid set of apartments. The sitting room was decorated in shades of blue with touches of white, including the low, simple Adam fireplace, where a cheerful fire welcomed her. No sooner had they entered from the corridor, however, than Meg Hardy appeared at one of two opposing doors that led off the sitting room.

"Miss Cicely!"

"Meg!" The butler's eyes warmed at their greeting, and he turned away as they rushed toward each other. But at the doorway he turned back again.

"My lady?" She turned. "I shall send a footman to fetch you in ten minutes, ma'am, else you might chance to lose yourself in our corridors."

"Thank you, Mawson." She turned excitedly back to Meg. "What a lovely home this is!"

"Indeed, m'lady. Not so big as what we are accustomed to, of course, whatever that Mawson says about losing yourself, but nice enough in its way." She gazed speculatively at her mistress. "Be you angry, Miss Cicely? He gave me little choice in the matter."

Cicely grinned. "You deserve a diet of bread and water for not telling me what was in the wind, traitor, but I quite understand how it came about. Don't bother your head about it now. 'Tis over and done."

Clearly relieved, Meg Hardy bustled about, and before the footman arrived to fetch her, Cicely was rigged out in a fresh, shell-pink gown with her hair neatly dressed in a plaited crown, à la Didon. She accepted a light scarf of silver Albany gauze to drape across her elbows, and as she adjusted it her gaze fell upon the high, wide bed with its tall canopy and crocheted lace spread.

"Where are his lordship's rooms, Meg?" she asked carefully. There was a pregnant pause. She gazed directly at her tirewoman, now endeavoring to avoid her eye. "Meg?"

"His dressing room be the other side of the sitting room, m'lady," Meg murmured.

"And his bedchamber is beyond that?" There was heavy silence. Cicely looked back at the wide, lace-covered bed. "His bedchamber is not beyond, is it?"

"No, m'lady."

Before she had time to digest this information, the footman was at the door. As she followed the tall young man down the spiral stair, Cicely forced her mind to dwell upon the impressive array of Lynsted family portraits that lined the walls on either side of the stair. It could do her no good to dwell upon the thoughts that struggled to gain possession of her mind. By the time they reached the library and Ravenwood had poured her a small glass of Madeira, she thought she had herself well in hand.

The library was truly magnificent. It was a vast room, opening off the stair hall, with one long wall of tall windows giving a view onto a torchlit colonnade. There was a fireplace in the center of the opposing wall, flanked by seventeenth-century shelved cupboards, or book presses, as they had been called at that time. The doors and joinery were elaborately marbled and painted with grotesques views of the house and surrounding landscape, as well as portraits of the family. The

Lynsted family tree, magnificently illuminated and complete with appropriate coats of arms, was given a place of pride over the chimneypiece.

The furniture was comfortable, rather than formal, and Cicely could tell by looking that this was a room enjoyed by the family and not one kept merely for show, despite the elaborate presses, which Ravenwood explained had been part of an older house and had been stored in the attics for many years before being incorporated into James Wyatt's renovations some two decades before.

"Originally, I believe, they filled a much smaller room," he added.

"Why were they ever removed? They are beautiful."

He smiled at her. "They were not designed to store books in the same fashion as we do so today, which is why Lynsted's father ordered the additional shelving you see here. Our ancestors were very haphazard about that sort of thing. The presses were meant to store manuscripts, papers, and books— mostly piled atop one another. Not very convenient. A good many books were also stored in chests. Not until their sons had seen the Bodleian at Oxford did it occur to landowners to store books in vertical, tiered stacks. Now we think nothing of tiers, ladders, and galleries. Nearly every great house has something like that. This one has been kept simple by comparison."

"Does Ravenwood Hall boast a large library?"

He nodded. "And my house in London has a good one, too. Do you like to read, Cilly?"

Why on earth, she wondered, feeling warmth rush to her cheeks, did his use of that absurd nickname send her nerves galloping? "I like to read very much," she replied, keeping her voice, at least, under firm control, "but I daresay my tastes won't agree with yours. I confess to a veritable passion for romantic novels."

"Well, you'll not be disappointed. My mother likes them, too, and I am on the subscription list for nearly everything that is published, so I daresay you'll find something to amuse you." He glanced toward the double, pedimented door in the north wall, and she followed his gaze to discover Mawson standing there respectfully.

"Dinner is served, my lord."

"Ah, good work, Mawson. Shall we, my dear?"

She let him take her arm, and they followed the butler into a formal, crimson-and-gilt drawing room, then through a spacious marbled anteroom, to a splendid, candlelit dining room. The long table was draped with white damask, and places had been set at either end with heavy silver, matching liners, and exquisitely cut crystal glassware. A centerpiece of ivy and evergreens occupied space between two splendid candelabra. Ravenwood frowned.

"I had forgotten how big this table is, Mawson. I've no wish to begin my marriage by shouting at my bride."

"Of course not, my lord." He gestured, and one of the stiffly starched footmen leaped forward. Seconds later, Cicely found herself seated at her husband's right hand, sampling oyster patties, turkey, haricot of mutton, and roast chicken. The removes for this first course included vermicelli soup, sweetbreads à la Daub, and broccoli, among others. Truly, Lynsted's servants had exerted themselves to please their master's guests.

For once in her life Cicely felt nearly tongue-tied. She almost wished Ravenwood had left her at the foot of the table, where he might not have expected her to speak to him. Thus far their conversation had been limited to his suggestion that she try the sweetbreads and her comment that the turkey was uncommonly tender. But no matter how hard she tried to concentrate upon her food, her thoughts kept flying back to that wide, lace-covered bed upstairs. It had been possible, in the magnificent library, to force such thoughts to the back of her mind, to play the role of a guest being entertained or some such thing; but now, sitting so near to him, conscious of each bite he took, even more conscious of each bite she took herself, Cicely could seem to think of little else. Her thoughts dwelt stubbornly upon that bed and what would undoubtedly take place there later on. She trembled a little at the thought.

"Are you cold? Shall I tell them to build up the fire?"

She started, feeling suddenly very hot as though he had somehow intercepted her thoughts. "No! That is," she amended, struggling for calm, "I—I'm perfectly comfortable, thank you, sir. Are these oyster patties not delicious?"

"Excellent," he agreed, watching her more closely than was compatible with her comfort. She wondered if she might have got a piece of broccoli caught between her teeth. Chewing her food seemed to require an enormous effort suddenly, and she set down her knife and fork, swallowing carefully, her eyes directed at the centerpiece.

Her silver-crested china plate was immediately taken away to be replaced by a clean one. The platters of turkey and oyster patties were swept off to the kitchens to make way for the prawns and apple puffs of the second course. Absently Cicely accepted a few slices of duckling, some fresh asparagus, mushrooms, and a rib of lamb, before she realized she could never eat so much as all that and waved away the scalloped oysters and Pompadour cream.

Ravenwood made no attempt to press her into conversation but began instead to tell her something of the history of the house. She heard of its comparatively humble beginnings in the early sixteenth century and even managed to take in some of the subsequent developments of the seventeenth and eighteenth centuries, during which the Lynsted family had somehow come into its own, despite ructions between Stuarts and Cromwells, as well as various religious difficulties. But when he mentioned the refurbishing of the state apartments to house King Charles II, Cicely found her mind drifting to beds again.

She would see Ravenwood without his clothes on. Nibbling a prawn and nodding absently to make him think she was listening, she considered the fact. Somehow she had not considered it before. She had persuaded herself that they would keep a proper distance between them. Indeed, she had persuaded herself so completely that she had quite failed to consider whether she could successfully maintain that distance twenty-four hours a day. It had been foolish of her, she realized now, not to have thought of this before.

Of course their sleeping arrangements had no doubt been arranged by the servants or even by Lynsted. Regardless, they had been arranged before she had made her position clear to Ravenwood. Perhaps he could be convinced—

"You are not eating, my dear, nor do I flatter myself that you are attending to my prodigiously entertaining monologue. Perhaps you would like some fruit and cheese?"

"No, thank you, sir," she answered quickly, her thoughts recalled to the present. "I fear I am no longer very hungry, although it was all most delicious."

"Perhaps, then, you would care to retire," he suggested gently.

"Retire?" Her eyes flew wide at that, but then she had another, more comforting thought. "Oh, you mean that I should leave you to your port now. Of course, if you wish it, sir." She began to push back her chair, but he shook his head.

"That is not what I meant. I find I have little taste for port tonight."

"Oh! But 'tis early yet, quite early, Ravenwood."

"There is nothing to fear, Cilly."

"Is there not?" Fighting sudden panic, she looked around the room, telling herself defensively that it was not panic at all but embarrassment because of the servants. But for the moment the room was empty. No one else had overheard the exchange. She looked back at Ravenwood to find that he was smiling, but for once there was no deviltry or mockery in the smile. She returned it weakly. "Does that mean, sir, that you do not intend . . . that is, that we—" She broke off, blushing and hating the telltale color, then began again, hoping she sounded a great deal more sure of herself than she felt. "Well, we have agreed to go our separate ways, have we not?" A glint of amusement leaped to his eye, and she bit her lower lip. She was behaving idiotically, she told herself angrily. Nonetheless, she held her breath, waiting for him to speak.

"I meant nothing of the sort," he said at last calmly. "You are my wife now, Cicely, and the sooner we consummate this union, the better, I think. You have expressed a desire for a certain amount of freedom within the marriage, and I can see no reason as yet why you should not be granted that freedom. But I am your husband, and I do not propose to waive any of the rights of that position."

"I—I see." She swallowed with difficulty. He had spoken quietly and without a trace of anger, but she still felt as though she had been given a setdown. And why, she asked herself, watching him, did she feel as though it had been well deserved? Could it be that she didn't want him to waive any of his rights?

He was certainly very handsome. The dark jacket set off the whiteness of his shirt and neckcloth, the texture of the silk-embroidered waistcoat However, it was not his clothes that fascinated her so, but the hard-muscled body beneath them. Ravenwood smiled again, and she noted the fine, even white teeth, the tanned face and deep blue eyes, the way his eyebrows seemed to bristle. She remembered what it had felt like to have his arms around her, to be kissed by him. A tremor stirred deep within her. She wondered what it would be like to let him lead her on an exploration of those delightful mysteries of love that until now had been little more than the subject of halting and no doubt naive discussions with Brittany. A footman entered, breaking into this intriguing train of thought.

"Shall we go up, my dear?"

Taking herself firmly in hand, she nodded, and the footman sprang to hold her chair. Ravenwood offered his arm. By the time they were halfway up the spiral stair, though still nervous, she was tingling with anticipation of what the night would bring. When they reached the blue-and-white sitting room, Ravenwood looked down at her.

"You did well enough with ten minutes to prepare yourself for dinner. Do you think you can manage with fifteen now?" She nodded, her gaze meeting his quite easily. "Very well," he continued in a tone that was nearly caressing now, "but don't get to gossiping with that Meg of yours. I shall send her away if she is still there when I come to you."

She watched, rather dazed, as he disappeared into his dressing room, then, recollecting his parting words, hurried into the bedchamber to find Meg waiting for her. Hurrying, she stripped off her dress and washed her face and hands before donning the lacy nightdress Meg held ready for her. Then she sat at the candlelit dressing table and tried to relax while Meg brushed out her hair.

"Stir up the fire a bit, Meg," she requested in a voice that sounded oddly unlike her own when the woman had laid the silver-backed brush upon the dressing table. "Then you may take yourself off to bed."

"As you wish, ma'am." Meg bent quickly to the task and put another log on the glowing coals in the grate. Just as she was getting to her feet again there came a light tap on the door and Ravenwood entered, wearing a dark red woolen dressing gown. Meg wiped her hands quickly on her apron, bobbed a curtsy, and smiled at him, then bade them both good night. Ravenwood held the door for her.

Once she had gone, he turned to face Cicely. "You look lovely," he said quietly. "Your hair is like a silver cloud."

"Thank you, my lord."

"Gilbert."

"Thank you, Gilbert," she repeated obediently.

"Come here, Cilly."

Her emotions seemed suddenly to churn within her. She felt shy and a little frightened, but there was also a sort of tension and a sense of excitement. Even before she moved into his waiting arms she could anticipate his touch and the delightful tingling sensation it would bring.

A candle burned by the bedside, and Meg had left the two on the dressing table, but otherwise there was only the fire's glow to light the room. Ravenwood leaned over and snuffed the two tapers on the dressing table.

Cicely began to turn toward the bed then, but he stopped her. "Not yet, Cilly." He put a hand under her chin, tilting her face up just as he had done in the bookroom at Malmesbury.

The kiss was all that she had remembered it to be, and what followed was a good deal more than even her vivid imagination had ever led her to expect. The very touch of his hands on her body seemed to stir passions that she had never dreamed lay within her. She responded easily to his every move, letting him guide her and teach her, then, encouraged by his tenderness, learning to follow her own instincts as well. By the time he led her gently to the bed their clothing lay in a heap upon the floor, and she was more than ready for the delights that lay ahead.

Ravenwood held back the quilt for her, then slipped in beside her, holding her close to him, smoothing the fine hair away from her face. Then, without speaking, he kissed her, at first lingeringly, then more possessively as his passions began to build again. His hands teased her, caressing her lightly, until by her own movements Cicely seemed to be begging him to possess her. When he moved over her at last, his caresses became gentle again, and she knew he feared to hurt her, but she urged him on, gasping at the brief, aching pain when he penetrated her at last, then feeling weak with near-blissful relief when it was over. She looked up at him, her eyes wide, reflecting the light from the nearby candle.

"It will be better next time, Princess," he murmured. "It will not hurt you again."

"It was not so bad this time, sir," she said, smiling.

Later, as she lay with her head on her pillow, listening to his even breathing, punctuated by the crack of an occasional spark from the dying fire, Cicely thought there might possibly be an advantage or two to marriage aside from the freedom it would afford her in London. In fact, there had been a moment or two during the past hour when it had occurred to her that it might be possible for her to fall in love with her husband.

She stirred at the thought. It would never do, of course. He had said absolutely nothing about loving her, and therefore it would do her little good to be so foolish as to let her emotions carry her beyond the line of what was pleasing. Lovemaking was a requirement of marriage, the only means by which her father's wish for an heir of his own blood might be attained. And as for Ravenwood, he was but exercising his connubial rights. For her to think in terms of love could only result in heartache. He had said and done nothing to belie the fact that he expected exactly the sort of marriage that she had been led to believe was commonplace within their circle. In fact, although she had insisted, it had nevertheless been an act of generosity on his part to agree that he would not play the heavy-handed husband while she enjoyed the same, or nearly the same, benefits of a marriage of convenience that he would enjoy himself.

He stirred beside her, and she wondered what he would do if she woke him up. Would he be angry, or would he want to make love again? Would she ever come to know him well? He had seemed different again today and tonight. He had seemed a good deal more approachable in some ways, more enigmatic in others. He did not seem to share his feelings. But, then, what could she expect, she asked herself, when their relationship was based upon a matter of convenience and nothing more?

8

Cicely felt shy when she awoke the next morning, thinking to find Ravenwood still in her bed, but it was Meg Hardy who wished her good morning when she stirred. The master, she said, had been up for some time and wanted to be on the road as quickly as possible. Deciding she wanted nothing more for breakfast than a roll or two with her chocolate, Cicely was able to present herself, ready for travel, rather more rapidly than he might have expected. She read approval in his expression when he greeted her, but little more. If she had expected comment upon their activities of the previous night, she soon found she had mistaken her man. His greeting was polite, but he seemed rather sleepy and a bit preoccupied. At least there was nothing in his manner to make her feel self-conscious, but she was oddly disappointed when he did not behave in a more romantic manner.

It was a beautiful day for the drive to London. They left Lynsted Manor a little after ten o'clock and twenty minutes later had reached Linan and the Cambridge turnpike. Ravenwood made little effort to maintain a conversation in the coach beyond pointing out an occasional object of interest. Once they were past the turnpike, the pace was increased, and the noise from outside increased accordingly. Perhaps that was the reason he seemed disinclined to speak, Cicely thought. Besides, she scolded herself as she glanced at that handsome face opposite with its lazy, bored expression, what did she expect? She herself had set the ground rules, had she not? She could scarcely demand a modern relationship and then sulk when he did not behave like a hero from one of her favorite romances.

They stopped for a tidy nuncheon at the George in Bishop's

Storford, changed horses again at Epping, and by half past four Cicely was enjoying the sights, if not the smells, as the coach made its way through Hoxton into the streets of London by way of Shoreditch Highstreet. Then the coach passed along Old Street to Coswell and Aldersgate, past St. Bartholomew's and the Smithfield Market, up Holborn Hill to Broad Street, St. Giles, and into Oxford Street. From there it was but fifteen minutes before they reached Mayfair and Ravenwood's elegant house in Charles Street, just off Berkeley Square.

Cicely looked up at the tall house on the south side of the pleasant street and felt a small quiver of excitement at the thought that this was her new home. It was wider than most of the other homes along the street, with a brick front and wrought-iron trim. The window frames and the massive front door were dark wood, which was as highly polished as the heavy brass knocker and the matching lanterns at either side of the entrance. A liveried boy stood at the foot of the steps waiting to open the carriage door and help them to alight. Cicely's excitement showed in her posture and contrasted markedly with his lordship's leisurely descent from the carriage. He smiled at the linkboy

"Well, Harry?"

"Very well, thank you, m'lord. Welcome home, sir."

Ravenwood nodded and drew Cicely forward, his grip light at her elbow. "This is your new mistress, Harry, the Lady Cicely." He smiled at her. " 'Tis the easiest way," he said. "Otherwise we shall have two ladies Ravenwood whenever Mama comes to visit." Cicely nodded. She had no quarrel with that. As a duke's daughter it was perfectly proper for her to retain her own title, and it would certainly make matters easier whenever she and the dowager chanced to be in the same place at the same time.

Harry had bowed low, his color rising at such condescension from his master, and she smiled at him, increasing his confusion. His head bobbed with relief when the front door opened and two tall young footmen, followed by a stately, middle-aged butler, emerged from the house.

Ravenwood gave orders for his valise and Cicely's jewel box to be taken upstairs, then turned to his butler. "This is the Lady Cicely, Wigan. I should like her to meet Mrs. Steele and the other servants as soon as it may be arranged. We passed up our baggage coach somewhere about a mile south of Harlow, but when they arrive, send her ladyship's abigail up directly. We are dining out this evening.''

"We are? Oh! I beg your pardon, sir,'' she added quickly as she glanced at Wigan and then back at her husband. "You neglected to mention that to me. ' daresay it slipped your mind what with all our other conversation. With whom do we dine?''

"Lord and Lady Ribbesford,'' he responded smoothly, ignoring the barb. "She has invited a select group of friends, which to her ladyship means nearly everyone of her acquaintance who chances to be in Town. It is to be dinner, with what she calls 'little entertainments' afterward. That usually means card tables and possibly some dancing. It will be a good opportunity for you to meet some of my friends and to announce the fact that we have arrived in Town. Have you met Carolyn Ribbesford?''

"Indeed, I have,'' Cicely responded, following him up the steps and into the entry hall as she spoke. From the highly polished parquet floor to the crystal-decked chandelier and the exquisite friezework, it was a lovely room, a fine introduction to what appeared to be a beautiful house. "I've met her several times,'' she added, peeping curiously through an open door into a small saloon. "I thought her a kind and generous woman.''

"I daresay she is at that,'' Ravenwood mused, watching her. "Never gave it much thought myself. Has an excellent chef, though. It will be a good dinner.'' He lifted his quizzing glass and peered at her thoughtfully. "Daresay you'd like to rid yourself of some of that dust, my dear. Wigan, a bath for her ladyship.''

Cicely opened her mouth to protest that she would much rather meet the housekeeper and have a tour of the house before Meg Hardy arrived with her clothes, but looking down at her crumpled skirts, she realized he was in the right of it.

"What time are we expected tonight, my lord?''

"Dinner at nine, I believe,'' he replied, moving toward a side table and extracting a silver-edged card from a pile of similar articles in a Sèvres basket. He glanced at it, then handed it to her. "As I thought.''

Cicely took the card and read it through. There was a gracious note written in stylish copperplate on the reverse, ordering Ravenwood to bring his new bride, but it was a small notation engraved in the lower right-hand corner of the invitation itself that caught her eye: "Mr. Townsend will attend."

"Who is Mr. Townsend?" she asked, wrinkling her brow. "The name sounds familiar, but I cannot place it."

"John Townsend is Prinny's tame Bow Street Runner," Ravenwood answered. "I daresay he's been invited because of the rash of robberies over the past months. No one seems to be immune. He's quite a character, however. I think you will enjoy meeting him."

"But why has Lady Ribbesford put his name on the invitation?"

"Makes folks feel safe, I expect. Knowing their money and jewels will be under the guardian eye of Mr. Townsend himself. You'll come to find, my dear, that the ladies and, indeed, even some of the gentlemen think nearly as highly of John Townsend as he does himself."

Cicely chuckled, but she was looking forward to meeting the illustrious Mr. Townsend and couldn't deny it, even to herself. A moment later a tall, slender, brown-haired woman, dressed neatly in black bombazine, entered through the green baize door at the back of the hall.

"My lord, welcome home. I was informed of your arrival only moments ago. I expect, however, that you will find everything in order."

"I have no doubt of it, Mrs. Steele. Cicely, this is our housekeeper. You will come to treasure her as I do, for I daresay she is one of the most efficient of her ilk in London."

Cicely nodded as the woman made her curtsy. She had already been pleasantly surprised by the apparent order of the household, having somehow thought to find more of a bachelor's establishment with few servants and much clutter. She had expected the task of bringing such a household into order to fall upon her own shoulders. But although she had been bred to handle just such a task, she could not deny she would be grateful to leave things to the trim, clearly capable Mrs. Steele.

"Would you like me to show you to your apartments, my lady? Wigan will order a bath. I know you must be longing to relax and refresh yourself."

Willingly now, Cicely followed her up the graceful, carved

staircase, then through a well-appointed drawing room to another, less decorative stair that took them to the second floor and a charming bedchamber. The walls were white, pin-striped with silver; the carpet was an Aubusson with a muted floral pattern in soft greys, lavenders, and pinks, and the curtains and bed hangings were pale lavender velvet. A maid knelt before the fireplace stirring coals into low flames. She jumped up at their entrance, then made a low curtsy.

"This is Betty, my lady. She can help you until your own abigail arrives. Her ladyship wishes to bathe, Betty. The men will be bringing the tub shortly."

"Very good, mum," Betty replied, her cheeks pink with pleasure. "I be right glad to do fer 'er ladyship."

"I am sure you will do very well, Betty," Cicely said to her. Then she turned back to Mrs. Steele. "There is just one thing, Mrs. Steele." The woman smiled, looking quite friendly. "If my clothes have not arrived, and I don't see how they can have done so soon, I've not a stitch to put on but what I stand in."

Mrs. Steele's smile broadened. "His lordship thought of that, my lady. There are clothes in the wardrobe, including I'm sure, some sort of dressing gown."

Curious, Cicely stepped to the tall, carved wardrobe and pulled open the doors. Two evening gowns, a simple peach-colored frock, and a pale blue wool dressing gown hung there. "My gracious!"

"His lordship likes to be prepared for unexpected events," Mrs. Steele said. "He seldom leaves matters to chance. His bedchamber, by the by, is just through that door to the right, and your own sitting room is through the left-hand door. Will there be anything else now, ma'am?"

"No," Cicely answered absently, still staring at the dresses. Then she realized Mrs. Steele was on the point of leaving and turned quickly. "There is something else." The woman turned back. Cicely thought she had never seen anyone so calm, so placid. No wonder Ravenwood liked her, she thought. Mrs. Steele was regarding her curiously. "I'd appreciate it if you would show me over the house after I've bathed. And do you suppose you could send up some fruit and cheese. I'm starving, and I'd just as soon not show it at Lady Ribbesford's table this evening."

Real humor lit Mrs. Steele's eyes. "At once, my lady.

And when you wish for me to attend you, simply have Betty ring for me."

The hot bath was refreshing. Afterward, wrapped in the wool dressing gown and toasting her toes before the fire, Cicely relaxed, nibbling on an apple while Betty brushed her hair dry. Deciding she could not with propriety wander over the house in a wool dressing gown, she put on the peach frock before asking Betty to ring for the housekeeper.

By the time she returned to her room she had decided she liked both the house and the housekeeper very much indeed. The house was a good deal smaller than anything she had previously lived in, but it was exceedingly comfortable and elegantly appointed. Clearly Ravenwood was not completely without a shirt. This had not been accomplished at three weeks' notice. Besides, according to Mrs. Steele, she had been housekeeper here for nearly twelve years, which meant she had worked for Ravenwood's father. Indeed, she mentioned that the dowager Lady Ravenwood had spent the last Season in the house while Ravenwood was on the Continent.

"Will she be staying with us, do you think?" Cicely had asked her. But Mrs. Steele couldn't say. It would be Lady Ravenwood's decision.

Cicely had liked the fragile dowager, and when she and Ravenwood were leaving for Ribbesford House, she asked him whether his mother would pay them a visit.

"As she chooses," he replied. "Will you mind?"

"Of course not. I liked her."

"That relieves my mind considerably," he responded promptly. "Mama does as she pleases, I fear. If I invite her, she is sure to say she has a palsy or an ague or the gout or some such thing."

"Not gout!"

"Gout," he repeated firmly, but the twinkle lurked in his deep blue eyes. "Don't interrupt. I was about to add that though she never comes when invited, she inevitably arrives just when you least expect—or want—her to arrive." There was a deeper gleam in his eye now, which led Cicely to suspect that Lady Ravenwood had arrived at an inopportune moment at least once. She longed to ask him about it but, fearing a setdown, held her tongue. "You're looking quite fetching tonight, by the by," he said after a brief pause.

She was pleased. Having nearly given up hope that Meg

and her own dresses would arrive in time, she had asked Betty to fetch out one of the evening gowns in the wardrobe. Unfortunately, though the fit was adequate, it was not what she was used to, so when Meg walked in five minutes later, she practically fell upon her neck in relief.

"I am sorry not to wear one of those exquisite gowns you provided," she said now. "It was thoughtful of you."

"Daresay they didn't fit properly. I was afraid of that."

"Well . . ." She remembered Meg's scandalized comments and stifled a chuckle. "I am certain very little alteration will be required. 'Tis simply that you overestimated one portion of my anatomy and slightly underestimated another." She shot him a mischievous look. "I hope the former was not by wishful thinking, sir. There is very little I can do to make myself grow."

He grinned appreciatively. "Only wait until you begin to increase, my dear. I'm given to understand that that's practically the first area to grow and the last to return to normal."

"You're joking!"

"Not a bit of it. Lynsted's wife told me all about it. You'll like Sally. She's a good wench."

"If she spoke to you about such matters as that," Cicely retorted swiftly, "I daresay my mother would take issue with you on that head, sir."

"Don't be such a Lady Fidget, Cilly."

The words came with a smile, though, and Cicely smiled back. She supposed she was being prudish, but he had surprised her again. He did not seem to be the same person two hours running. Would she ever come to know him?

Once they had reached Ribbesford House, however, she forgot all about analyzing him and thoroughly enjoyed herself. The dinner was as good as Ravenwood had promised it would be, and she met a number of interesting people. Sir David Lynsted and his wife, Sally, were among the first, and she promptly expressed her thanks for their hospitality the previous evening. As the evening progressed she discovered them to be kindred spirits. Sally was bubbly, and Sir David was possessed of a dry wit. At one point he put up his own gold-rimmed quizzing glass and surveyed Ravenwood, who had drifted away to speak to a plump gentleman in a blue coat that fit like a sausage casing.

"Damned if I can think how he manages to stay awake

through these things," Sir David murmured. "He's always half asleep when he comes through the door."

Sally, a pert brunette with plump arms and a full bosom that threatened to spill over the top of her dress, chuckled. "He's awfully sweet, Davy, and you know it. He only looks sleepy, but I for one believe he's awake upon every suit. Why, he's the only one who even realized poor Faringdon was in—"

"Hush, Sally," said Sir David sternly. "Neither Ravenwood nor Faringdon would thank you for telling that tale out of school."

"Oh, pooh," retorted Sally, grinning impudently, but when her husband's gaze did not falter, she shrugged a pretty shoulder and changed the subject. A few moments later, however, when Sir David turned to acknowledge an acquaintance, she leaned closer to Cicely with a confidential air. "Towed Faringdon right out of River Tick and no one else even knew he was in the suds." Cicely glanced at Sir David, and Sally chuckled again. "Never mind Davy—he's merely being fusty. The old school tie and all that. No reason you shouldn't know your husband's capable of generosity. I'll wager you don't know him very well yet."

"I did know him some years ago," Cicely said, "but I've scarcely laid eyes upon him since he returned from the Continent, and he's changed a good deal from the boy I knew."

Sally nodded wisely. "Something happened to all of them over there, I think. They were all so full of fun and gig before, but since they've come home, they're quite different."

"All? Then Sir David—"

"Oh, Davy was there, all right, but he sold out after they put Napoleon on the shelf the first time. Gil and the others stayed for one reason or another, though Gil did come back briefly when his father died, of course."

"Who are the others?"

"Oh, their cronies. You know—that is, I daresay you don't—but most of them were at Eton and Oxford together, then purchased their colors together. The Inseparables, their parents were used to call them. There's Gil and Davy, of course, and Faringdon, and Roger Carrisbrooke, and Inglesham—though we don't see so much of him now, of course. His father's been seriously ill these past months and isn't expected to see another summer.''

"I'm sorry," said Cicely, and meant it, though she hadn't the slightest notion who either Inglesham or his father was.

"We all are, of course." Sally knitted her brow. "Who've I forgotten? Oh, there's Blakeney and Wensley-Drew and Tom Lacey, though he was killed at Waterloo, so you won't meet him. And Lord Toby Welshpool. I daresay you know him—everyone does—the Duke of Horncastle's younger son.''

Cicely did indeed know Lord Toby and, repressing a smile, was grateful to have a topic to discuss. "Do you mean to say he is in London now?''

"Oh, yes. He always likes to get to Town the moment Parliament opens. They've all been here for some time, actually, now that I come to think of it. I couldn't imagine why Davy wanted to come up so soon, but he said it was on account of all the fuss and bustle over the Princess Charlotte's wedding.''

Sir David turned back just then and informed them that Lady Ribbesford was organizing a set or two for a country dance in the next room. "Would you care to join me, Lady Cicely?''

"Why, I'd like that very much, sir," she replied, smiling.

"Well, I call that shabby treatment, Davy," scolded his wife with a twinkle in her blue eyes.

"Nonsense, m' dear. If you wish to dance, here's Faringdon delighted to partner you. Here, Tony," he called. "Sal wants to dance.''

"Right you are. My pleasure, Lady Lynsted." A rakish-looking gentleman, with auburn hair skillfully styled à la Brutus and wearing a dark coat and pantaloons with a neat, rather plain waistcoat, made a leg and then grinned impudently at Sally. She made a moue.

"He will tread upon my toes, Davy. You know he always does.''

" 'Twill teach you to be lighter on your feet, m'lady,'' retorted her fond spouse. "Lady Cicely, have you met the Earl of Faringdon?''

Cicely searched her memory, thinking he did look familiar. "I don't believe so," she said doubtfully.

"Well, that's put me in my place," replied Faringdon with a wry grin. "I offered for your hand not two years ago, my lady. Got turned down flat, too,'' he added for the others' benefit.

"Oh, dear!" Cicely looked up at him ruefully. "I'd quite forgotten, my lord. You see there were—" She broke off, blushing to think how conceited she would sound if she were to finish the sentence, but it was finished for her whether she liked it or not.

"You must forgive my wife, Tony," murmured the familiar voice at her shoulder. "There were so many, I fear she cannot remember them all."

Pointedly ignoring Ravenwood, she turned her candid gaze upon the earl. "I should blush, my lord, for that was what I nearly said myself, and 'twas not well done of me to speak so. If I was rude to you two years ago, I apologize for that as well and hope you will have the generosity to forgive me."

"Not at all, ma'am. Nothing to forgive. Assure you."

"I protest, Tony," put in Ravenwood on a near-querulous note. "Let her apologize. It will no doubt do her a great deal of good. All young girls in their first, and certainly in their second, Seasons are rude. And cruel."

Cicely drew herself up indignantly, only to hear Sir David chuckle behind her. "Behave yourself, Gil, or I'll have to call you out. You are insulting my partner for the dance. I hear the musicians tuning their fiddles, Lady Cicely. Shall we?"

Gratefully Cicely put her hand upon his arm and, with a chilly look at her husband, let Sir David lead her into the next room. She decided that if she was to begin flirting, she might as well begin with him. His easy responses let her know he was only too happy to oblige her, and when Faringdon appeared at the end of the first set to suggest an exchange of partners, she agreed to it immediately, favoring him with her most charming smile. He responded with exaggerated gallantry, and she soon found that she was enjoying herself hugely, laughing gaily, and entering into the spirit of the fast-paced dancing. When the music paused, they drew up, breathing heavily but grinning at each other.

"That was fun, my lord," she said. "I liked it prodigiously."

"Dare I solicit your hand for another, my lady?"

"Indeed you may, sir. You did not tread upon my toes even once." She laughed, looking up at him from under her lashes. "If you are a friend of my husband's, I daresay we shall come to know each other much better."

"My pleasure, ma'am." His look grew a shade more serious. "Perhaps I should return you to him now before he comes to search for us."

"I doubt he would exert himself," she said, chuckling. "Moreover, my lord, we have agreed that we shall not interfere with each other."

"Indeed." He sounded slightly skeptical and looked around as though he expected to find Ravenwood descending upon them. Instead there was a heavyset young man with curly, light brown hair who stepped forward eagerly.

"Cicely!"

"Toby! How nice to see you!" she exclaimed. "Sally said you were in Town. You know Lord Faringdon, of course."

"Unfortunately," Lord Toby agreed with a mock grimace. "Trying to cut Gil out already, Tony?"

"I've no death wish," chuckled Faringdon. "I leave you in good hands, my lady." He took himself off, and Lord Toby guided Cicely toward a set of chairs, thoughtfully placed against the wall for the weary and the aged.

She was truly glad to see him. She had met Lord Toby at the beginning of her first Season, when he had been recovering from wounds sustained in battle and had been temporarily assigned to London. He had been one of the few who had never offered for her hand. Indeed, Lord Toby was quite the despair of the matchmaking mamas because, although a younger son, he was nevertheless eminently suitable husband material. But Lord Toby clearly had no wish to settle down upon one of his family's vast estates. For the moment, at least, he much preferred the company of men to that of a wife.

"Have you been in Town long?" she asked.

"Oh, merely a week or so." He gazed at her critically. "Marriage suits you."

"Does it indeed? And how can you tell, sir? I've been married only two days, after all."

"Well, it seems to do so, at any rate. You seem more relaxed than I remember."

"Does it show so readily?" He nodded. "Well, I can tell you, Toby, I intend to enjoy the freedom of being married," she said frankly.

"Freedom?"

"You know what I mean," she said quickly. "Married ladies are not nearly so hedged about by rules and propriety. I shall no longer require a chaperone everywhere I go, and I shall be able to choose entertainments for myself without having to submit them to Mama or Aunt Uffington for approval."

"Aren't you forgetting one small detail?"

She chuckled. "If you mean Ravenwood, sir, he is scarcely small. But I assure you, he quite agrees that ours shall be a modern arrangement. He does not mean to keep watch over me, nor do I intend to make any difficulties over his amusements."

Lord Toby cocked an eyebrow, and she read the same skepticism in his expression as she had heard in Faringdon's tone earlier. "I daresay the two of you will know what you are about," was all Lord Toby said, however.

"Of course we do." She glanced up at that moment and caught Ravenwood's eye upon her from some distance across the room. He lifted his wineglass in a gentle salute, but even with the distance between them, she could not miss the glint of lazy amusement in his look. She turned to Lord Toby, smiling sweetly. "Do you know, Toby dear, my throat is fairly parched. Do you suppose we might find the punchbowl together?"

He agreed with alacrity, and sipping punch, she quickly found herself being introduced to other friends of her husband's. Of the group of Inseparables, only Ravenwood and Lynsted had married so far, the others remaining quite happily unattached. Two of the gentlemen—one the slightly tipsy Roger Carrisbrooke, the other the morose-looking Philip Wensley-Drew—mentioned that they had attended the wedding, but Cicely did not remember them. No one seemed to think anything about that, however, so she was spared any embarrassment and merely enjoyed being the center of an admiring group of young gentlemen.

A few moments later Lady Ribbesford herself, a plump matron in billowing chiffon, stepped up to the group. "For shame, gentlemen," she tittered behind a gloved and beringed hand. "You must not monopolize my special guest. Though, to be sure, my dearest," she added, putting the hand lightly upon Cicely's shoulder, "you are in splendid looks tonight."

"Thank you, my lady. 'Tis a charming party."

"Well, that's what we like," pronounced her ladyship. "I was telling Ribbesford only this morning that we like nothing better than to provide good, wholesome entertainment for our dearest friends."

"Since when does that Townsend fellow number amongst your friends, Carolyn?" demanded Faringdon with one of his impudent grins.

"Rascal!" If Lady Ribbesford had had the foresight to carry a fan, Cicely was quite certain she would have rapped his knuckles with it. "Mr. Townsend, as you know perfectly well, is a most experienced fellow, and it gives me such a feeling of safety, don't you know, when he is here to protect my guests and their valuables."

"Persuaded you the place would be run over with felons and other such improper characters without his attendance, no doubt," laughed the irrepressible Faringdon. The others laughed with him, but their laughter didn't faze Lady Ribbesford. She turned enthusiastically to Cicely.

"Wouldn't you like to meet him, my dear? He's such a fascinating man. Moreover," she added, glancing to one side of the room, "he is conversing with your husband just now, so it would be the most natural thing in the world for me to present him to you."

Fascinated, indeed, Cicely allowed herself to be led away from the group. "I don't blame you for being cautious, my lady," she said as they walked together. "I have been given to understand that there have been numerous robberies throughout the city."

"Oh, indeed, it has us all in a twitter, my dear. The patrols seem to have no effect, you know. Indeed, one sometimes fears the officers themselves . . . but I should say nothing. Ribbesford says my tongue has a hinge in the middle, and there has been no proof against anyone, and one knows the Bow Street people, at least, are above reproach. But here we are. Ravenwood, I've brought your lovely wife to meet Mr. Townsend."

Cicely found herself face to face with a portly, smart little man, as neat as paint, if a little peculiar in his costume. He wore a very tight suit of light green knee breeches and a yellow coat, short gaiters, and a white hat with a very broad brim. He doffed this last article as the introductions were

made, then plopped it back upon his head and surveyed her
gravely from beneath its brim.

"You would be wise, m'lady," he said quite seriously,
"to hand over them beads yer awearin' t' my safekeeping."

Cicely stared at him. "Surely that isn't necessary here, Mr.
Townsend!" she exclaimed, putting a hand to her pearls.

"There be nips and files where we least expect them, my
lady," he answered importantly, gripping the lapels of his
jacket and rocking back and forth on his toes. " 'Tis best to
be safe. Even the Regent hands over his rhino and gewgaws
whenever he attends a thing like this. I never allow him to
keep above five guineas in his pocket. The rest—sometimes
as much as fifty or sixty pounds, mind you—and his watch I
keeps in my own pocket, where few people would think to
look for them."

"Do you, sir?" Cicely replied, amused. "He must trust
you a good deal."

"I say, Townsend," interrupted a young sprig of fashion
from the group gathering around them, "I wish to ascertain a
fact but, 'pon my honor, I do not wish to distress your
feelings." He had spoken with considerable hauteur and now
paused to take a pinch of snuff. Townsend nodded tolerantly
for him to continue. "Well, then, man," the lordling went
on, "in the early part of your life, were you not a coal
heaver?"

"Yes, my lord," answered Townsend, making a bow with
the most profound respect. "It is very true. But let me tell
your lordship," he went on dulcetly, "that if you had been
reared as a coal heaver, you would have remained a coal
heaver up to the present hour."

In the general laughter that followed Ravenwood drew
Cicely to one side. "If you are becoming weary of this, my
dear, I am quite prepared to take you home. It has been a
long day."

"Oh, no, please, sir! I am having a wonderful evening.
Pray, do not say we must leave."

"As you wish, of course," he replied politely. "We shall
remain as long as you like."

"Good. Tell me, my lord, is it true he was a coal heaver?"

"I believe so. It is said he used to attend all the trials at the
Old Bailey and kept a detailed list of who was acquitted and
who was found guilty. Became a sort of oracle, I daresay.

with all that information. Gave him a certain notoriety, at any rate, and he was eventually appointed a police officer because of it. It wasn't long after that before his name alone became a terror to the criminal element. Now it is not at all uncommon for great personnages to nod at him and say 'how do' in passing. I think he's a bit of an imposter myself, but there's no denying he's made something of himself.'' He smiled. ''He certainly prefers not to be reminded of his roots in the coal cellars.''

Cicely chuckled, glancing back to where Mr. Townsend was holding court. He seemed to be relating an anecdote now to the group of avid listeners, but the musicians were striking up again and the handsome Mr. Reginald Blakeney, another of Ravenwood's friends, whom she had met but a few moments past, stepped up to beg the honor. With a casual farewell to her husband, Cicely accepted willingly, and Ravenwood watched her go, a speculative gleam in his dark, hooded eyes.

9

They returned to Charles Street at last in the small hours, and Cicely went straight to her bed, exhausted, falling asleep the moment her head touched the pillow, without another thought for her husband. If he came to her room at all that night, she was unaware of his visit.

The next thing she knew, Betty had pulled back the curtains and stood by her bed, ready to serve her chocolate. Cicely sat up slowly, rubbing sleep from her eyes, willing the painful throb in her head to perdition.

"What time is it, Betty?"

"Half after ten, m'lady. Miss Hardy said you would be wishful to be wakened now."

Miss Hardy, Cicely thought with amusement. Meg had come into her own. "Ring for her, if you please, Betty."

"At once, m'lady." The girl bobbed a curtsy, straightened her mobcap, and tugged the bell cord. "Will that be all, m'lady?"

"Yes, unless Miss Hardy has errands for you. But if she has, she will ring. You may go now."

Meg Hardy bustled in a few moments later, took one look at her mistress, and threw up her hands. "If you haven't got one of your headaches, Miss Cicely, you may call me a Dutchman."

"I'm sure I shouldn't do anything so uncivil," Cicely began mildly, but she might as well have spared her breath.

"Wearing yourself to the bone and only in Town the day. It won't do, my lady. Indeed, and it won't. Getting home at four in the morning, too, after all the hustle and bustle you've been through down at Malmesbury these past weeks!."

"Oh, Meg, have mercy!" Cicely moaned. "Don't scold

me. It makes my head pound unbearably. A cold cloth, if you love me, and no more harsh words.''

Meg muttered under her breath but scurried to fetch the compress. She was laying it tenderly upon her mistress's brow when the door to the adjoining room opened and Ravenwood stood upon the threshold, his eyes narrowing a bit at the sight of Meg in the role of ministering angel.

"What's amiss?" he demanded, striding into the room. "Is she ill, Meg? What's wrong?"

Cicely had leaned back gratefully against the headboard and closed her eyes to let Meg put the cold cloth on her head, but at the sound of his voice, she straightened, snatching it away, her eyes widening at the obvious concern in his.

"'Tis only a headache, Ravenwood," she said. "Nothing serious, I assure you. Here, Meg, move this tray before I spill chocolate all over myself."

"Stayed up too late," Meg muttered, obeying. "Near burnt to the socket, what with preparations for the wedding and all, then to go off dancing after a long journey like that—"

"Hush, Meg," Cicely ordered. "You'll have his lordship thinking I must be wrapped in cotton wool if you go on like that. I'm perfectly all right, Ravenwood."

"Perhaps so," he returned on a doubtful note, "but you'll stay in bed today, my dear. It will do you no good to make yourself ill.'

She raised her brows at that. "I shall do no such thing. I mean to call upon Sally Lynsted this afternoon."

"I am persuaded that to do so would be unwise," he said gently, moving to sit beside her on the bed. "Leave us, Meg." Meg turned away, obedient to his command, but her mistress's next words arrested her midstep.

"You shall not go, Meg. You stay right here and fetch out my clothes. Really, my lord," she said when she noted a tightening in the muscles of his jaw "have neither the need nor the inclination to remain in bed I am not such a mollycoddle as to be undone one late evening.' He still looked unconvinced and she rested a hand upon his knee. "Please, my please, Gilbert. 'Tis merely a small headache. If I stay here quietly with the cold cloth upon it for half an hour, I shall be right as a trivet, I promise you " She smiled at him.

"The role of heavy-handed husband does not sit well upon you, sir. Will you not trust my judgment in this?"

He returned her smile and lifted her hand to his lips. "You know your limits better than I, I suppose, and of course Meg will be with you when you go to Lynsteds', so I will defer this time."

"Meg! Why should I take Meg, sir?" Her headache was momentarily forgotten. "I need no chaperone."

"I have deferred to you, Princess, and now you must return the favor. It does not suit me to have my wife traveling through this city alone."

"But I will not be alone! I shall have Tom Coachman and a footman with me. Surely 'tis enough, my lord."

"It is not the same as having another woman with you," he said, his tone still gentle. When she continued to look mulish, however, the tone altered somewhat. "I must insist, my dear."

Hearing the implacable note, she swallowed a retort that sprang to her lips, despite the fact that she would have dearly loved to come to cuffs with him. She would not do so with Meg as an audience, however. "Very well, sir. Today I shall do as you request."

"Thank you." He kissed her hand again, watching her as he did so. "I shall leave you to rest now, but I trust you will not go out until you are feeling more the thing."

"I won't." Silently she watched him go, striding back across the room, so large and yet with a catlike grace, thigh muscles rippling under tight, buff stockinette breeches, top boots gleaming. She had a sudden wish that he would not go, that instead he would come back and talk with her until her headache went away. But what, she wondered, would they find to talk about? He treated her kindly, but more like a new possession he had purchased to amuse himself than like a companion. It struck her suddenly that she would rather like him for a companion. Already she missed the easy camaraderie of her sisters. She had no one to confide her thoughts to, no one who was the least interested in her opinions or in her flights of fancy.

She thought back to the previous evening. Now, that had been most amusing and definitely a vast improvement over any of the entertainments she had suffered through during her come-out. The feeling of being on view to potential bidders was quite gone. She had been able to relax, to be herself, as she had never been before in a social situation. But it was still social, and she felt a strong need for something more intimate. It had been only a matter of days, but already she missed having the opportunity to talk things over with someone who cared.

There was Sally Lynsted, of course. She had liked her enormously, so perhaps they could become close friends. With that thought in mind, she began to look forward to her visit even more enthusiastically.

The Lynsteds had a handsome little house in South Audley Street, and Cicely could feel the stamp of their personalities the moment she set foot in the spacious entry hall cluttered with pictures and bric-a-brac. A footman showed Meg to the housekeeper's room while the butler himself led Cicely to an Egyptian drawing room on the first floor, where she found her hostess curled up on a claw-footed sofa with a slim, leatherbound volume in her hand. With a squeal of delight, Sally flung the book aside and jumped to her feet.

"I am so glad you came!" she cried. "You've no notion how dull I've been." She gestured toward the book. "I am reduced to Shakespeare for company, if you can believe it. Davy and I had the most dreadful row this morning." Astonished, Cicely looked quickly toward the hovering butler, but Sally only laughed. "Never mind Abingdon. He heard the whole, and it wasn't of vast importance anyway. But afterward Davy gave me that book to read." Her eyes twinkled. " 'Tis *The Taming of the Shrew*. He is persuaded it will improve my mind."

Cicely laughed. "And will it do so?"

"Well, I've not read enough to know yet; however, I believe I shall commit some of Kate's better remarks to memory. For future use, you know. I wonder what Davy would do should I threaten to 'comb his noddle with a three-legged stool.' I truly liked that phrase. So picturesque, don't you know."

With a chuckle, Cicely shook her head. "I'm sure I've no idea what he would do. I daresay Ravenwood would merely recommend some less strenuous activity. But I fear I don't know Sir David well enough to hazard a guess."

"Well, I know him," Sally said, "and I can tell you it would be as well for me if I didn't speak so to him in company." She grinned. "Do let Abingdon take your cloak, then sit here with me. I was just thinking how deliciously wicked it would be to indulge myself in a cup of tea. Do say you will join me."

Cicely agreed, and the butler soon left them to their privacy. "Must you truly read that entire play?" Cicely asked, indicating the slim volume.

Sally grinned at her again. "No, I am doing so to show Davy what a properly submissive wife I am."

"You don't seem very submissive to me," Cicely said frankly. "Is that the sort of wife he wants?"

"So he says, whenever I displease him," Sally laughed. "But he fell in love with me just the way I am, so I daresay he doesn't know his own mind."

"Love!"

"Yes, is it not wicked of us? And it was love at first sight, too. My mother nearly suffered an apoplectic seizure. Luckily his family is a very good one, and he's got a private fortune as well. Not as much as Papa might have wished for me, but respectable nonetheless. We were lucky."

"But I thought everyone here in London was quite casual about marriage, that love was . . . was—"

"Found elsewhere?" Sally supplied delicately. Cicely nodded. "I daresay you're quite right in nine cases out of ten, but we are the tenth case."

"Nevertheless, Sally, Sir David . . . that is, last night . . . well—" She broke off, appalled at what she had been about to say, but Sally took it in stride.

"He flirted with you," she said matter-of-factly. "Yes, of course. I saw it. But he means nothing by it, of course, any more than I daresay you do, if you would but consider the matter. You may flirt with him as much as you like, with my goodwill. 'Tis perfectly safe. Toby, too, is quite safe. But I'd have a care with Tony Faringdon, if I were you. Roger Carrisbrooke, too. They might read more into flirtation than you mean for them to read. Moreover, I daresay Gil wouldn't like it above half. I know Davy didn't." She smiled reminiscently.

"Well, I don't live in Ravenwood's pocket," Cicely said confidently, "but I'll have a care if you think it necessary."

"I do." There was little chance for further confidences after that because first their tea was served, and almost immediately afterward a trio of gentlemen callers arrived, including the aforementioned Faringdon and Carrisbrooke, plus Mr. Philip Wensley-Drew, the tall, rather forlorn-looking gentleman whom Cicely had met only briefly the night before. They made their bows, agreed that a glass of Madeira would be most welcome, then Faringdon turned to Cicely, his dark eyes atwinkle.

"Been searching high and low for you, my lady."

"Indeed, my lord, how flattering," she returned archly. "I trust not too low, however. I've a reputation, after all."

He grinned. "Only at the bottom of Charles Street, ma'am. That pokered-up butler of Ravenwood's directed us here. I say, though, have you heard the news? Someone made off with the Ribbesford emeralds last night!"

"Lady Ribbesford's jewels!" Cicely exclaimed, shocked. "Not when we were all right there in her house!"

"Precisely, ma'am. Right under Townsend's long nose, too," said Roger Carrisbrooke. "I daresay he's out of twig today."

"I shouldn't blame him if he was," Cicely said sincerely. "Lord Ribbesford has called in the Runners, of course."

"He has, much good may it do him," answered Mr. Wensley-Drew pessimistically.

"You don't have faith in their capabilities, sir?"

"Oh, Philip and Reg Blakeney agree with the reformers who want to upend the system." Sally laughed. "You know about the select committee, of course." The others looked at her in surprise. "Oh, I'm no expert," she chuckled. " 'Tis merely that Davy must find *something* to discuss besides his dinner. He thinks there might even be the taint of corruption at Bow Street."

"Surely not," Cicely protested, but that evening, over a tête-à-tête dinner with her husband, she produced the matter as a topic of conversation.

Ravenwood's eyebrows lifted lazily. "Are you intrigued by politics, my dear? I confess I never suspected it of you."

"Not politics precisely," she replied. "Just the matter of corruption amongst the police, and the need, as Mr. Wensley-Drew suggested, to reform the whole system. Do you think there is such a need?" She waved away a footman offering scalloped veal and watched her husband interestedly.

Ravenwood leaned back in his chair, dabbing at the corner

of his mouth with his serviette. "I daresay there is always room for reform. Did you know, for example," he added with a wry grimace, "that a man may be hanged for such things as eloping with an heiress, for associating with Gypsies or impersonating a Chelsea pensioner, even for carving his initials on Westminster Bridge? Yet, another may frame an innocent victim for robbery, claim a forty-pound reward when his victim is hanged, and go scot-free even if his plot should be discovered."

"You're joking! That must be murder!"

"Ah, you see that as clearly as I do," he replied approvingly. " 'Tis a pity the law is not so wise. In law that is deemed conspiracy, and conspiracy is not a capital offense." He smiled at her. " 'Twould seem we both favor some sort of reform."

Cicely thought that must be an understatement of her own feelings, and as she came to know more about the matter, she wondered more and more why nothing constructive had yet been achieved. Ravenwood said only that the men in position to alter the laws had never been brought to understand the need, and with that, for the moment, at least, she had to be satisfied.

With the approach of Princess Charlotte's wedding, members of the beau monde began flocking to the metropolis. The first of her own family to arrive, as predicted, was Lady Uffington, who lost no time in dispatching an invitation to Charles Street that was nothing less than a command. Cicely and her husband were to dine at Uffington House that very night. Ravenwood, who had planned to dine at White's, changed his intention without comment, merely smiling when Cicely said she supposed she must send a note to tell Lord Toby Welshpool she could not attend the play in Drury Lane with him.

"Why not invite him to accompany us instead?" Ravenwood asked reasonably.

She glanced at him curiously. His expression was mild, and he seemed perfectly sincere. "Very well," she said, "I shall. Aunt won't mind another gentleman at her table. Only extra females overset her." Ravenwood nodded and departed, volunteering the amazing information that he could be found after two at Jackson's Boxing Saloon. Cicely supposed idly that he must go there to visit with his friends. The notion of

Ravenwood, no matter how much to advantage he might strip, trying to pop one under the great man's guard himself could only make her smile. The smile faded, however, when she remembered his attitude toward Lord Toby.

To be sure, since their arrival in London, he had kept his word, saying nothing when she danced and flirted with other men. Not by so much as the twitching of an eyebrow did he betray annoyance when she informed him that she had made plans of her own for an evening and could not go out with him. Though she knew she ought to be grateful for such tolerance on his part, it was, quite perversely, beginning to annoy her.

She didn't know why she should find his attitude irritating. Certainly he didn't flaunt his own amusements, whatever they were. If there was indeed an opera dancer, no one had breathed a word of it to her, and she had come to know Sally Lynsted well enough by now to realize that if Sally knew of such a liaison, she would be incapable of keeping the news to herself. He spoke to other ladies, of course, whenever they were out for an evening, but he rarely danced, and she could hardly accuse him of flirting. He was charming, even witty, and always polite. But she found herself wondering upon more than one occasion why, if he did not care for such amusements for himself, he did not object to her flirtations.

To be sure, she had limited her experiences to flirting only with his particular friends. More than once she had found herself automatically reverting to Ice Princess when some sprig of fashion allowed himself too much familiarity. Once, when that had happened, she had no sooner frozen the man where he stood than she had looked up to find her husband's eye upon her, the glint of amusement that so annoyed her dancing wickedly. She had promptly given him a fine view of her back, but the memory lingered.

No doubt it was because he trusted his friends that he had allowed her to go about with them. Then she remembered Sally's warnings with regard to Faringdon and Carrisbrooke. Why had Ravenwood not seen fit to issue a similar warning? She had gone out once with Carrisbrooke and more than once with Faringdon, whose irreverent attitudes amused her. Not that either gentleman had put so much as a toe out of line, of course. But still, there it was.

She thought little more about the matter, however, when

she greeted her aunt in the large house in Mount Street that
evening. Lady Uffington was an upright dame with stiff gray
curls and a large figure ruthlessly contained in corsets. Her
bright pink dress clung a little tightly in places, but her
appearance did little to detract from the grande dame manner
with which she greeted her niece, her niece's husband, and
plump little Lord Toby Welshpool. After informing the latter
that of course he must always be welcome, she turned to
Cicely.

"How well you look, my dear," she pronounced. "You're
looking well, too, Ravenwood." She turned, gesturing to
someone just beyond Cicely's view through an open doorway.
"I don't know if you are acquainted with my son."

An extraordinarily handsome, conservatively dressed young
man of some five-and-twenty summers strolled into the entry
hall from the drawing room beyond. His smile showed big,
even white teeth in a face that some men said turned women's
senses to porridge. Cicely had never been particularly suscep-
tible to his charms, but she greeted him warmly nonetheless,
holding out her hands.

"Good evening, Cousin Cicely," he said, gripping them.
"May I say you become more beautiful each time I see
you?"

"Thank you, sir. I feel as though I must return the
compliment. I know that you know Lord Toby, but are you
acquainted with Ravenwood?"

"Not really," he said offering a hand. Ravenwood shook
it. "I've seen you at Jackson's, my lord, and Cribb's Parlor,
but we've never been introduced."

"Fond of the sport, are you?"

"Oh, yes, sir. Mere cross and jostle work myself, but I
find it provides exercise. Can't claim entrance to the inner
circle, of course." He glanced back at Cicely. "You have
improved beyond all expectations, little cousin," he said.

"You may converse later," stated her ladyship firmly.
"Show them into the drawing room, Conrad. We've other
guests, you know."

Cicely remembered Sir Conrad's having been something of
a nuisance during her previous sojourn amidst the beau monde.
And, too, he had been known to bully his cousins when they
had been younger. But he seemed to have outgrown such
tendencies, and no one could deny he was quite the handsomest

gentleman present. Deciding he would augment any young
lady's credit, she promptly added him to her mental list of
harmless flirts.

She sat next to Lord Toby during dinner and thoroughly
enjoyed his amiable conversation, scarcely casting so much
as a glance at her cousin. That made it all the more flattering
when he sought her out immediately after the gentlemen had
finished their port. "Will you favor us with some music,
cousin?"

"You've got me confused with Tani," she chuckled. "If
you've a wish to empty this room, however, I shall certainly
play for you."

He laughed. "I remember. You were the one who was
always in the stables. Quite a hand with the horses, too, as I
recall. Have you got a decent mount here in Town?"

She shook her head. Nothing at all had been said about
riding, and she was nearly certain no arrangements had been
made to bring Conabos down from Malmesbury.

"Well, that won't do," he said firmly. "You won't like
London at all if you cannot ride in Hyde Park at the fashionable hour."

"I don't know that I worry overmuch about being seen in
Rotten Row," she smiled, "but I confess I have missed my
horses."

"Then say no more. I have what I believe to be some
excellent stock in my stables, and I should be interested to
know your opinion of them. Suppose I take you riding some
fine morning."

"Tomorrow?" Her tone was wistful, and he laughed again.

"If you like. Tomorrow it is."

Conversation soon turned to the Ribbesford robbery, and
there were several comments made with regard to Mr.
Townsend's failure to stop the thief. Sir Reginald Blakeney,
taking snuff, pointed out that Townsend himself had claimed
to have identified no fewer than seven pickpockets and one
jewel thief at a single masquerade. "And if he can do it when
the rascals are disguised, why can he not see them when they
come as they are?" he demanded.

Clearly Mr. Townsend's reputation had suffered as a result
of the rash of robberies plaguing London, and many feared
matters would become worse as more and more of the beau
monde returned to the city. When Cicely saw Bow Street's

finest at a rout several nights later, she thought she detected signs of strain.

The rout was at Lady Jersey's home in Berkeley Square, and since her ladyship was Cicely's own sponsor for admission tickets to Almack's, she had thought there could be no way to refuse the invitation. However, Ravenwood had a prior engagement with Roger Carrisbrooke and Sir Reginald Blakeney and could not go with her. He had said to extend his apologies to her ladyship, who was known to be a stickler for the proprieties, and had said nothing further about it. Since he was still at home when the time came for her to depart, he walked downstairs with her to meet her escort. Sir Conrad Uffington stood to greet them.

"You look charming as always, cousin," he said, smiling. "Good evening, my lord."

"Good evening." To her astonishment, Ravenwood's greeting was nearly curt. Cicely glanced at him in amazement, then turned her gaze toward her cousin, who was still smiling blandly. It occurred to her then that Sir Conrad was the first of her cicisbei who was not a particular friend of Ravenwood's. And since the night at Uffington House they had been several times in each other's company. As promised, he had taken her riding the very next day, and on subsequent days as well, although after the first morning Ravenwood had observed rather pointedly that she had only to ask to have a suitable mount provided from his own stables. She thought about his attitude now. Was it possible that the viscount was disturbed by her friendship with her cousin?

In Sir Conrad she had found someone who seemed profoundly interested in her and who could converse easily upon any number of topics. She certainly found his attentions far more flattering than those of Ravenwood's friends, and if he sometimes went a tiny step beyond what was pleasing, she was willing to attribute such behavior to their family relationship. But the thought that Ravenwood might not approve of their friendship somehow made it all the more exciting. She smiled brilliantly at Sir Conrad.

"Shall we go, sir? The sooner we arrive, you know, the sooner we may depart."

"Do you plan to go elsewhere, my dear? Perhaps I might join you once my business is done." Ravenwood's tone showed no further sign of discontent. He merely sounded interested.

"I thought my cousin might enjoy visiting a gaming establishment where they allow ladies to play," Sir Conrad said.

"Hougham's in Cockspur Lane?"

"The very same."

Ravenwood gazed thoughtfully at his wife. "I do not think you would find pleasure in such an establishment, my dear. My own advice would be to make an early night of it. You have been out late every night these past two weeks, and you cannot wish to make yourself ill. Of course," he added when she opened her mouth to protest, "you must decide for yourself."

"I think it would be fascinating to visit a gaming hell," she said firmly. "We must go now, sir. I hope your business does not tire you."

With that as her parting shot, she took Sir Conrad's arm and departed. The rout at Lord and Lady Jersey's was like any rout, with people coming and going constantly, seeming to make little difference in the total numbers at any given time. Nonetheless, they had no sooner paid their respects to their hostess than they came face to face with the very man Cicely had been hoping to see.

Mr. Townsend promptly recognized her and doffed his wide-brimmed hat. "Good evening, my lady," he said quietly.

"Good evening, Mr. Townsend. I was shocked to hear of the incident at Lady Ribbesford's house."

"Would that it had been the last," he said morosely.

"There have been more?"

"Indeed, ma'am. Several more."

"I have heard it said," put in Sir Conrad in dulcet tones, "that some thieftakers may well be involved in a conspiracy of sorts that is hampering the apprehension of the villains."

Mr. Townsend gave him a straight look. "I have heard that," he said, "and I cannot deny the possibility, sir. We at Bow Street abhor the practices of certain private thieftakers. They give the profession a bad name. But it is not, in all fairness, a matter of a few bad men but of a rotten system, I fear."

"Rotten, Mr. Townsend?"

"Indeed, my lady. So long as police officers continue to work for reward money, the temptation toward corruption cannot be denied. An officer must be paid well to be kept honest.''

"But what is the alternative to offering rewards?"

"A salaried, organized, uniformed force, ma'am. Men with a sense of duty rather than an itch for a reward.''

Sir Conrad laughed. "Much chance we have of seeing that in this country, man. The English have been fighting against such a force for centuries. Too much power given to what amounts to a military force in peacetime. That notion has been laughed out of Parliament more times than you or I can count. We've no wish to see the sort of thing here they've seen on the Continent and in Russia, thank you all the same.''

Townsend raised himself up on his toes and looked at Sir Conrad with his usual knowing expression. "Someday, sir, wiser minds than yours will recognize that there is room for a compromise between what we have now and what caused the problems you allude to so glibly.''

Sir Conrad bowed with a sardonic lift of his eyebrows and suggested to Cicely that they seek refreshment. She went with him willingly enough, but she continued to contemplate the things she had heard. Not that she had not heard similar arguments before. The topic was a common one, especially since the forming of the Parliamentary select committee to study the problem. It had been pointed out many times that this was not the first such committee and that no committee had ever succeeded in effecting much in the way of change. But, she thought, if they could find a way to curb the number of robberies in London, surely they would have done some good this time. And if there truly were police officers involved in the wicked business—if they were actually encouraging robberies in order to apprehend the robbers for the reward money—well, that was downright frightening.

They left Lady Jersey's house soon afterward and made their way to Cockspur Lane to the plain house known only as Hougham's. It looked quite unremarkable from the outside, but inside all was gaiety and a good deal of noise.

10

Hougham's was indeed a fascinating place, and Cicely enjoyed watching others placing their bets at *rouge et noir,* and faro, and even piquet. She indulged herself by placing a bet or two, but she found that she was not particularly interested in gaming. Instead her gaze kept drifting, whether she willed it to do so or not, toward the front entrance, and she realized before long that she was not merely interested in learning who patronized the establishment. She was watching for the appearance of a large, sleepy-eyed gentleman.

She wondered if it would annoy him that she had come to the gaming house against his advice, and it occurred to her that she would like very much to know his reaction. But when he had not arrived after an hour or so, her head began to ache from the constant noise and laughter, as well as from a seeming lack of good fresh air to breathe. Her escort seemed to have deserted her. People jostled her, and a variety of strangers seemed to be assessing her appearance. One man unabashedly leered. She gave him her best icy stare, but it seemed to have very little effect. She looked around for her cousin. At first she had a rather panic-stricken fear that he might really have disappeared, leaving her to her own devices altogether, but at last she saw him.

He was seated at one of the faro tables, and he seemed to be completely engrossed in his game, though he looked up cheerfully enough when she approached him.

"I hope you will not think me a complete spoilsport, sir, but my head is beginning to ache dreadfully, and I think I should like to go home," she said quietly.

A gleam of mockery appeared briefly in his eyes. "Not fearful of a scold, are you, dear coz?"

"Of course not," she retorted. "You heard him yourself. He said I was to make the decision." She smiled at him then, forcing herself to remain calm, knowing that for a reason she could not fathom she had come close to snapping at him like a fishwife. "He was right about one thing, you know. I have been overdoing it of late. An early night will do me a great deal of good."

"It would no doubt do all of us a deal of good," he said, folding his hand and nodding farewell to the others at the table. "Come along, then. 'Tis against my nature to be so accommodating, but if you insist upon it, it shall be my pleasure to see you safely back to Charles Street. Will you ride with me tomorrow?"

"Of course," she replied, glad he had not protested more about taking her home. Her head was beginning to pound.

At home there was still no sign of Ravenwood, and she realized she was disappointed. He had not come to her bed for several nights now, and she missed him. Sometimes, when she returned from a night's carousing, she would find him in his bookroom reading, and they would share a small glass of brandy in front of the fire while she told him about her evening, before going upstairs together. She looked forward to these quiet times, but even more did she look forward to what followed them, for Ravenwood was a gentle, experienced lover who seemed to delight in their lovemaking. There was nothing sleepy or lazy about the man then, she thought now, wistfully. But, of course, it was too much to expect that he would have returned home so early.

She went upstairs to find Meg Hardy awaiting her, and was forced to endure a scold before being tucked up with a posset and a cold compress to her head. Ravenwood had still not returned home when Meg took away the cloth and the empty cup, and Cicely curled up in the bed, feeling lonely and rather neglected, and drifted into sleep.

The next morning she felt quite herself again and perfectly ready to ride in Hyde Park with her cousin. She was a bit surprised, however, when she discovered one of Ravenwood's grooms standing on the flagway, the reins of his gelding in one hand and those of the little mare Ravenwood had provided for her use in the other. Sir Conrad stood with him. Cicely approached the groom.

"What is it, Nat?" she asked.

''Beggin' yer pardon, m'lady, but the master give orders,'' he said, touching his forelock.

''What orders are those, if you please?''

''I'm t' ride ahind of ye, m'lady.''

She glanced up at her cousin, who favored her with a mocking smile. ''He was waiting here when I arrived, sweet coz. Seems the master thinks you have need of a guardian angel.''

''Well, I don't. You may return to the stables, Nat. I don't need you today.''

''Please, m'lady. 'Tis as much as my place be worth an I go back now.''

She stared at him, but he seemed to believe the truth of his words. Sir Conrad's smile was beginning to annoy her. She glared at him. ''We'll just see about this,'' she said, turning on her heel and reentering the house. According to Wigan, the master had not come downstairs yet, so she hurried up to his dressing room, entering without so much as a tap at the door. ''If you please, my lord!'' she began angrily. Then she fell silent, realizing it would do no good at the moment to continue.

He was seated at his dressing table, engaged in the careful arrangement of his hair, and he did not so much as glance at her until he had finished. His valet had turned one scandalized look upon her at her entrance, and then he, too, had returned his attention to the task at hand. At last Ravenwood set down his brush and turned to face her.

''You may leave us, Pavenham,'' he said quietly. ''What is it, my dear?''

Cicely restrained herself only until the door was shut behind Pavenham before turning upon him furiously. ''You know perfectly well what it is, my lord! Why have you set Nat to spy upon me?''

''Dear me, is that what I have done? Won't you sit down? You'll wear yourself out with so much agitation.''

''No, thank you!'' she snapped. ''And you have not answered my question, sir. Why have you ordered poor Nat to attend me like a Cerberus?''

Real humor lit his eyes. ''Once again I must admire the aptness of your mythological allusions, Cilly, though I can safely assure you that Nat won't eat Sir Conrad. Nevertheless, I'm afraid you must take him with you.''

"You have never insisted upon such an escort before, my lord, and I have ridden several times with my cousin."

"I had not realized it, however."

"But you knew when I rode with the Earl of Faringdon!"

"The cases are different."

"And when I rode with Roger Carrisbrooke in his carriage."

"Again, a different case entirely."

"And Lord Toby?"

"Likewise."

She paused, regarding him quizzically. He met her gaze with placid good humor. "I see," she said slowly. "It is Conrad. He is my cousin, sir. You've no reason not to trust him."

"I have not indicated a lack of trust."

"Then what?"

Ravenwood sighed. "I told you at the outset that I would countenance this play for freedom only until I could see a reason to stop it, Cilly. There has been some talk. Nothing important yet, but talk nevertheless. You see, of late the two of us have so seldom been seen together that people are beginning to wonder if something is amiss. Therefore I must ask that you take a little more care not to be seen quite so often, alone, with other men."

She bit her lip self-consciously. It was true that the only place she had gone with him recently had been the dinner at Uffington House. It had seemed as though their paths just never met. More often than not she had made plans for an evening before he mentioned that he would like her company, and she had never felt that she could cry off once she had given her word to go with someone else. Ruefully she put her hand upon his shoulder.

"Perhaps we might contrive to be seen together more often, Gilbert."

He smiled. "Perhaps."

"Yes, well, after all, Mama and Papa and the girls arrive tomorrow, and then there will be the princess's wedding and Almack's first assembly. You know we must attend those events together. And then there is Brittany's ball the week following. I daresay we shall not find it so difficult, after all."

"And tonight, Cilly? I had thought I might take you to that

play you missed seeing last week. And then to the Clarendon for dinner afterward. What would you say to that?''

"Well, Conrad did suggest that we might return to Hougham's tonight. But I confess, sir,'' she added hastily when he began to turn away, "I should much prefer the play. I . . . I found I did not care particularly for the gaming house.''

"Did you not, my dear?''

"No, and anyway, I daresay Conrad won't mind if I cry off. Good gracious,'' she added with a guilty laugh. "I've left him standing in the street with no one but Nat to keep him company. You will agree that I must leave you, sir.''

"Will I, indeed?''

"Indeed, yes,'' she chuckled. "Why, you are the same man who said it would be an ill fate to be left with only a coachman for company, and Nat is not nearly so lofty a companion as Tom Coachman must be.''

He smiled at that. "Piqued, repiqued, and capotted, I think. Run along, my dear.''

She found Sir Conrad waiting none too patiently in the street below, but he said nothing when he helped her to mount. They rode on ahead of Nat and had gone some distance before her escort remarked, "I see you were outgunned, coz.''

"He said people are beginning to talk,'' she said with a smile. "One could not expect him to like that.''

"No, of course not, but it's just my damned luck that they should put off their talking until my arrival on the scene.''

Though she could not know whether he had intended it so or not, his words sank deep. She had not considered it before, but now that he had put the thought into her mind, she remembered that Ravenwood had agreed that she did not need an escort with any of his close friends. It was odd. At least, as he pointed out, the timing was odd.

So lost in her own thoughts was she that it took a moment before she realized Sir Conrad was saying his own mother had been the latest victim of the robbers plaguing the area.

"*What!* Did you say Aunt was robbed? When?''

"Last night. I blame myself for it. She had asked that I accompany her to her party, but I had other plans, as you know. Had I known, however, that she meant to take a chair,

I'd certainly have insisted upon the coach at least. She said she was merely going from Mount Street into Grosvenor Square, however, and could not conceive why she should roust the coachman and footmen out for such a short journey. On her way home, the ruffians overpowered her chairmen and took both her money and jewels.''

"How frightened she must have been!"

"Not a bit of it," he chuckled. "Said she'd like to have their heads for washing."

Cicely smiled but found it difficult to imagine how he could see any humor whatsoever in such a situation. "You will call in the Runners, of course."

"No. Why should I? They've little interest beyond catching the thieves, and they've had precious little success in that direction of late. Only one or two very small fish."

"But how will you find her jewels again if you do not tell someone they have been stolen?"

"Ah, but that's the point, don't you see? The Runners are interested only in the reward, just as friend Townsend pointed out only last night. And the reward is given only for seeing the thief hanged. Nothing is said about recovering the goods, and more often than not they are never recovered. But Mama was wearing a very distinctive set of rubies, so if they haven't been removed from their settings already, I think I know a way to get them back."

"How?"

"A fellow I know of, named of George Vaughan. Not a Runner, but the next best thing to it. A member of the Bow Street Foot Patrol who wants to become a Runner. Motivation of the highest sort to make a name for himself in high places. And he can make that name by recovering the goods when others fail to do so. He knows what he is about, too. He's already recovered stolen property in more than one case. As a matter of fact, I've been given to understand that he is in a way to recovering the Ribbesford emeralds."

Cicely repeated that conversation to Ravenwood over a delicious dinner at the Clarendon Hotel that evening after the play, adding, "Do you not think it would be wise for them to call in the Runners, Gilbert?"

" 'Tis not my decision to make, I'm thankful to say."

"Well, it seems odd to me," observed Cicely, helping herself to another slice of succulent roast beef. "Why would he prefer a mere member of the foot patrol to an experienced Runner?''

Ravenwood lifted his quizzing glass to peer curiously at a dish presented for his inspection, then shook his head. The dish was promptly removed. ''I daresay he knows what he is about if his primary goal is the recovery of his mother's rubies,'' he said. ''He's quite right when he notes that the Runners are mostly interested in capturing the thief. The reward, after all, is forty pounds. Of course,'' he added, thoughtfully swirling the dark red liquid in his wineglass ''one may quite properly offer a reward to a Runner for the recovery of the goods as well.''

Cicely looked at him, thinking she had detected an odd note in his voice, but he only looked thoughtful. Then, catching her eye upon him, he smiled and changed the subject by asking her if she had enjoyed the play. The topic proved a felicitous one, occupying them through the rest of their dinner. In the carriage, on the way back to Charles Street, they observed a companionable silence, and Cicely found herself wondering why they had not done this sort of thing more often.

There would be little time for it in the weeks ahead, she thought almost sadly. Her family was arriving the following day, and with the princess's wedding and the opening assembly at Almack's, the Season would be in full swing at last. Already invitations were piling up in the Sèvres basket on the side table in the front hall. It was all she could do to keep up with them from day to day. As if it had not been hectic enough these past weeks, she thought as they turned into Charles Street.

When they entered the house, Cicely began to move automatically toward the bookroom, but Ravenwood stopped her, a gleam of unmistakable intent in his eye.

''Go upstairs, Cilly. Meg Hardy is waiting up for you.''

A tiny thrill shot up her spine at the caressing note in his voice. ''Very well, sir,'' she murmured, her words seeming to catch low in her throat.

Meg was indeed waiting and expressed approval over her mistress's good sense in returning whilst she might still have time for a proper sleep. Cicely merely smiled at her, rejecting the simple nightdress she presented in favor of a low-cut lacy dressing gown that fastened with two sets of narrow lavender ribbons.

Meg chuckled. ''Like that, is it?'' Cicely blushed and her henchwoman shook her head. ''I'll tell that Betty to let you sleep late in the morning,'' she said.

''Thank you, Meg,'' Cicely replied pointedly. ''You may go to bed now.''

''You'll want that fire stirred up a bit, Miss Cicely.''

''I'll tend it myself, then. Go to bed, Meg.''

Still shaking her head in undisguised amusement, Meg extinguished all the tapers but the one nearest the bed, then took herself off as ordered. With one eye alert for movement from the adjoining room, Cicely knelt in front of the tile-framed fireplace and used a poker with an experienced hand. The coals crackled and a sparking flame jumped to life. She stirred a bit more, then set a small log from the woodbasket carefully in place.

The low chuckle from behind startled her. She had become so engrossed in her task that she had forgotten to keep watch for his arrival.

''You should not creep up on a person like that, sir,'' she scolded, looking up at him.

''I didn't want to disturb so entrancing a scene,'' he replied, holding out a hand to help her to her feet. She rose to face him, warmth from behind attesting to the fact that the flames had suddenly taken hold of the new log. Then warmth crept into her face when she realized her husband's gaze was traveling downward, taking in her appearance.

''I like that thing you're wearing,'' he said softly as his smoldering eyes met hers. '' 'Tis a most attractive dress, my dear.''

''By the look of you, my lord, I fear I shall not be wearing it long,'' she whispered, her eyes downcast. She saw his hand move to the first tie, then looked up into his eyes again, only to gasp as the ribbons parted and his fingers caressed her smooth skin. The second tie parted but a moment later. Still she kept her eyes on his face. His own gaze drifted lower now, following the movement of his hands upon her silken body.

A low moan escaped her when those warm hands moved across her breasts and upward to slide the garment from her shoulders. With a hushing sound it slithered down her bare legs to the Aubusson carpet. His own brocaded dressing gown soon followed, and Cicely found herself scooped unceremoniously into his arms. He carried her to the bed and laid her down upon it, pulling the quilts up over them as he slid in beside her. There was a brief pause while he extinguished the lone candle. Then, exploringly, his lips met hers, and while the fire crackled, casting a golden glow across the room and setting shadows dancing on the pale walls, they made love together, gently, slowly, deliciously, letting their passion build as they rediscovered each other's secret pleasures until that passion reached new and unsuspected heights. When it was over, they lay in each other's arms and watched the dying embers together. Cicely's last waking thought was that a world wherein one might find such safety and security as she felt at that moment must surely be a magical place.

11

When she awoke the following morning, he was gone, as usual, and Cicely felt momentarily bereft until she remembered that today was the day her family would arrive in Town. Since the duchess always traveled by easy stages, she knew they would have passed the night no farther away than Harlow, and would not be surprised to learn that they had been as close as Epping. As she discovered shortly after noon, the latter was indeed the case. A note, informing her that the duchess was in residence at Malmesbury House, was delivered by a pageboy wearing the Malmesbury green livery.

Without pausing to do more than find a cashmere shawl to fling about her shoulders, she ordered the carriage and, after a journey of but a quarter hour, was set down in front of the huge ducal mansion, which, together with its grounds, occupied an entire city block in the center of Mayfair. Hurrying up the broad stone steps to the colonnade with its high, pedimented portico, she flung open the front door herself, without waiting to make use of the crested brass knocker, and rushed up the grand, swooping staircase to her mother's favorite drawing room, on the first floor. There she found them all, the duchess, Brittany, Arabella, Alicia, and Amalie. Flinging her arms around each one in turn, she grinned, hugged, and kissed them much as though, observed the duchess faintly, she had never expected to lay eyes upon them again.

Amalie was dancing with excitement. "Cicely! Miss Fellows said she will take me to the Tower this year. And we will drive in Richmond Park and even make an excursion to Hampton Court. She says it will be educational, but I want to see the Maze!"

"To be sure, love, and you will like it exceedingly," Brittany laughed. "But don't shout at poor Cicely. You will deafen her."

Arabella and Alicia made their greetings, too, and there was much excited chatter until Miss Fellows appeared briefly a few moments later to whisk the younger girls off to the schoolroom, whereupon the duchess said wearily that she knew Cicely and Brittany would wish to have a comfortable coze.

"I shall leave you to amuse yourselves, my dears. I am very pleased to see you looking so well, Cicely. We have missed you." She smiled, then added rather vaguely, "I trust Ravenwood is also well, but of course he must be or you would not be here." She moved toward the door, then turned back, seeming a bit distracted. "Your father is in his library, dearest. I know you will not be remiss in your duty to him and will pay your respects before you go."

"I will see him, Mama." She grinned at Brittany when the duchess had gone. "Kind of her to grant us some moments of privacy, was it not?"

Brittany chuckled appreciatively. "If she is not sound asleep in ten minutes' time, I shall be surprised. The girls nearly drove her distracted with their chatter."

"But surely there were two coaches!"

"Of course, but it was thought best to keep Amalie and Lissa separated. They seem to be at a point where they irritate each other constantly, which is prodigiously wearing to those in their company. Consequently Mama allowed one at a time to ride with herself and Papa. Of course, neither finds it possible to keep a still tongue for more than a moment or two."

Cicely grimaced. "How is Papa?"

"Well enough. He bellowed at each of them once, Mama said, then retired into a pretense of dozing for the greater part of the journey. Oh, Cicely! How glad I am that we are here. Are you happy? Mama was quite right, you know. You look to be in a splendid way. Is Ravenwood kind to you?"

"Yes," said Cicely slowly. "He is very kind. But I think . . ." She went on in a rush of words. "I think a modern relationship lacks something, Tani, though I am not perfectly certain what it may be."

"Does he have a great many . . ." Brittany paused, clearly searching for a delicate way to put her thought. ". . . amusements?"

"Not that I know about," Cicely admitted. "I suppose it is only that I had hoped to have the same habit of easy intercourse with my husband that I have been accustomed to enjoy with you."

"Well, I expect that sort of thing takes some time," Brittany said reasonably. "Surely you talk with him."

"Yes, of course," Cicely agreed, "but always upon some specific topic or other. Well," she amended, remembering certain odd things they had said to each other the previous night, "nearly always."

Her blushes betrayed her, and Brittany's eyes lit with amusement. "Is that part of marriage nice, Cicely?"

"Oh, Tani," she answered quickly, " 'tis much better than 'nice.' I expect you'll take me for a judy, but I quite like it. 'Tis beyond anything great. Only wait until you love someone!" She clapped a hand over her mouth when she realized what she had said.

"Do you love him, Cicely? I think that must be wonderful."

Cicely stared at her sister blindly, turning her own words over and over again in her mind. Did she love him? And if she had truly fallen in love, what could she do about it? And what, precisely, was love anyway?

It was too much to ponder at that moment, and for the next week things moved entirely too fast for her to take stock of her own feelings. First came the royal wedding.

The Regent and His Serene Highness, Prince Leopold, came up to London from Brighton at last, and the royal couple once again became the primary topic of conversation everywhere. The Regent had been treating his daughter badly for years, but things seemed to come to a head with the wedding when he took the opportunity to lay down certain rules for her future conduct. Her highness was not to be allowed to use the scarlet royal livery but must use the so-called Kendal green instead. She was not to live in a royal palace but must acquire her own residence, and she would not be permitted to hold her own royal drawing-room receptions.

"I think it is disgraceful," Cicely said, not for the first time, as she and Ravenwood were preparing to depart for the ceremony. It was only two o'clock, but the streets between Berkeley Square and Carlton House were already teeming, and the crowds would only grow worse. "How can a man be so cruel to his own daughter?"

Ravenwood smiled at her. "He has never been particularly kind to her, my dear, but you know the reason he gives upon this illustrious occasion as well as I do."

"That he may yet have a son? That to set the princess up in royal state as heir apparent to the throne would be improper, when by such an event she might later be disappointed?" She gave an unladylike sneer. "Stuff! Time enough for him to set her aside if that very unlikely happenstance ever comes to pass. He must first either rid himself of the Princess Caroline or allow her to return home from Italy."

"There has been talk of a divorce."

"There has been such talk for at least two years and more, sir, and well you know it. Yet he has not lifted a finger to effect such a thing. And whilst he dithers, the Princess Charlotte is the heir apparent whether he chooses to grant her the formal title or not. He behaves out of nothing more than petty spite, sir, and I say again, 'tis a disgrace!"

"Gently, my dear." He smiled again and handed her into the landaulet. "You have said so many times, but saying so does nothing to alter Prinny's behavior. Perhaps the princess will find her happiness with her handsome prince. That is far more important, is it not?"

She could only agree with those sentiments, and as he settled himself beside her she wondered briefly if Ravenwood was happy with her. He did not seem unhappy, to be sure, but she was beginning to hope very much that he was pleased with his marriage.

So crowded were the streets that the drive to Carlton House was nearly frightening, but they arrived safely at last, and the wedding itself was wonderful to behold. Afterward Cicely had little memory of Prince Leopold, remembering only that he had worn something blue with military decorations. It seemed that hers was a general reaction, however, for the London *Times* reported the following day that he had greeted the citizenry from his balcony, wearing "a blue coat and a star." Rather scanty attire for a prince of the realm, she thought when she read that.

Her eyes, and very likely those of whoever had penned the report for the *Times*, had been firmly fixed upon the bride and old Queen Charlotte. The princess, beaming with happiness, wore a white gown with silver lamé trim, but although she looked as beautiful as any girl does upon her wedding day, her gown had been as nothing when compared with that of the Queen. Her majesty wore gold tissue trimmed with a mixture of gold and silver. The magnificent gown had two flounces of silver network, bordered with silver lamé and richly embossed with stripes of gold lamé. She had presented a grand sight indeed.

After the ceremony the royal couple had departed for Oatlands, the country mansion of her uncle, the Duke of York, while their guests enjoyed an elegant dinner at Carlton House, hosted by the Regent himself, who sat with his foot propped up and enjoyed the fussing attentions of a good many attendants.

The very next night, Almack's opened its doors for the first assembly of the Season. Ravenwood and Cicely attended together, as they had planned to do, in a party with the duchess and Lady Brittany, but although he stood up with her for the opening set and danced once with Brittany as well, Cicely saw little of Ravenwood after that. She and Brittany were rapidly surrounded by her admirers, and though Brittany proved to be as much of a success as everyone had predicted, Cicely never lacked for a partner. She and Sir Conrad, along with Lady Brittany and her partner, a young baronet who gazed at Brittany with sheep's eyes, went down to supper just before midnight, and she caught a glimpse of her husband a few tables away, sitting with Sir David, Sally, and several others. He nodded politely but made no attempt to join them. She glanced away again when Sir Conrad brought her a plate of canapés and a cup of orgeat.

"I've not had an opportunity to mention it before," he said as he seated himself beside her, "but you will be pleased to learn that George Vaughan has recovered my mother's rubies."

"So soon! Have they caught the thieves, then?"

"Not so much as a clue."

"Then how did he manage to recover the gems?" Brittany asked as she received her refreshments from her bashful escort.

Sir Conrad shot Cicely a humorous look. "I'm afraid I didn't think it politic to inquire further into the matter."

"Dear me." She frowned. "Then do you think he is in a league with the villains?"

"Oh, no," he denied, looking slightly alarmed. "Nothing like that! I do think perhaps he spread the word through the criminal community that the owner would pay more highly for the recovery of the jewelry intact than a fence would pay for the gems alone."

"A fence?" Brittany looked puzzled. "Pray, sir, what might that be?"

Sir Conrad smiled. "A fence is a receiver of stolen goods, my lady. He either purchases the things outright or sells them for a percentage of the take. A lucrative profession, I've been given to understand."

Cicely's attention was still upon his original statement. "Does the sort of action you've indicated not encourage the villains in their work?" she inquired.

He shook his head, with a somewhat superior smile. "They need no encouragement, sweet coz. They are, by their very nature, bad men."

She glanced toward the other table as she thought about his words. Ravenwood was watching her. She remembered the way his eyes had always seemed to twinkle when she was in the company of another man. They did not twinkle now. In fact, if one were the least bit fanciful, one might think them a trifle sad. But she was not fanciful, she told herself sternly, and it was perfectly childish of her to want suddenly to go to Ravenwood when she was with one of the handsomest men in the club, a partner that nearly every female present would give her best lace to have at her side. She straightened, favoring Sir Conrad with a brilliant smile.

He was at his best tonight, too, she thought a moment later, laughing at some sally he'd made. He was so extremely good-looking and so well set up. He looked particularly well in the knee breeches that were the required male attire at Almack's. But more than that, he was charming, witty, and able to make her feel charming and witty, too. Acknowledging to herself that she found it flattering when he chose to spend so much time with her, she sighed and let her gaze drift absently back to Sir David's table. Sir David and Sally were still there and appeared to be having one of their arguments. The others had gone.

"Pardon me, my dear." The familiar voice startled her, and she turned, her eyes lighting, to find him standing just behind her. "The next dance is a waltz, and I'd like it very much if you would favor me as a partner."

"Oh!" She glanced at her dance card. "I'm sorry, Gilbert," she said sincerely, "but I've promised this dance to Lord Faringdon."

"Tony will no doubt agree that I have a greater claim to your company, my lady, and though I daresay he will be prodigiously disappointed, he will survive the loss."

She stared up at him, her eyes widening with surprise. Such an attitude was unlike him. He looked perfectly normal—relaxed and slightly bored. But she had the oddest notion that he would not be sent away even if she were inclined to attempt it. She smiled uncertainly. "In that case, sir, I should be happy to dance with you."

He offered his arm, and she stood to take it, making her farewells with slightly forced laughter to the others. The musicians were just returning to their box when they entered the main ballroom, and while they waited for them to tune their instruments Cicely looked up into her husband's face.

"You seem very grim, sir. Do you mean to scold me?"

He glanced down, his expression lightening considerably. "I had not thought of it, my dear. Do you deserve a scold?"

"No, of course not! I only wondered because you looked so serious."

"My apologies. I was preoccupied, I expect. But it is nothing of importance and surely has nothing to do with my feelings toward you."

She was on the verge of asking him just what those feelings might be, but the musicians struck up the waltz at that moment, and Ravenwood swung her deftly onto the floor. It was the first time she had waltzed with him. In fact, she had not even thought he did waltz. But he did, and very well, too. Her excitement at being held in his arms in so public a manner drove all thought of inquiring about his feelings from her mind. She felt like a feather, light and graceful. Smiling up at him confidently, she discovered a warmth in his expression that she seldom saw in public, and it occurred to her suddenly that his actions might very well have been prompted merely by his wish to quell any gossip about her. Though it took the edge off her enthusiasm, she determined to do her part. He was her husband, after all, and all thought of a modern relationship aside, she did not want anyone to imagine she was unhappy in her marriage.

In the days that followed, the social pace increased. Though it had been common for her to be out most evenings in the weeks that preceded the official opening of the Season, it now became necessary to fit a number of entertainments into any given evening. It was not uncommon, in fact, for her to plan to attend as many as five or six functions before returning, exhausted, to fall into bed. Meg Hardy scolded and threatened, but to no avail. Cicely was enjoying every moment.

Ravenwood said little, but he showed no inclination to follow the fast pace himself. Often he would escort her to one affair, only to relinquish her to one or another of her cicisbei when she mentioned a desire to go on to another.

The constant late hours did take their toll, however, and she began sleeping later and later into the mornings. This meant she had to decline Sir Conrad's frequent invitations to ride early in the park, but that did not mean she saw much less of him. He often served as her escort in the evenings, and was nearly always present when she paid a call upon her aunt at Uffington House. Meg Hardy accompanied her on those latter occasions, of course, and was also with her when she chanced once to meet Sir Conrad while shopping in Bond Street.

Sir Conrad was handing some parcels up to a servant on the box of his coach when they saw him. Just before Cicely moved to hail him, however, she heard the young woman beside her make an unladylike sound very much in the nature of an indignant snort.

"What is it, Meg?"

"That's that upstart Alfpuddle with him, Miss Cicely. I've told you about *him*." As indeed she had. The man Alfpuddle had seen Meg on one of their visits to Uffington House and had evidently taken a liking to her. But Meg, considering herself quite beyond his touch, would have none of him, and her indignation over the man's continued advances provided a good deal of amusement for her mistress.

She chuckled now. "I'll protect you from him, Meg."

"That's as may be, my lady, but who's to protect you from his master? Like man, like master, I always say."

Cicely was astounded. "Whatever do you mean, Meg? What a thing to say! Sir Conrad is my cousin and every inch a gentleman. Moreover,'' she added with a touch of irritation, ''you've got the thing wrong way round. 'Tis supposed to be 'like master, like man.' ''

''Well, that's true enough where Mr. Pavenham is concerned, I'm sure,'' announced Meg Hardy, undaunted. ''Mr. Pavenham has a great deal of character. He is as much a gentleman as that Alfpuddle there is an underbred gapeseed.''

Diverted, Cicely stared at her. ''Pavenham! Oh, Meg, you rogue. Never tell me you've designs on Pavenham! He's as starched up as one of Ravenwood's neckcloths.''

''Mr. Pavenham,'' stated Meg with great dignity, ''is a high stickler and no doubt, Miss Cicely, but he's as kind as the master is and no mistake.''

So Meg thought Ravenwood a kind master, Cicely thought, regarding the other woman fondly. And so he was. Kind and generous and tolerant. And able to set her nerves tingling just by looking at her. The mental list of his qualities might have grown a good deal longer had Sir Conrad not caught sight of her just then and come to join them. If he had hoped for private conversation, however, his hopes were dashed, for Meg stood quite close to her mistress, and for all the attention she paid to the wiry, gap-toothed Alfpuddle's come-hither gestures, the man himself might have been so much air.

The next day was the day scheduled for the Malmesbury ball. Cicely had promised to help with the last-minute details and so was forced to arise earlier than had become her habit. Bleary-eyed, she watched as Betty approached with her chocolate and laid the tray gently across her knees.

''You look fagged nigh to death, m'lady. Be you certain sure you'll not stay abed the morning?''

''I'll be right as rain once I've had my breakfast, Betty. Ring for Miss Hardy, if you please.''

Meg Hardy was more outspoken than Betty, scolding and telling her mistress that the proper place for her that morning was bed. ''And no mistake, Miss Cicely. Your mama has a houseful of servants and four other daughters to help her. She's got no call for an extra pair of hands, and so I shall tell the master if you don't lie straight back down in that bed this very minute. Betty, draw those curtains again. Her ladyship is going back to sleep.''

''No, Meg, her ladyship is not,'' Cicely said calmly but with a note of unmistakable authority in her voice. ''And you will say nothing to Ravenwood about it, either. I promised Mama I would help, and she is depending upon me. You know how she gets before an affair of this sort. I cannot let her down. Now, say no more about it, if you please. I shall wear the sprig muslin with the green sash.''

Meg gave her a sharp look but responded to her tone, and Cicely was soon dressed and ready to go downstairs for a proper breakfast. She found Ravenwood in the breakfast parlor, reading the *Times*. When she entered, he folded the paper and laid it beside his plate before rising to greet her. His glance was nearly as penetrating as Meg's had been, but he made no reference to her appearance. A footman entered.

"Coffee for me, please, Michael," she said, "and tell Cook I should like a baked egg and some of that Yorkshire ham with my breakfast." The footman bowed his way out, and Ravenwood held her chair. "Thank you, Gilbert. 'Tis a fine morning, is it not? What news had the *Times* to offer?''

"You are up quite early, my dear," he replied, taking his seat.

"I promised to assist Mama today."

"Ah." He nodded. "I see."

"Was there anything of interest in the newspaper, sir?" she repeated, not wishing to discuss her early rising further.

"Not very much. Now the princess is safely wed, there seems to be little to write about. There was a mention of that Vaughan fellow your cousin sets such store by. Seems he's recovered more items recently. Must be quite a fellow."

"We shall see for ourselves tonight, sir. Mama is never behindhand with the fashions, and she has invited not only Mr. Townsend but Mr. Vaughan as well. Conrad convinced her that he could only be an asset, since so many people will be attending the ball." Ravenwood returned a neutral response, and she looked up at him curiously. "Conrad says Mr. Vaughan offers to pay more for the jewels than a fence would pay," she said, smiling delightedly at his startled reaction to her use of the cant term, then turning serious again when she continued. "I do not think things ought to be done that way, do you? It seems dishonest somehow. Why cannot the police capture the thief *and* recover the goods?''

"I daresay they do sometimes, though it is very likely more difficult than one might suppose," he answered. "Is there anything I can do to help at Malmesbury House, do you think?''

''Oh, no,'' she replied vaguely, her mind still taken up with the police and the recovery of stolen goods. ''There are all of us and plenty of servants besides. You need not interrupt your plans for the day.''

''I would be glad to help.''

''Thank you, sir.'' She smiled, her eyes twinkling now. ''I know you mean that, and I thank you for your thoughtfulness, but there is truly no need for you to subject yourself. Mama tends to become a trifle overset by these affairs. She would very likely set you to three tasks simultaneously and then decide all three either didn't need to be done at all or needed to be done all over again in an entirely different and more difficult manner. Papa will be at his club all day, just as he has been nearly every day this week, and I think you would be wise to do the same. Gentlemen, in my experience, have very little patience with such capriciousness.''

''I daresay you're right,'' he responded, looking appalled. ''Very well, I shall take your advice. I doubt I shall spend the entire day at my club, but if you have need of me, a message sent to White's will find me eventually.'' He sat with her while she ate her breakfast, then handed her into the landaulet and saw her on her way to Malmesbury House.

12

As expected, everything in the ducal mansion was at sixes and sevens. When Cicely stepped into the entry hall, the first thing she heard was the Lady Alicia shrieking like a banshee, just off the gallery, that someone, unseen, was a precious, mealymouthed brat. Next, Amalie's voice was heard, nearly as loud but rather more controlled, as she pronounced her sister to be all about in her head and jealous besides just because she was not to attend the ball. At that opportune moment Lady Arabella stepped into the entry hall through the green baize door leading to the housekeeper's rooms and the kitchens beyond. An arrested look showed that she had heard what was taking place above them.

"Where on earth is Miss Fellows, Bella?" Cicely demanded.

Arabella grinned. "Polishing the crystals of the chandelier in the dining room. You know how anxious she is to please, and Mama was persuaded they were smudged and said she knew dear Miss Fellows would know precisely which cleaning mixture would set things to rights. Nothing would do but that Miss Fellows must try to mend the matter herself. No one can tell her that such a task or any task that will please Mama is beneath her. Never mind those two," she added, gesturing upward. "I'll attend to them. Tani and Mama are in the sun-room. Do you go and see if you can put Mama in better spirits. She has managed to convince herself that all is in a way to ending in disaster."

Chuckling companionably, they went upstairs together, and as Cicely made her way toward the rear of the great house she could hear her sister saying in her patient, practical way, "This will not do, Alicia, you must apologize. You are the elder and ought to have set a better example."

Cicely smiled to herself. Arabella would make a fine wife and mother someday. She was still smiling when she entered the cheerful sun-room. The duchess looked up from the lists she was perusing near the well-swept hearth, and Brittany called a greeting from the window embrasure, where she sat upon a French seat, brushing the golden hair that hung damply to her waist. The windows were open, and birds could be heard singing in the sun-drenched garden below.

"Cicely, I'm so very glad you've come at last," said the duchess fretfully. "My new French chef says he will not be told what to serve, and he was affronted when I informed him that I had ordered ices from Gunter's. Everyone orders ices from Gunter, do they not? People would be disappointed not to find them. But I've not the slightest notion what Alphonse means to serve my guests for *dinner*, never mind what he will produce for the supper later!"

"But, ma'am, surely he presented a menu!"

"Well, of course he did, but 'tis all in French, and I never know what the things are, and when I asked him, he became offended again and said he never divulges his receipts!"

"Miss Fellows could—"

"Cicely! You cannot expect me to ask my daughters' governess to read the menu to me!"

"Very well, Mama, but one of us could very well have read it. You must have seen it days ago. Why did you say nothing then?"

The duchess looked slightly embarrassed. "Well," she said hesitantly, "Sally Jersey was here when Alphonse brought in his menu, and I didn't want to say I couldn't read it with her sitting right there. You know what a chatterbox that woman is. The tale would have been all over Town in a twinkling. So I merely looked it over and said it would do nicely. And now I can scarcely demand to have it back. If only Jacques were still here! Alphonse is not nearly so conciliating."

What her mother meant, Cicely knew perfectly well, was that her former chef had flattered her and catered to her whims much more easily than did the presiding tyrant of the ducal kitchens. She smiled encouragingly. "Mama, you know you may trust Alphonse to do the right thing. He is an excellent, very experienced chef."

The duchess agreed reluctantly, and the matter was laid to

rest, but similar small crises presented themselves one after another until Cicely felt at last that she simply had to get back to Charles Street if she was to have sufficient time to dress before returning to Malmesbury House for dinner.

Wearily she called for her carriage, and when she got home she went straight up to her bedchamber and rang for Meg Hardy.

Meg said very little, but her disapproval was all but palpable. She had ordered a bath before coming up, and the men soon arrived with the tub and hot water. Meg ordered one of them to light a fire, then sent the hovering Betty for a pot of hot tea for her mistress.

"Now, Miss Cicely," she said gently when the others had gone, "just you get yourself into that tub and relax whilst I wash your hair. I only hope there's time enough to dry it before you must depart. And how you managed to get cobwebs in it from a house that's supposedly been harboring an army of cleaning folk for an entire week," she added more tartly, "I should like very much to know." Cicely smiled weakly and, having been stripped of her clothes like a child, climbed into the tub. "That's it now, dearie," said Meg. "Just you settle in." While she worked Meg chattered idly, and when her mistress's hair was clean and her body glowed from head to toe, she held out a huge, fluffy towel. "Now, then, Miss Cicely, out you come, and step over to the fire, where it's warm. Here's Betty with your tea now. I'll just fetch out a warm dressing gown."

Obediently Cicely moved toward the fire, wrapped in the towel. Soon, however, she was seated in a comfortable chair in the light-blue wool dressing gown, her feet propped up on a footstool, her back to the cheerful fire, with a cup of hot, sweet tea in hand. She sipped while Meg brushed her hair dry by the warmth of the fire, and the rhythm of the strokes in the heat of the room was nearly enough to put her to sleep. But once her hair was dry, it was time to dress.

Her ball gown for the evening was of pale-gold shimmering silk, cut high at the waist and low at the bosom. The puffed sleeves were trimmed with lace ruffles at the cuffs and lace caps at the shoulder line, while matching lace edged the ornately embroidered flounce. Meg styled her hair in the plaited coronet that was so becoming to her, and when Ravenwood tapped at the door to discover if she was dressed, she had just fastened her pearls and was stepping into a pair of gold satin slippers.

"You may come in, Gilbert," she said, smiling when he peered around the door. "I'm nearly ready to depart."

He looked perfectly splendid himself, she thought. He wore dark knee breeches with ornately clocked stockings and a brilliant gold-and-silver–brocaded waistcoat under the snugly fitting dark coat. He carried a blue velvet box, which he presented to her with the confident air of a man expecting to please his lady.

"I thought you might like to wear these," he said. "Not so magnificent as the Malmesbury jewels, of course, but these were purchased just for you, Cilly."

She opened the box and gazed raptly at the exquisite sapphire necklace and bracelet resting side by side on white satin. The magnficent, glowing stones were set in delicate filigreed gold. She gazed up at her husband with sudden tears welling into her eyes. "They are beautiful, Gilbert." She rose on tiptoe to kiss him gently on the cheek. "No one ever gave me anything so beautiful before."

"I thought they would suit you," he said almost gruffly. "You wear your pearls so often, people will begin to think you have nothing else."

"I like my pearls," she replied simply.

He smiled. "I'm glad, Princess. But take them off now, and let me put the necklace on for you. Tonight you should be very grand."

Obediently unclasping the pearls, she turned, trembling when first his fingers and then his lips brushed the nape of her neck. Silently slipping the bracelet out of the box, she let him fasten that as well, and he held her wrist a moment longer than necessary, looking searchingly into her eyes. "The jewels are lovely," he said, his voice still a bit husky, "but you are lovelier still, my dear. 'Tis proud I am to be your husband tonight." Then, before she could say anything at all, he practically demanded her wrap from the silent Meg, flung the deep-gold, fur-trimmed velvet cloak around her shoulders himself, and urged her toward the door.

Torches lit the entrance to Malmesbury House, and link-boys scurried to direct the disposal of the carriages already lining the street. Although the vast majority of the guests had not yet begun to arrive, it was clear that the attendants at least expected the ball to be a sad crush. No hostess could ask for more.

The duke and duchess sat down nearly fifty people to a magnificent dinner, and the duke was polite for once, while his duchess was as charmingly placid as she always was in company. Cicely had expected no less. It never seemed to matter how unsettled the duchess became in the hours before an affair such as this one. Once the first guest had put his foot across the threshold, she became the perfect hostess.

Cicely wished she could think herself the perfect guest. But before dinner was half over, she realized that her long day and the short nights preceding it were beginning to take their toll. It was all she could do to concentrate when one or the other of the gentlemen flanking her attempted to engage her in conversation. And although she had been quite curious to discover what, in fact, the temperamental Alphonse had elected to serve, she scarcely noted the contents of a single dish, mechanically accepting and then toying with whatever was offered to her.

She sipped her wine, then set it down, realizing too late that it was giving her a headache. Requesting a glass of water in its place, she glanced down the table to discover Ravenwood watching her, a crease between his brows. Though she smiled at him, the crease did not go away, and once dinner was over, he came to her side immediately.

"What is it, my dear? Are you ill?"

"Oh, no," she replied, striving for a light tone. "It was just a trifle stuffy in the dining room. With a breath of fresh air I daresay I shall do very well."

"I am persuaded that I would be doing better to take you home, Cilly. You don't look well at all."

Alarmed, she put a hand on his arm. "Really, Gilbert, I shall be all right. Only think what a stir it would cause if you were to take me away before the dancing has even begun. There is a balcony off the ballroom. Take me there whilst Mama, Papa, and Tani are greeting the new arrivals. I'm sure it will help prodigiously."

He agreed, as she had been certain he would. For her to leave now would be to disturb the others far too much for them to enjoy the ball. It mustn't be thought of.

As they passed through the ballroom she noted that the musicians were already in place. Then she saw Mr. Townsend standing perfectly upright, rocking back and forth upon his toes near the door to an anteroom, a strange, rather slim man in an ill-fitting dark blue coat and yellow breeches lounging gracelessly next to him. She and Ravenwood paused to greet them, and Mr. Townsend presented George Vaughan, albeit none too enthusiastically. Ravenwood chuckled as he guided her onto the moonlit balcony a few moments later.

"It seems that Townsend does not appreciate assistance from such a quarter as that one."

"He is merely being fusty," Cicely replied, breathing deeply of the crisp night breezes.

The fresh air did revive her, and by the time the musicians were striking up for the first set of country dances she was sure she would do nicely. Ravenwood, still visibly skeptical, led her inside to join their set. Her dance card had been filled for days, and as the evening wore on she began to feel as though she were two separate people, the first dancing with one man after another, with no memory of which was which, and the other already asleep and observing the first as in a dream. But when her headache returned, it did so with a vengeance, establishing itself directly behind her eyes, setting her temples throbbing.

She glanced around the ballroom, instinctively looking for Ravenwood, but it was Lord Faringdon who approached, intent upon claiming his dance.

"Just been talking with Townsend," he chuckled. "Damned amusing fellow. First he wanted to keep my fobs in his pocket. Then he ups and says he's arrested dukes and marquesses in his time and thinks it's demeaning that folks should desire him to arrest a common thief."

"Tony, please," she muttered wretchedly. "Will you be a love and forgive me? I've got the most miserable headache. I don't want to spoil anyone's evening, but I must get out of here. Will you find Gilbert and tell him I've gone upstairs to lie down? Tell him I'll be in Tani's bedchamber. I shall ring for her woman to fix me a posset or something. And, Tony," she added more firmly, "tell him he is not to worry. He knows perfectly well the headache will go away if I but lie down and let it take its course."

"Your servant, my lady," he replied, frowning with immediate concern, "but dashed if I think Gil's going to like this much. Don't mind telling you, he's more like to collect you and carry you off home, where you belong.''

"I depend upon your resourcefulness to prevent that, sir. My mother would never forgive us if we both deserted her at such an early hour."

"Do my best, ma'am."

She thanked him profusely and left the room immediately to make her way up the nearby service stairs, grateful for the relative peace and quiet of the empty corridors on the second floor. Suddenly, however, as she passed the duchess's bedchamber, its slightly open door revealing darkness within, she heard a sudden scraping noise and a muffled masculine oath. She hesitated just outside the door, listening.

Surely there was movement within, then a clinking sound as though two glass receptacles had collided. Next there came the unmistakable metallic jingling of chains. *Someone was rifling her mother's dressing table!* Only trinkets of little value would be found there, of course, for Fortescue had no doubt locked up her grace's jewel case and hidden it away in one of the many cupboards, but if the thief were left to his own devices, he would surely find it before long.

Her headache forgotten, Cicely turned on her heel, then thought better of the action and moved slowly to open the door wider. There was truly very little light within, but there was a small glow from the dying fire, and she could catch a glimpse of a shadowy figure near the dressing table. At that moment there was a sudden burst of flame from the fireplace. The sneak thief, startled, turned from the dressing table toward the fire, and she had a brief but clear profile view of a narrow, foxlike face, with long side-whiskers and a prominent, hooked nose. She had never seen him before, but she was quite certain she would recognize him if she ever saw him again.

She was not so foolish as to challenge him herself, of course, but, having seen as much as she dared, she hurried back down the corridor the way she had come. A moment later she was on the first floor, intent upon alerting Mr. Townsend to the thief's presence in the house. However, even before she reached the ballroom, she recognized the thin, ill-dressed, slouching figure crossing the anteroom toward her as the man who had been lounging at the Runner's side earlier in the evening.

"Mr. Vaughn! Thank goodness!" she exclaimed, relieved to think she would not have to search through the stuffy, overcrowded ballroom for assistance. "You must come with me, sir. There is a thief in my mother's bedchamber. You must capture him at once, before he finds her jewels!"

Mr. Vaughan regarded her curiously. "How do you know he is there, my lady?"

"Why, I saw him, of course. Don't stand there discussing the matter. We must stop him."

" 'Tis my duty t' stop 'im, ma'am, and no place for you t' be, I assure you," he added gravely. "You would be much better occupied in discovering the whereabouts of Mr. Townsend, who will be wishful to know what is what."

Assuming that he must know his business best, Cicely agreed, taking time only to give him directions to her grace's bedchamber before setting off herself to find the Bow Street Runner. As it happened, however, she found her husband first.

"Cicely! I was just coming for you. Faringdon says—"

"Never mind that now, Ravenwood. I discovered a sneak thief abovestairs, and we must inform Mr. Townsend."

"*What?* Where?"

"In Mama's bedchamber. But Mr. Vaughan has gone to intercept him, so we must find Mr. Townsend at once."

"Nonsense, you'll do no such thing. You'll let me handle this, and you will find a quiet corner in which to await my return. Here, Uffington!" he called when Sir Conrad entered the anteroom at that moment. "Take her ladyship to a place where she may sit quietly, then find Townsend. There's a thief upstairs. I must alert the servants."

Sir Conrad asked no questions, merely accompanying Cicely to a nearby sitting room, where she might await her husband. He smiled down at her as she wearily took a seat. "You look as though you ought to be in bed, sweet coz."

She smiled wanly. "I daresay I shall be quite soon, sir, but you mustn't stay to bear me company, you know. Ravenwood will expect you to find Mr. Townsend."

"There is truly a thief in the house?"

"Yes, indeed. I saw him myself, pawing about through Mama's trinkets. I told Mr. Vaughan."

He looked relieved. "Ah, then there is little need to worry, you know. Vaughan is as shrewd as can hold together. He'll have the villain in a trice.''

But that was not to be the case. Although the servants quickly manned all the obvious exits from the huge mansion, and a general search was made, it was Mr. Townsend's expressed opinion an hour later that the villain had made good his escape. His presence did not become a matter of general knowledge, however, so the dancing went blithely on. But the duchess, informed that her bedchamber had been invaded, insisted, albeit in fainting accents, that Cicely take her upstairs at once that she might discover for herself what had been taken.

Once candles were lit, a quick search of the dressing table revealed that a number of trinkets were missing, but this fact did not alarm the duchess particularly, since most were of little value. What did set off a crisis of nerves was the discovery that her jewel case was also missing from its customary place of concealment. The duchess moaned and immediately demanded that someone ring for the estimable Fortescue to support her through this tragedy. Cicely moved quickly to obey, putting an involuntary hand to her head when it protested the sudden movement. No sooner had she given the requisite number of tugs to the cord, however, than she felt a gentle touch on her shoulder and turned to find her husband gazing down at her, concern clearly imprinted upon his countenance.

"Let me take you home, Cilly."

His tone was so gentle that she felt an odd urge to cry. "I must stay with Mama," she said, looking away from him.

"She does not need you," he said quietly. "Her woman will soon be here, and she has others to support her as well if necessary. But you, my dear, are in no shape to be of much assistance to anyone. We will collect your wrap and be on our way. I ordered the carriage when I spoke to the servants earlier. It will be waiting for us."

There seemed to be nothing further to say, so without another word, she let him take her away. It was blissful to sink back against the plush squabs, to rest her head against his shoulder and, a moment later, to feel his arm around her, drawing her closer. With a sigh, she snuggled against him, and despite the briefness of their journey, she was sound asleep before they reached Charles Street.

She scarcely stirred when he lifted her from the carriage and carried her effortlessly up the steps and into the house. Nor did she hear him, a few moments later, when he dismissed Meg Hardy with the simple explanation that he would tend her ladyship himself and that she was to be left alone to rest undisturbed until either she rang or he gave orders to the contrary the following day. She did open her eyes briefly when, having discarded her cloak, he began the more difficult task of disrobing her, but if she noticed any difference between his dimly outlined shape and that of the much shorter, plumper Meg, she was too sleepy to make comment upon it, merely shutting her eyes again with a tiny sigh. Ravenwood made no attempt to coax her into a nightdress, simply laying her naked upon her bed and drawing the heavy quilts gently over her. Then he stripped himself of his own clothes and slipped in beside her. When he drew her protectively into his arms, she made a sound low in her throat, much like a purring kitten, stretched a bit, then snuggled closer, her head comfortably nestled in the curve of his shoulder.

When she awoke late the following morning, her first thought was that the room was very dark. She was used to being wakened by Betty when she opened the curtains to admit the morning light, and at first she supposed it must still be early. But there was sufficient light to see by the little jeweled clock on the night table that it was nearly eleven o'clock.

Memory of the previous night's events began floating back, and her next thought was to wonder why she was in bed without her nightdress. Not that it really mattered much, she thought. With a smile to think how wickedly idle she had been to sleep so late, she stretched her legs languidly, then tensed when her big toe came into contact with another human leg.

"Good morning, my dear. I trust you are well rested."

"Gilbert!" She turned over to find him smiling lazily at her. "What on earth, sir? I know you rarely appear in public before noon, but you are generally up and about long before this."

"I was afraid I might disturb you," he answered. Then, with a rueful grimace, he reached out to brush a strand of hair from her cheek. "I'm afraid I didn't brush your hair out last night. It will be most dreadfully tangled."

She chuckled. "One of the very few advantages of having fine hair, sir, is that nothing can tangle it. Generally that is a disadvantage, mind you, since it will lend itself to no fashionable hairstyle. If I were to have it cropped, it would merely hang straight, regardless of the most ruthless attempts with a curling iron."

"You must never have it cropped, Cilly. I like it long." His voice deepened, and he raised himself up to rest upon one elbow, his expression growing tender as he gazed down into her eyes. His free hand moved to stroke her, and she gasped at the sensations coursing suddenly through her body. It was not long, however, before she was moving sensuously against him, using her own hands to stir him as he stirred her. His mouth came down against hers suddenly, almost brutally, as though he would devour her. But her response was nearly as passionate, and it seemed to become almost a contest between them to see who could stir the other more, to determine who would be subdued first. At last, however, she fell away from him, gasping, ready to beg him for release if he did not possess her soon. But as though he had known instinctively when that moment would come, Ravenwood moved over her, claiming her once again as his bride, his wife, his cherished possession.

13

They were discussing a light nuncheon in the breakfast parlor when Lady Brittany entered, smiling brilliantly. She wore a deep green sarcenet walking dress with a matching bonnet, which she promptly removed, automatically sweeping wisps of golden hair back into place even as she spoke.

"What a cozy scene you present," she said. "Wigan said he didn't think you'd mind if I came straight on in."

Cicely looked up, glad to see her. "Is Mama in better twig today, Tani?"

Brittany laughed, taking a seat. "Well, she is in a bit of a pelter yet over the fact that a strange man actually invaded the privacy of her bedchamber and touched her things. But since it turned out to be not so bad, after all, she is in prime—"

"Tani!" Cicely interrupted. "What do you mean, 'turned out to be not so bad'? Did they find Mama's jewels, then?"

"Why, didn't you know? I thought you did, although no one thought to inform me that anything exciting was happening at the time. Mama said you were there until Fortescue came to support her spirits."

"No, we departed before she actually arrived," Cicely explained, glancing at her husband. He smiled, and she turned back to Brittany. "What had Fortescue to do with anything, anyway?"

"Fortescue had Mama's jewel case with her," Brittany said simply.

"Had it with—"

"Of course. You know the woman is a very dragon where Mama is concerned. She said she'd never have dreamed of leaving her duchess's precious jewels at risk, and couldn't imagine why we had made such a fuss."

"Oh, dear," Cicely chuckled, "I can almost hear her saying the words. And she must have been more upset than Mama at the thought of a strange man in the bedchamber!"

"Not a bit of it," retorted Brittany, straight-faced. "She said she had expected as much, what with all the 'sorts' Mama had invited to her ball. Looking very down-the-nose when she said it, too, as you might think. You know she thinks anyone of lower rank than an earl is of no account, begging your pardon, Ravenwood."

"Oh, never mind Gilbert," Cicely advised kindly. "He will come about. Just as soon as poor Papa . . . What was the charming phrase Lissa used that day? Ah, yes, just as soon as he cocks up his toes."

Brittany giggled, but Ravenwood merely recommended that his wife try for a little more conduct.

"Yes, you must," Brittany agreed, "for you will be a duchess one day, Cicely, and your Meg Hardy will grow to be just as high in the instep as Fortescue is now."

"Grow to be! You cannot have seen her of late," Cicely laughed. "She will have none of Sir Conrad's man, Alfpuddle, because she thinks she is too good for him. Not that I can blame her for resisting a man with such a name as that. Only imagine her as Margaret Alfpuddle! Now, mind you," she added wickedly through the others' chuckles, "if he were in service to a marquess, it would no doubt be a different matter altogether."

"Not by comparison to a duke's man," Ravenwood murmured, irresistibly drawn into the foolishness.

"A duke's man?" Cicely regarded him quizzically. "Who—" Then her brow cleared. "Then she *has* got a case. You've seen it, too."

"Offhand, I'd say the case is mutual," he returned. "Pavenham actually forgot to warn me to have a care for my boots this morning. It must be the first time since he came to me. But I think you underestimate your Meg. I believe if she truly cared about a man, she wouldn't care a jot about his station in life."

"How noble you make her sound," Cicely said, grinning. "But if she will not even speak to a man she thinks to be beneath her touch, how could she ever fall in love with one?"

"Pavenham is your valet, is he not?" Brittany asked Ravenwood. He nodded. "Well, I think that's sweet," she said. Then she turned back to her sister. "Have you got plans for this afternoon, Cicely?"

"Yes, I must call upon Lady Jersey," Cicely said, making a small face. "I never know what to say to her. When one knows one's every word will be repeated everywhere her ladyship goes, it rather stifles conversation. But she procured my vouchers to Almack's, so I am obliged to her."

"She procured mine as well," Brittany admitted. 'Shall I go with you?"

"Oh, if you would! We can walk over from here, you know. She lives just across Berkeley Square."

"You shall certainly not walk," Ravenwood interposed with mock sternness. "Sally Jersey is the very one who makes such a fuss over ordering out her carriage to take her to pay a call three doors down the square. She says it would be easier to walk, but it would look so common. No, no, my dears, you must order up the carriage."

"Pray, Ravenwood, do not be absurd. 'Tis only a step."

"Nonetheless," Brittany put in, "we may as well take the carriage. Oh, no, sir," she said quickly when Ravenwood put a hand to the bell. "I have my mama's. The coachman is walking the horses, but he will come by presently, and we shall signal him to stop." She smiled at her sister, who had opened her mouth to insist upon walking. "I shall have to go home afterward, Cicely, and 'twould be easier to go on from there. Though, of course," she added as an afterthought, "we shall be pleased to bring you back here first."

"No need of that. I can walk."

"I shall send the landaulet in half an hour to fetch you," Ravenwood said, smiling. "If Tani brings you back, you'll very likely sit chattering until she is so late getting home as to bring your father's wrath down about all our ears. And as for walking, my girl, you may put that notion straight out of your head. Not only does it not suit my consequence, but I countenance this visit at all only because you promised Sally Jersey you would pay her a call. Otherwise I should tuck you up with one of your romances to read. You were meant to rest today, you will recall."

"Yes, my lord," said his wife in a tone that was meant to sound meek but succeeded only in sounding long-suffering.

He chuckled. "And you will take Meg Hardy to bear you escort on the return journey."

"Yes, my lord." She raised appealing eyes to the ceiling.

A few moments later, in the duchess's carriage, sitting opposite Meg Hardy and Sarah Basehart, Brittany looked her over closely.

"Are you in better frame today, Cicely? Mama was distressed by your illness last evening."

"Oh, yes, of course. I am in prime twig today, Tani. I was merely tired last night. I have been going it a trifle strong, I'm afraid."

"But does Ravenwood fuss over you like this often?"

"Fuss? No, of course he doesn't." She considered a moment. He did seem to be very concerned about her well-being. The thought gave her a warm glow. "He persuaded me to cancel my engagements for the evening," she mused aloud. "We are to dine together and have an early night for once."

"Well, I expect that's an excellent notion," Brittany said approvingly. "From the sound of it, you're well nigh burnt to the socket."

Cicely gave her a look but made no reply, for they had arrived at Lady Jersey's town house. Brittany's footman opened the carriage door and let down the steps. He held out a hand, first to his mistress, then to Cicely, and escorted them up the steps to the front door, where he manipulated the heavy brass knocker to good purpose before returning to the coach.

Sarah Basehart and Meg Hardy were left to sit in the front hall of the elegant house while a footman guided Cicely and Brittany to her ladyship's sitting room. Lady Jersey was in an excellent mood, and she, whom the beau monde referred to as Silence, entertained her two visitors with a running monologue of anecdotes, making it almost unnecessary for either to say a word. Thus the visit passed harmlessly, and when the requisite half hour had passed, they rose to their feet to make their adieus.

Out in the hall, they found Meg Hardy alone. "That Sarah says she has a cousin working here, if you please," she said tartly. "No sooner did that footman return than she asked to be taken to some Polly or other. Said I wouldn't mind waiting alone. Such manners!"

Cicely knew that Meg assumed Sarah had been taken off to enjoy a cup of tea and was merely jealous. The same obliging footman was sent to fetch her, however, and the party soon separated on the flagway outside.

Cicely settled back in the landaulet, glad now that Ravenwood had insisted upon it. She yawned delicately behind her hand and saw Meg give her a sharp look.

"Yes, Meg, I'm still a little tired. You needn't scold, however. Ravenwood and I are staying at home tonight. I shall be in bed at quite an early hour, I expect."

"And a good thing, too," muttered Meg, still out of sorts over her treatment in Berkeley Square.

When they returned, Cicely decided to take Ravenwood's advice and curl up with a good book. Consequently she sent Meg on upstairs with her cloak and went to have a look in the library.

It was not the first time she had been in the room, of course, but it was the first time she had entered it to find a book. She thought about how often she had read down at Malmesbury, and it seemed impossible to realize that she hadn't read a single book since coming to London. Doing the pace too fast and furious, my girl, she scolded herself.

The shelves had been arranged in order of subject matter, so it was not long before she found what she sought. From there it was but a step to a large, overstuffed chair near the south window, and within moments she had seated herself, slipped off her sandals, and curled up with her toes tucked warmly under her in the large chair. Both the duchess and Meg Hardy would have roundly condemned such a posture, but neither was present, and she did not think Ravenwood would mind in the slightest.

The story was lurid enough to hold her attention easily, and the hours slipped away unnoticed. So engrossed was she that she did not hear the click of the latch when the door opened, but she sensed Ravenwood's presence and looked up before he spoke. The expression on his face warned her, and her smile of welcome faded into a worried frown. "What is it, sir?"

"You must come with me, Cicely."

"But why, sir? What has happened?"

"I can say nothing, my dear. But I ask you to trust me."

"Of course." She put her hand in his and let him assist her from the chair, then paused, shooting a guilty look in his direction as she slipped her sandals on. He did not smile.

Her curiosity well aroused, she followed him to the small saloon just off the main hall, where unknown or unworthy visitors were often kept waiting while the servants ascertained whether or not the master or mistress was "at home." The first person she saw there, however, was none other than Meg Hardy, white-faced and clearly furious, wringing anxious hands one moment and dashing angry tears from her eyes the next. Two men were with her, one wearing the red vest of the Bow Street Patrol and the other dressed in near-gentleman's clothes and carrying the tiny baton with the gilt crown on top that proclaimed him to be a Runner. Both men peered searchingly at Cicely, then glanced at Ravenwood. He shook his head, and the Runner seemed to relax.

"What goes on here?" Cicely demanded, hurrying to Meg's side. "Meg, what is it?"

"Beggin' yer pardon, m'lady, but the wench 'as been ordered not t' speak, just as we hopes 'is lordship were kind enough t' honor 'is word. You will oblige us, howsomever, if y'll deign t' answer a question or two."

"What question?" Thoroughly alarmed now, she glanced anxiously from the Runner to the viscount, standing against the doorjamb with his hands gripping his lapels. "Ravenwood, what is this?"

"Just answer Mr. Fowler's questions as well as you can, my dear."

"Very good advice, sir, and more 'n' what we bargained fer, I don't mind tellin' ye. Nobbut what John Townsend said ye was a man of sense." Fowler turned back to Cicely. "Now, then, me lady, just ye mind yer lord and answer me proper."

Cicely stiffened at his patronizing tone, and his expression promptly grew a trifle meeker. "Ask your questions," she said icily.

"Very well, me lady, and I'm sure no offense was meant. Did ye not call upon m' Lady Jersey in Berkeley Square this very afternoon?"

"I did."

He nodded, withdrawing a well-worn black leather occurrence book from an inside coat pocket and scribbling rapidly with a stub of pencil. "And did ye not be accompanied by yon wench?"

"*Miss Hardy* did accompany me, as she generally does. My sister the Lady Brittany Leighton and her maid, Sarah

Basehart, also accompanied us. Whatever is all this in aid of, if I may ask?''

"Was the wench . . . ah, Miss Hardy, that is," he added with near sarcasm, "left alone in that house at any time?"

"No, of course she was not!" But then she remembered, and it required an enormous effort and all her experience as the so-called Ice Princess to school her features, but it was no use.

"Ain't the way I heard tell," Fowler said simply. "Ye'll understand, me lord. Consequent of our findings here, the wench'll 'ave t' come along o' us." To Cicely's astonishment, the viscount only nodded.

"Ravenwood!"

"They can do nothing else, my dear. Sally Jersey's house was robbed this afternoon, apparently at the very time you were present. And some of the missing jewelry, as well as several trinkets missing from your own mother's dressing table, were found among Meg's effects upstairs."

"*No!* I won't believe it. Meg *wouldn't!*" She turned, meaning to fling herself between the patrolman and Meg, to protect her from the consequences of this dreadful mistake.

"Cicely." Ravenwood's low tone stopped her in her tracks. "I am persuaded that you ought to retire to your sitting room, my dear. These proceedings can only distress you."

She turned to face him. "Distress me? Indeed, they distress me! You must do something, my lord. She is innocent."

"I can do nothing at the moment, my dear. Nevertheless, I shall see to it she lacks for nothing."

"They will put her in prison!"

"Go upstairs, Cicely. There is nothing you can accomplish here."

She glared at him, then looked back to see the burly patrolman grasp Meg's arm in an ungentle grip. Angrily she swept from the room, but not without first favoring her husband with a devastating look of contempt.

Upstairs, Betty practically came running in answer to her summons. "Oh, m'lady, ain't it awful! They looked ever'wheres, and then they come across them jewels in Miss Hardy's own portmanteau, the one at the foot o' her bed. Ain't it dreadful? It was pretty stuff, too, ma'am. I seen it. Chains and baubles and one bracelet as looked like real diamonds, too. Least, I thought they was real."

But Cicely was no longer listening. She had remembered something she ought to have remembered earlier. "Never mind, Betty. I don't need you, after all. I am going back downstairs."

Hastily she ran back down to the saloon, but it was empty. The library was likewise empty. Finally she found the young footman generally on duty in the front hall.

"Michael, where is the master?"

"Gone to White's, I expect, m'lady. At least, he said a message sent there would fetch him."

"Then I must send a message at once," she declared. "You shall take it yourself, Michael. 'Tis exceedingly important."

She scribbled a brief note, sealed it, and watched him run off with it. Then her temper began to rise. How dared Ravenwood just wander off to his club as if nothing of consequence had occurred? Angrily she paced back and forth for some two or three minutes, then, recognizing the futility of such an expenditure of energy, she went back upstairs to her sitting room and rang for a pot of tea.

It was nearly two hours before Ravenwood returned. By then she was furious, ready to flay him no matter what he might say to her. He was smiling when he entered the sitting room.

"I had your message, my dear. Poor Michael has been all over Town, I fear. How may I serve you?"

"Ravenwood, how could you leave at a time like this?" she demanded. "How could you?"

"My dear, I protest. I fail to see what I might have achieved by remaining here."

She stared at him but willed the pain she felt at his words not to show in her eyes. That he could ever ask such a question astonished her, particularly after his tenderness the previous night and his concern for her well-being earlier. Surely he must realize that Meg's arrest would be a shock to her, that she would need his support in order to bear such a crisis. And that was only if he believed Meg to be a criminal. That he could care for her and think such dreadful things about someone she loved was reprehensible. But that he could think such things and still go off, leaving her to cope by herself, was monstrous. This was a side of modern marriage she had not foreseen and one, morever, that she did not like at all.

She felt a calmness creeping over her. She no longer cared what he thought. She must help Meg. "Ravenwood, listen to me. Meg is innocent."

"She was alone in that house long enough to take the jewels, Cicely. I could see that by your own reaction to the Runner's questions. And they caught her red-handed with the stolen goods."

"But they found Mama's trinkets as well," Cicely said desperately. "Don't you see, Ravenwood? Meg was nowhere near Malmesbury House last night. She was right here, and there is no way by which she might have got into Papa's house without being seen and recognized. How could she possibly have got her hands on Mama's jewels?"

"If she is in league with the thief or with the receiver, she could easily have the jewels," he answered calmly.

"But she had only baubles, Betty said! Why only those and not more expensive stuff?"

"There was a diamond bracelet," he reminded her.

"I don't care! She didn't take anything. I *know* her. Meg would *never* do such a thing. Oh, why won't you listen?"

"I think you are overwrought, my dear," he said gently. "Perhaps a nap before dinner would—"

"I don't *want* a nap! I want Meg. Only you are too cork-brained to see what is before your very face. I shall go myself to Bow Street and tell the magistrate she is no common criminal. I shall—"

"You shall do no such thing," he interrupted, still calm. "It does not suit my dignity to have my wife creating a public display. I fear you are rapidly becoming hysterical, and as I've no wish to cope with a fit of the vapors, I shall ring for Betty to attend you. If you are wise, Cicely, you will collect yourself before you come downstairs for dinner."

He spoke blandly enough, but there was a note of finality that told her as well as words would have done that he would prevent her from leaving the house if necessary. No doubt he meant to intercept Betty to give orders that she not leave her room. Silently vowing that she would starve before she had dinner with him, she watched helplessly as he turned on his heel and left.

What manner of man was he, that he could behave so

callously? He had always seemed to like Meg Hardy. Surely he could not mean to abandon her to her fate. But, no, she corrected herself, he would not do that. He had promised to see she lacked for nothing. Nothing but freedom, anyway. She turned to stare out the window at the back garden. Perhaps he merely preferred to take the line of least resistance. Certainly he had done so with regard to her upon more than one occasion. Whenever she had really taken a stand for something, until now, he had given in. He seemed to balk only when his consequence was threatened. She sighed again. She had really thought he would help her, but once again he had proved to be too lethargic to exert himself. She would have to help Meg herself somehow. Perhaps Sir Conrad would have a notion.

Betty did stay in the room with her, but Cicely quickly decided that sulking would gain little for herself or for Meg, so she dressed carefully, did the best she could with her hair, and went down to have dinner with her husband.

She found him in the library, and when she entered he got to his feet with a smile of approval. She returned a chilly look, straightening her shoulders and lifting her chin. "I believe Wigan is about to announce dinner, my lord."

"Then shall we adjourn to the dining room, my lady?" he answered with exaggerated formality. She could discover no hint of mockery in his attitude, however. It was more as though he were metaphorically walking on eggshells instead. Dinner was an extremely polite exercise. Topics for conversation were limited to the weather and the delicacies placed before them, and Cicely was exceedingly relieved to see Wigan enter with the viscount's port.

"I shall leave you now, sir," she said with great dignity, letting Michael assist her with her chair. Ravenwood made no protest, merely getting to his feet until she had gone.

Cicely wished now that she had not canceled her engagements, for this would have been a perfect night to forget her troubles in a whirl of social pleasures. But it could not be. Depressed, she turned toward the drawing room. She had no particular wish for the solitude of her own company, but it was entirely too early to go to bed, and she had no wish to stare at the walls of her sitting room. She had had enough of that already today. Even the slight change of scenery would be better than nothing.

There was a copy of the latest *Monthly Museum* on the table in the drawing room. She picked it up and sat down to leaf aimlessly through it, wondering if Ravenwood would dare to join her when he finished his port. He could simply decide to return to his club, after all. The canceling of engagements meant little to gentlemen. They could always find entertainment of one sort or another. She sighed.

"Sir David and Lady Lynsted, my lady." Wigan stood upon the threshold, a grinning Sally moving swiftly past him. Cicely's eyes brightened considerably.

"Sally!"

"The very same, and don't say you aren't overjoyed to see us, or Davy will wring my neck."

"Of course I'm overjoyed. You've no notion how dull I was feeling just now."

"Well, of course I know. Didn't I tell you, Davy? He saw Ravenwood this afternoon and heard how you had determined to spend an evening at home, and he seemed to think you would like the change of pace. But I knew better. I was sure that after all that has passed today, you would want company. So here we are!"

"I am delighted to see you, but I hope you do not expect me to be very good company, Sally. Just the thought of poor Meg languishing at Bow Street makes my blood run cold."

"What on earth do you mean, 'languishing'? Surely you heard what happened after she left here!"

Cicely stared at her. "After she left? Whatever do you mean? The Bow Street people had her in custody. What could have happened other than that they carried her to Bow Street and cast her into one of those dreadful cells one hears so much about?"

"Why, my dear, I was certain you would have heard. Six masked men on horseback stormed the coach at the bottom of Longacre Street and rescued your Meg from the very clutches of those dreadful Bow Street men!"

14

Cicely stared at her friend. "You cannot mean it," she whispered. "Who on earth would do such a thing?"

Sally came quickly to sit beside her, taking the magazine gently from between limp fingers. "Cicely, it may be nothing—only a jest. Please, dearest, I never meant to distress you so."

"A jest! How could such a thing be done in jest?"

"Sal means it may have been some young jackanapes, enjoying a lark," explained Sir David, moving to warm his hands at the fire. " 'Tis a practice in similar favor with 'boxing the watch.' Surely you're acquainted with that charming game?"

She nodded, collecting herself with difficulty. "That is when young gentlemen tip over the night watchmen's shelters with the watchmen trapped inside, is it not?"

"Aye. They pull the guard hut over face first, and most of the Charlies are so old they cannot lift the boxes to free themselves."

"I wouldn't call the men who do such disgraceful things 'gentlemen,' myself," Sally said tartly. "Some of those poor old men have been grievously injured in such frolics, and one or two have even died."

"Be that as it may," interposed her spouse, "robbing the Bow Street coach provides some rascals with the same sort of low thrill as boxing the watch provides. "Ah, Ravenwood, good evening," he added as the viscount strolled in. "You behold in us a leavening to the unalleviated boredom Sal is persuaded you would suffer with only each other for company. A sad commentary upon her opinion of your poor servant as a boon companion," he concluded morosely.

Sally grinned. "Pay him no need, if you please. He often pities himself this way, and I have discovered it does no good to show sympathy for him when he is in such a state. Come and join us, Ravenwood."

"Were you planning an evening out?" Ravenwood inquired smoothly. "I heard a reference to 'boxing the watch' as I came in. Low sport, I always thought it."

"We were telling Cicely about the men who abducted poor Meg Hardy," Sally explained with dignity. "Davy suggested they might have done it for sport."

" 'Tis possible, I suppose."

"You *knew* of this, Ravenwood?" Cicely shot him another icy glare, but he met it calmly.

"I did. The news was brought to me just before we dined, but as I thought it would do little to lift your spirits, I thought it best not to mention it immediately."

Though Sir David seemed to find something fascinating in the crackling fire, Sally glanced uncertainly from Cicely to the viscount. "But I thought Cicely would be grateful to know Meg is not stuck in that awful place. And if some young bucks did it for sport, surely they will have set her free. Well," she demanded when no one spoke, "will they not?"

"If she had been freed, she would have come home," Cicely said dully.

"Home is the last place she would come, I'm afraid," Ravenwood said. His tone was gentler now than it had been.

"But why?"

He was not required to answer, however, for at that moment Wigan entered and spoke to him in an undertone.

"Show them in, Wigan," the viscount said wearily. He gazed at his wife, his expression enigmatic. Not a moment later the door opened again, to admit the Bow Street Runner and his patrolman. Both looked considerably the worse for wear.

"M'lord," Mr. Fowler said brusquely, "we come on a bad business."

"Well, out with it, man! Have you found Miss Hardy yet?"

"Ye 'eard about the incident, then?"

"Of course we've heard. And I might add," Ravenwood

continued sardonically, "that I expected to find you on my doorstep before now."

The Runner's face reddened, and his henchman looked studiously at his own boots. "We . . . ah, that is, m'lord, we were detained on business at Bow Street," the former said stiffly.

Sir David regarded them searchingly. "I am acquainted with Sir Nathaniel Conant's temper, gentlemen," he said wryly. "I daresay he would have had a thing or two to say about your mishandling of a rather simple business before he sent you out again to pursue your inquiries."

The patrolman grimaced, showing that Lynsted had touched a nerve, but the Runner was made of sterner stuff. "Have y' seen the young woman in question, m'lord? I remind ye that it is yer duty to give 'er into our custody if ye 'ave knowledge of 'er whereabouts."

"I know my duty, man," Ravenwood replied calmly. "She is nowhere on the premises."

"I believe 'e, m'lord, and it don't surprise me. No, sir, it don't surprise me at all. That 'ere wench be long gone b' now, I'm afeared."

"Why does it not surprise you?" Cicely asked, controlling her temper with difficulty. They were discussing Meg as though she had no meaning to anyone but Bow Street. "I assure you, if Miss Hardy were able to do so, she would come home."

"Now, that she wouldn't, me lady. Not if 'twas 'er own 'enchmen what sprung 'er."

Cicely gasped, but before she could dispute the matter with them, Ravenwood cut in suavely to ask if there would be anything else.

"Nothing, m'lord," replied Fowler. " 'Cept, o' course, in the unlikely event ye 'ave word from the wench. Like as not, she could lead us t' the rest o' them villains. Don't mind tellin' 'e, we'd like t' lay 'em by their 'eels. Been calls fer an arrest from the 'ighest quarter. Mr. Conant be losin' 'is patience, as I'm sure ye'll understand."

"Quite right, too," put in Sir David. "Disgraceful how long this business has been let to go on."

Wigan entered just then in answer to Ravenwood's summons, and the viscount requested that he show the men to the door.

There was silence in the room when they had gone. Then Cicely looked at Ravenwood, her gaze accusing.

"Is that what you meant when you said this was the last place she would come, sir? Because you, too, believe she was rescued by her cohorts in crime?" Her gaze dared him to answer in the affirmative.

"It is a possibility which must have occurred to them at Bow Street," he replied, "but I meant only that Meg would never be so foolhardy as to come here when it must be one of the first places they would seek her."

"She would communicate with me if she were able to do so," Cicely repeated stubbornly. "What if Sir David is right, and some stupid young men did it for a lark? What if they are holding her against her will? What if . . ." Her words failed her when a harsh vision of the possibilities invaded her mind. She saw Sir David and Ravenwood exchange glances and glared at them both. "I won't be kept in cotton wool! That's what you have feared from the outset, isn't it?"

Ravenwood stepped forward as though he would comfort her, but her icy, demanding glare froze him halfway. "Meg is in much less danger now than she was in, Cilly," he said suddenly. "I know it. You must not work yourself into such a lather. Think only that she has been spared the experience—a humiliating one, I assure you—of being hailed before a magistrate and incarcerated in a noisome cell at Bow Street. The ensuing trial would be worse yet, believe me." He paused, then added gently, "You have never seen that courtroom, but I have. The magistrate is like a great bird of prey, glowering at the poor prisoner while filthy, toothless old women and flea-ridden reprobates jeer from the public seats. And if she was to be found guilty, she could be publicly whipped, transported, even—and most likely in this instance, when there has been so much public outcry—hanged."

Cicely swallowed carefully, aware that her stomach was churning at the images his words produced in her mind. "You are right, my lord. Whatever has become of Meg, it cannot be so bad as that." The admission did nothing to put her in charity with him, however, and the rest of the evening passed without much evidence that she relished her role as hostess. Indeed, she greeted the arrival of the tea tray with undisguised relief and saw Sir David and Sally on their way shortly afterward with a good deal more enthusiasm than was commensurate with good manners.

Knowing she had behaved rudely, she expected at least a reproof from her husband, but when she announced somewhat defiantly that she meant to retire at once, Ravenwood made no demur, merely remarking that he hoped she would sleep well. If there was so much as a gentle barb in the words, she ignored it and went upstairs.

Betty's assistance was no substitute for Meg's, and as a consequence, the girl's very presence depressed her, so she sent her away as soon as she could reasonably do so. Then, extinguishing her candles, she banked the coals in the fireplace, and with a last, speculative glance toward the door to the adjoining bedchamber, she climbed into her bed. He would not come to her tonight.

It began to rain during the night and continued steadily into the next day. There was still no word from Meg, and Cicely racked her brain for something she could do to help. She considered approaching Pavenham but rejected the notion when she saw him, for he seemed more starched up and unapproachable than ever. No doubt, she decided—remembering that Meg herself had called him a high stickler—he had washed his hands of her, believing her to be guilty of the charges.

Then she remembered her cousin. She had thought before that he might have a notion how to help Meg, but the notion had slipped her mind until now. Accordingly, despite the weather, she set out at once to pay a call upon Lady Uffington.

Her aunt was at home and relatively pleased to see her; however, it was rapidly brought home to Cicely that her ladyship merely wished for an opportunity to animadvert upon the evils of harboring a viper in one's bosom.

"I shall not pretend I ever thought badly of her, of course, my dear," she stated magnificently. "She has managed to cozen us all with her encroaching manners and sweet tongue. I know your dear mother, especially, set great store by her before all this. Well, live and learn, as they say."

Cicely gritted her teeth in order to stop herself from saying something rude and disrespectful that she would later regret. It was all she could do, however, to put a good face on it until she could divert her outspoken relative to a safer topic. Even then, she was forced to endure the occasional side comment in reference to the incident.

"I tell you I was never more shocked than when Sir Conrad brought me news of your Meg's arrest. And to have had the nerve to steal from Sally Jersey, of all people!"

"Sir Conrad told you of it, ma'am?"

"Indeed, yes. And of that subsequent business as well. No doubt, my dear, she is in league with a whole raft of rogues. You may thank the fates that saw her unmasked before you were murdered in your very bed."

"I have not seen Sir Conrad for several days, ma'am," Cicely said evenly. "Not since I saw him briefly at Mama's ball."

"That was merely two nights ago, Cicely."

"So it was." She was surprised. It seemed much longer ago than a mere two nights. "Is he at home now, Aunt?"

"Who, Conrad?" Cicely nodded. "Oh, no, I never know where he is from one moment to the next, of course. But, then, a mother never does."

"Surely he is a very good son, ma'am?"

Lady Uffington looked skeptical. "Is he? Well, I expect he is as good as most."

Cicely rose to her feet. "Will you tell him I called, ma'am, and was disappointed to find him from home?" It was the most she could do. If she were to offer to leave a note, her aunt would be likely to scold, saying it was most improper to address *billets doux* to any gentleman other than one's own husband. Which of course it was. Even her casual request brought a look of censure to the august dame's brow.

"I shall mention that you called, of course, my dear," she said unencouragingly.

It was enough, however, to bring Cicely a note later in the day from Sir Conrad himself, inviting her to ride in the park the next morning if the weather had cleared. The very thing, she thought, sitting down at the library table immediately to send him an affirmative response.

"Dare I hope you are writing to me, Cilly?"

She jumped. She had not heard Ravenwood come in, and she turned now, blushing, to face him. "No, sir, 'tis a response to an invitation." She glanced guiltily at Sir Conrad's missive, lying face up on the table near her left hand. The hand moved almost of its own accord to cover it, but Ravenwood nipped it smoothly from beneath the reaching fingers. He glanced at it almost absently while she watched him, nibbling unconsciously at her lower lip.

He looked at her apologetically when he had read it. "I hope you will not mind putting him off for a day or so, Cicely."

"But why should I, sir? Unless, of course, this stupid rain continues. I will take my groom," she added on a nearly bitter note.

"I had hoped you would ride with me," he said diffidently.

"But you never ride in the park, except during the fashionable promenade, of course. Even then you generally drive a phaeton or your curricle. Why should you suddenly wish to ride?" she asked suspiciously.

"Well, I have something I wish to discuss with you, my dear, and I had hoped to be able to discuss it then."

"Why not discuss it now?" she invited.

But he was not so easily caught. "I've a pressing engagement that I cannot avoid," he replied. "I only stopped to . . . ah, that is—"

"To ask me to ride in the park with you," she supplied, not bothering to hide her disbelief.

"That's it."

"We can talk tonight, my lord," she said firmly.

"I'm afraid I have other commitments. So do you. Is this not the night you promised to make up to Toby for missing that play? And are not Lynsted and Sally going as well?"

It was true. Lord Toby had got up a party for the theater, and she had promised not to fail him this time. "Later tomorrow, then," she suggested, knowing already that he would counter.

"I must go out of Town briefly, I'm afraid," he said ruefully. "And tomorrow night is the assembly at Almack's. You will not wish to miss that."

"Very well, my lord," she replied, knowing she had been outmaneuvered, "I shall ride with you in the morning."

"Excellent." He bent to kiss her cheek, then took his leave of her. After staring thoughtfully at the door he had shut behind himself, she turned back to her task, dipped her quill in the standish, and wrote, informing Sir Conrad that although she would be unable to accompany him to the park the following morning, she was in need of an escort to the assembly at Almack's. Then, feeling that for once she had outflanked Ravenwood, she dispatched the note and went upstairs to prepare for the evening ahead.

The rain had stopped by morning, and directly after she had had her chocolate and read the post, Cicely donned the grey velvet riding habit with emerald trim that she had worn the day she had met Ravenwood on the road near Malmesbury Park, then went down to meet her husband in the front hall. Ravenwood's eyes gleamed with reminiscent approval when he saw her, but she pointedly ignored the look and merely asked if he was ready to depart.

Nodding, he said he had already ordered the horses brought round, and once they had reached the flagway, he waved her groom aside and tossed her into the saddle himself.

"How was your evening?" he asked politely after a few minutes of silence.

"Very nice, thank you."

"The play was entertaining?"

"Exceedingly."

She stared straight ahead, but she was beginning, in spite of herself, to enjoy his struggle to begin a conversation. Not an inkling of her amusement showed in her expression, however. She would not make matters easier for him.

"I trust Toby provided a good supper?"

"Excellent."

"Tell me about the play," he suggested, a note of satisfaction showing that he thought he finally had her.

"I do not remember it well enough."

"Oh." He gave up for the moment, and silence reigned until they reached the park. The sun had come out and there were only scattered clouds, but the breeze was crisp, and there was a hint in the air of more dampness to come. Few people were in the park. "Cilly, I'm sorry," Ravenwood said suddenly.

"Sorry?"

"I should not have left you alone after they took Meg. You needed me then, and I failed you. There were matters that needed my attention, but I should have let someone else attend to them in order that I might have remained with you."

"Is this the matter you wished to discuss, Ravenwood? Because you would have done better to have said it yesterday," she replied, not giving an inch.

" 'Twould have been better to have told you that very night," he agreed. "But, no, it was not what I wished to discuss." He fell silent again.

"*Was* there anything to discuss?"

He glanced at her ruefully, then shook his head. He seemed to brace himself then, as though he waited for a storm to break. But she was not angry. Oddly, she was rather pleased by the thought that he would ride with her himself rather than let her ride with her cousin. The fact that he had every right as her husband simply to forbid her to ride with Sir Conrad made it all the more gratifying that he felt it necessary to go to such lengths to achieve his ends.

She was not amused that evening, however, when he came down the graceful stairway, looking very grand indeed, just as she and Sir Conrad were on the point of departing for Pall Mall. Ravenwood wore buff knee breeches, a dark blue coat, a gold Florentine waistcoat with numerous fobs and seals, and gold-clocked stockings. He paused just before reaching the bottom and lifted his quizzing glass to peer at them.

"Ah, good. You've not gone yet. What luck. Evening, Uffington."

"Good evening, sir."

"I thought you had to go out of Town," Cicely said accusingly.

"So I did, my dear, but I am, most fortunately, as I am sure you will agree, returned safely to you."

"Indeed, my lord." Noting that his expression held a hint of gentle mockery, she lifted her chin. "Do you go to the assembly, sir?"

"Does not the entire world go to Almack's on a Wednesday evening, my dear? Have you your carriage waiting, Uffington?"

"Of course." Sir Conrad's tone was carefully even, and Cicely glanced apologetically at him.

"Good," said Ravenwood with satisfaction. "Then I'll just send word around to the stables for Tom Coachman to call for us later, and we can go. You won't mind me as an addition to your party, will you, sir?"

"Not at all," replied Sir Conrad. But when Ravenwood turned away to speak briefly to Michael, he grimaced at Cicely. Oddly enough, it was then that her sense of the ridiculous stirred. Sir Conrad looked very much like a frustrated turkey cock. Or perhaps a peacock, she amended. He was so very handsome. Personally, of course, she preferred her men to show more strength in their faces, to look a trifle more rugged.

Ravenwood turned back, completely at his ease, and the three of them went out to Sir Conrad's waiting carriage. The viscount then took full advantage of his age and rank, preceding his reluctant host into the carriage and sitting next to Cicely, which left the forward seat for Sir Conrad.

Cicely did find an opportunity to speak to her cousin, for Ravenwood could scarcely stop them from dancing together, but the results were disappointing, for Sir Conrad had no notion where Meg might be or what might be done to help her. "Short of capturing the real thieves, of course," he added with a quizzical look that showed he considered the possibility a remote one.

"Then you don't think her guilty!"

He shrugged. "Oh, she may know the villains. I don't know her as you do. But 'tis my belief a maidservant simply couldn't be responsible for all that's been taken in these homes."

It was not all she might have wished to hear, of course, but it was much more palatable than what others had been saying. Even her family seemed more shocked than supportive, with the duchess seeming to accept Meg's guilt quite as readily as Lady Uffington did. And the fact that, with a good many people searching for her, no one appeared to have seen hide or hair of the girl nearly a full week later strongly reinforced her grace's belief.

"But, Mama, you have known Meg Hardy for years," Cicely protested when this was pointed out to her during an afternoon visit to Malmesbury House. "How could you think she would steal from you?"

"She had the stolen items, Cicely," the duchess stated reasonably, "and she has disappeared. You must face the facts."

Her father had declined right along to discuss the matter, but her sisters were less inclined to assume Meg's guilt. Amalie said simply that she liked Meg Hardy, and that seemed to be that. Alicia said that stealing when one was the only likely suspect was stupid, and to her knowledge Meg had never seemed to lack sense. Arabella agreed with Alicia, adding that no one who had managed to steal so many jewels as the London thieves seemed to have taken would be content to remain a maidservant, and she pointed out also that the thefts had begun long before Meg had reached Town.

"Yes," agreed Brittany, "I think the whole thing is a mare's nest. After all, we were there only half an hour, and how would Meg even know where to find Lady Jersey's jewels?"

This being unanswerable, Cicely smiled at her gratefully, then glanced at the little ormolu clock on the sitting-room étagère. "I really must be going," she said to the room at large. "We are expected to attend Lady Holland's musical party this evening."

"Do you go with Ravenwood?" Alicia inquired.

"Oh, yes," she chuckled. "I scarcely go anywhere without him these days. If I am engaged to attend a function in someone else's party, either he will decide at the last minute to go with us or he will already be there when I arrive." She grinned at her sisters. " 'Tis almost unsettling, but I find I am bearing up well enough."

Brittany's eyes lit with warm amusement. "I shall walk out with you," she said, putting her arm around her sister's waist.

On the flagway, she peered up at the greying sky. "It is going to rain again, I fear."

Cicely agreed, then bade her good day, and signaled Tom Coachman to whip up the horses. There was a little more traffic than usual, which slowed their pace, and Cicely gazed idly out the window amusing herself by imagining things about the various passersby. The tall, extraordinarily thin gentleman in the fur-trimmed coat was undoubtedly a Russian grand duke in disguise searching the world for a girl who would love him for himself alone. That plump lady in the grey cloak was an infamous courtesan, and the elderly dame walking by her side was none other than her invalid mother. The thin, fox-faced man with the long side-whiskers and hooked nose talking with the slender gentleman lounging against— She sat up suddenly, her gaze no longer idle. She recognized not only the two but also the wiry, gap-toothed man with them.

A moment later, she was stripping off her hat and gloves and banging a signal to Tom Coachman to stop the carriage.

As it rolled to a halt near the flagway she glanced back again, to see that the three men were still involved in their conversation. None so much as glanced her way. She could see their features well enough, however, to be certain she had not made a mistake. George Vaughan was talking to Sir Conrad's servant, Alfpuddle. That in itself she might have paid little heed to. However, the third man in their company, unless she was very much mistaken, was the sneak thief she had seen in the duchess's bedchamber!

15

Thinking quickly, Cicely stripped her pearls from around her throat and stuffed them into her reticule, but decided her wedding ring would attract no particular attention. Pulling her shawl up over her head, she pushed open the carriage door and jumped down to the flagway.

"My lady?" Tom Coachman gazed down at her anxiously, and Cicely wondered what on earth she could say to him. She decided to keep it simple.

"I have decided to walk, Tom. I've been wanting to do so for weeks now, and I have simply decided to take the opportunity now."

"But it's coming on to rain, m'lady."

She glanced up at the overcast sky. It was beginning to look threatening indeed, but she swallowed any worry she might have had and smiled at the coachman. "A little rain won't melt me, Tom, and I daresay it will hold off long enough for me to get home dry."

"But I've got no footman t' walk wi' ye, m'lady!"

"'Tis of no consequence. I don't need one."

"But the master—"

"Pooh to the master," she laughed, giving a snap of her fingers and hoping her coachman would have better sense than to repeat either the words or the gesture to the viscount. "You know he does not interfere with me."

"He'll not like this, I'm thinkin'," retorted the coachman stubbornly, shaking his grizzled head.

She did not choose to think about Ravenwood's probable reaction. It was of little consequence compared to Meg's well-being.

"Ye should not walk alone here, ma'am," said the coachman, making a last effort.

"Oh, don't make such a fuss, Tom!" she snapped, thinking that to look as if she might lose her temper might be the best thing at the moment. "We are scarcely ten minutes from Charles Street, and this is Mayfair, after all. What could possibly happen to me?"

"But, ma'am, I canna—"

"*I* cannot stand here debating the matter, Tom." She glanced over her shoulder to see that, although Vaughan had disappeared, the other two were still speaking. She didn't think the thief would know her, but Alfpuddle certainly would, and if Tom Coachman kept her standing here much longer, they would both be off and gone, or else Alfpuddle would recognize either herself or the crest on the door of the coach. "You are blocking traffic, Tom, and I do not intend to get back into the coach, so you might just as well go home. You needn't say a word to Ravenwood if you are worried about what he might do. He will no doubt still be at White's, in any case, and I shall be home long before he returns. Now go, do!"

Reluctantly he touched his hat and gave his horses the office to start. Cicely stood where she was for a moment, watching until she was nearly certain he would not look back. Then she glanced over her shoulder again to see that the two were still talking. Drawing her shawl closer to her face and shivering in the now-chilly breeze, she wished briefly that she had brought her fur-lined, hooded cloak instead of only her woolen shawl, but then she rejected the notion. Nearly anyone could have a wool shawl, and it would be difficult to tell, particularly in this light, that this one was cashmere. But the cloak, like her pearls, would call attention to her station in life and thus to herself, making it much more difficult to do what she meant to do. For Tom Coachman was right. Ladies of quality did not walk the streets, any streets, alone.

The two men ahead of her straightened, and for a moment she feared they would walk directly toward her. But they turned and strolled slowly away up the street. At the first intersection they paused, and Alfpuddle said something briefly to the other that made him laugh, then he clapped him on the back and turned away up the side street. From the direction he took, Cicely had no doubt he was returning to Uffington House. At any rate, she would know how to find Alfpuddle if she wanted him. And wouldn't Sir Conrad be surprised to hear about the sort of company his man had been keeping?

Of course it was possible that Alfpuddle had merely been sent by her cousin with a message to George Vaughan and had met the fox-faced man by accident. Anything was possible, she told herself, even things that were prodigiously improbable.

The fox-faced man crossed the street, and she hurried after him, only to walk straight into the line of fire as a passing carriage lurched into a muddy pothole and spewed wet mud all over her skirts. Suppressing a gasp of dismay, she told herself sternly that it would now be that much more difficult for anyone to recognize her.

Her quarry was moving more rapidly, and she saw him glance once or twice at the skies. It was certainly getting darker. She could match his pace easily enough, though she was glad she had chosen to wear half boots and not thin sandals when she had set out that afternoon. The rapid pace was taking her away from Charles Street and into streets she did not know well. Half an hour passed before she recognized the Holborn Hill Road, but that didn't help her much, because the little man only crossed it, skittering in front of first one carriage and then another coming from the opposite direction.

She realized she had to get herself across the busy road, and there was no urchin waiting to sweep the crossing, let alone to stop traffic for her. Finally, with her heart in her throat, she ventured off the flagway, then jumped back as a low-slung carriage flashed past. A glance across the way showed her quarry rapidly approaching a side street. When he turned into it, she nearly panicked. She must be miles from home! She could not lose him now simply for lack of a little resolution.

Lifting her chin and straightening her shoulders, she gave a quick glance in both directions before dashing across the traffic-laden road. Then, still running and holding the shawl close about her head and shoulders, her reticule banging against her mud-bedaubed hip as she went, she rushed after him, letting out a long sigh of relief when she finally caught sight of him again. The first drops of rain began to fall.

Her quarry turned again, and suddenly it was as though they had entered a maze, where little narrow, twisting lanes seemed to cross and recross one another. And despite the drizzling rain, there were a good many other people hustling along these same streets. It was gloomy and the smells were dreadful. As she tried to keep her man in sight Cicely shuddered at the thought of what the area would be like on a hot summer's day. The structures lining the streets seemed to be shops of one sort or another with residences above. But shops or not, she didn't think Ravenwood would approve of her visiting the neighborhood even if she had brought her coach and every footman in his employ.

The thought gave her pause, but then the fox-faced man turned another corner, and she hurried after him again, kicking against a pile of garbage in her haste. But as soon as she had her eyes fixed safely upon the man again, her thoughts returned to Ravenwood. It was true that he had interfered with her very little, and she could not remember that he had ever so much as raised his voice to her. A mild rebuke was the most she could remember, and that had happened only when her behavior had not suited his dignity, when he had worried about what others might think.

But there was no one who mattered to see her here. To be sure, it was not a particularly savory part of the city, but no one had attempted to speak to her, let alone molest her. She looked like any one of the other bedraggled women on the street. Ravenwood might be displeased if he learned that she had not ridden home in the carriage, might even scold her for walking unattended, but there was no reason he should even know she had come to a place like this or that he would be more than moderately annoyed if he did discover it. No doubt that sudden hesitation she had experienced just moments ago was due to her upbringing. The duke had always bellowed and blustered at the least little thing. She remembered that when she had visited the Haymarket during her second Season, he had even threatened to thrash her, and though he had not done so, he had frightened her a good deal.

But Ravenwood had never given her cause to fear him. In fact, she had thought him, for the most part, perfectly harmless. However, there had been a time or two when his jaw had tightened or there had been a certain glint of steel in the blue eyes—

Her quarry turned another corner, and she hurried again, forcing the disquieting thoughts from her mind.

It was far more important that she help Meg than that she

worry about whether or not Ravenwood would react unpleasantly if he found out about this little adventure. She knew perfectly well that Meg had never taken so much as a hairpin that did not belong to her. Therefore, someone else had to have put the stolen items in her portmanteau.

Someone else had to have known Meg had been in the Jerseys' town house. And that someone also had to have access to the house in Charles Street. She remembered the day Lord Faringdon and Roger Carrisbrooke had found her at the Lynsteds' house. Faringdon had said then that Wigan had sent him. No doubt Wigan would tell anyone he trusted where she might be found. Certainly he would tell Sir Conrad. And there was no reason to suppose Sir Conrad would not tell Alfpuddle. And if Alfpuddle had been angered enough by Meg's continual snubs, who was to say he might not arrange to implicate her in the thefts out of pure spite?

Had Mr. Townsend . . . No, it had been Sir Conrad himself who had told her about the forty-pound reward for capturing a thief. Could George Vaughan have located the thief for Alfpuddle? But then she realized things had to have happened too quickly. They had, as Brittany had pointed out, been in Berkeley Square for only half an hour, yet the goods—or some of them—had been found that same afternoon. Even if Sir Conrad had called while they were away, Alfpuddle could never have learned about the robbery and Meg's presence soon enough to have tracked down Vaughan and the jewels in time to see them into Meg's possession. The only way he could have done it—if indeed he was responsible—would be if he had had a hand in stealing the jewels himself!

They had turned into a wider street when the little man ahead of her suddenly disappeared, and since there was no intersection near where she had last seen him, it was not difficult to deduce that he had turned into one of the shops. Not certain which one it had been, however, she quickened her pace again, peering through one dirt-streaked window after another. But when she came to the right one, there was no possibility of mistaking it, for the windows were relatively clean and a number of candles glowed warmly inside, casting enough light for her to identify the fox-faced man in conversation with a plump, grey-haired woman behind a counter. With a nod, the woman gestured toward the rear of the shop, and the man turned away from the counter. A moment later he had passed from Cicely's sight through a curtain-draped doorway.

She stepped back away from the shop, peering upward into the gloom and drizzle to try to read the sign over the door. Though she could make out little more than the word "chandler," she knew that if she could discover the name of the road she was on, it ought to be enough to make Ravenwood listen to her and pass the information along to the proper authority, either Mr. Townsend or Mr. Vaughan.

No, she told herself grimly, not Mr. Vaughan. If, as she very much suspected, Alfpuddle was a thief, then the fact that he and the fox-faced man had both been with Mr. Vaughan made a very good case against Mr. Vaughan himself. It was a fact that some thieftakers cultivated thieves until they "weighed forty pounds." Perhaps Vaughan was merely waiting for sufficient evidence against the pair to see them hang. But they had all seemed very friendly, and she didn't think it would be wise to trust Mr. Vaughan.

She stood where she could watch the shop and still be somewhat protected from the rain, which was coming down more steadily now, but though she waited for what seemed a very long time, the man did not come out again.

Not being able to bring herself to stop one of the grimy-looking passersby to ask the name of the road, she began walking back the way she had come, hoping to find a sign that would give her the information. At least, she thought, she was no longer in the awful maze of narrow streets. This one was not only wider but fairly straight and possessed of a moderate number of moving vehicles, including hackney coaches. She stepped forward when she recognized a hack moving in the direction she hoped would take her back toward the Holborn Hill Road. But just as she lifted her hand to signal the driver, there was a flurry of motion, a silvery flash near her arm, and a tremendous hand pushed her back against the wall of the nearest shop with bruising force. As she tried to stop herself from sliding down the stone wall, she caught a glimpse of flying feet and realized her reticule had been snatched by one of those villains known to all and sundry as a cutpurse.

The hackney coach rattled past as she got painfully to her feet. She ached all over from the jarring crash against the wall, but more than that, it was suddenly brought home to her that she was wet, tired, and alone, and that her feet hurt. She had no idea where she was, except that she was a good deal too far away from Charles Street to attempt to walk the distance now, and night was approaching. She remembered that she and Ravenwood were supposed to be dining with the Lynsteds before attending Lady Holland's *musicale*.

Though she still didn't think he would be particularly angry with her once she told him all she had discovered, she knew he would be annoyed if she caused them to be late. And he would not be pleased if she made herself ill again, she thought more dismally. Had she had any notion how far the thief meant to take her, she doubted that she would have attempted to follow. But she had followed, and she had found the chandler's shop, which seemed to be at least a place with which he was familiar. The men at Bow Street, she was quite certain, had found success with less information than that upon which to act.

The problem now was to get back to Charles Street and to do so as quickly as possible. Clearly she would need a hack. Stepping to the curbstone again, she remembered she had no money. Then she remembered what else had been in her reticule, and her hand groped suddenly at her throat. Her pearls! The pearls Ravenwood had given her for a bride gift! They were gone.

She tood a deep breath. This was not the time to worry about it. She must first get home. But the loss of the pearls would annoy him, and it was rapidly dawning upon her that she did not wish him to be annoyed with her. Indeed, it would be most uncomfortable if he was even mildly displeased. She was beginning to think she had done a very foolish thing. And even if they caught the thief, she wondered, how would they prove he had also taken Lady Jersey's things? And how would that keep them from believing still that Meg was in league with him? And where was Meg, anyway? Surely, if she was alive, she must have sent word of her safety by now. A hack lumbered toward her, and she lifted a hand to hail it, feeling suddenly very depressed and on the verge of tears.

"Where to, wench?" the plump, oilskin-wrapped driver peered down at her through the steady rain. Instinctively Cicely stiffened at his insolent tone, and her own was chilly when she answered him.

"Charles Street, if you please." She waited, expecting him

to jump down to help her into the hack, but he merely stared at her.

"Ain't that where the nobs live? Over t' Mayfair?"

"Yes, of course."

"And just what might ye be thinkin' o' doing' there, luv? Settin' up housekeepin' fer a lord, mebbe?" He guffawed at his joke.

Cicely glared at him. "I live there, of course."

"Oh, out a course! A real flash mort! 'N' I be the Queen o' the Nile, meself."

"Look here, will you take me or not?" Cicely demanded icily.

"Take 'e anywheres 'e want if'n I like the color o' yer gelt, lass. Lemme cast me peepers o'er wot 'e got."

"I beg your pardon?" She hadn't the slightest notion what he was talking about.

"Gelt. Ye ken, luv. Lucre, the ready. Sport yer blunt, else I'll be off t' find me a payin' cove."

"You mean money, then." Cicely flushed. "Well, I haven't got any exactly, but—"

"I see 'ow it is, luv. Expectin' t' turn a wee trick fer the ride, were ye? Well, I don't 'old wi' it, not wi' flash morts, and not e'en wi' a prime bit sich as yersel'. Not that I don't think ye'd strip well enow t' gie a man 'is pleasure. Leastwise, not if'n ye was cleaned up a bit. But me missus'd snatch me bald'eaded, so run along wi' ye. Them lords up t' Mayfair ain't goin' t' be needin' a bit o' fluff like yersel' nohow. Best 'e stay wi' yer ain sort."

Cicely understood enough to stare at him with eyes widened by shock. Before she could collect herself to reply, however, he had flicked his whip and the coach rattled away.

"Wait!" she cried. "You don't understand." But it was no use. He didn't even look back.

She began walking miserably toward—she hoped—the Holborn Hill Road, watching for hacks as she went. Twice more she managed to hail one, only to be rejected as a passenger by both drivers. The first smiled knowingly when she began by insisting that he would be paid at the end of her journey, and the second laughed outright when she informed him rather tearfully that she was the Viscountess Ravenwood. When he drove off, she stood upon the flagway with tears and raindrops mingling on her cheeks. At least, she told herself, she had retained sufficient presence of mind with the second of the two to discover that she was in Gray's Inn Lane. That was something, but it was not enough to stem the tears.

Angrily she dashed them away with the back of her hand, only to scratch her cheek with the edge of her wedding ring. She stared at the ring stonily for a full minute, then drew a long breath and began to look for another hack.

This time the driver was fairly young. He, too, wore oilskins over his clothes, and he looked very broad and solid. He grinned down at her.

"Ye're a sight 'n' no mistake. Whither ye bound?"

"Please," she said desperately as she yanked the ring from her finger, "will this take me as far as Charles Street?"

He accepted the ring without looking at it, regarding her instead, his eyes curious and, surprisingly after her experiences with the others, even compassionate. Then he looked down at the ring, holding it flat in his palm, then moving it near one of the carriage lamps to see it more clearly.

"Aye, it will at that," he said at last, letting out a long, slow breath, "and a good bit farther if ye wish it, ma'am."

"No, just Charles Street. Number eight. And . . ." She paused, then went on in a rush. "I'd like the ring back when we get there. You'll be paid for your service, of course, but that is my wedding ring, and I'd like to have it back."

The driver gave her another long, piercing look. Then, with a grunt, he wrapped the reins around his brake handle and jumped down from the box. Opening the door of the hack, he said, "Just you climb inside, ma'am, and we'll have ye in Charles Street afore the cat can wink 'er eye."

She heaved a sigh of relief and let him help her into the coach. As soon as she was seated, he pulled a ragged blanket from under the seat and handed it to her.

"Wrap up in that, ma'am. Ye look chilled t' the bone."

She was, but she hesitated. "I . . . I'll get it wet."

"Never you mind about that. And put this gimcrackery bauble back on yer pretty finger, too. I don't doubt I'll get my blunt." So saying, he handed her the intricately twisted gold band, and with more tears streaming down her cheeks, she slipped it back on.

"Thank you," she said simply, then, "Do you think we might hurry? My husband will be . . ."

He grimaced reprovingly. "If that's where yer 'usband abides, ma'am—or is it m'lady?" She nodded. "Well, 'e's going t' be much as I'd be m'self if'n m' Suzy came home lookin' like yer la'ship does. I just 'ope someone else'll be there t' gie me what's owed, is all." He looked as though he'd like to say more, but he apparently thought better of it and slammed the door shut after adjuring her again to wrap up tight. Then she felt the hack rock with his weight as he swung himself back onto the box.

On the way back to Charles Street she alternately shivered and tried to put the pieces of the puzzle together without thinking about Ravenwood. But his image kept interfering with her thoughts. She had been so frightened when no one would believe her and she had thought she would have to walk home in the dark. How she had longed for his presence then! Big, solid, and reassuring, he would have put an arm around her shoulders, given a lazy snap of his fingers, and everything would have come right.

Not that she hadn't managed by herself, she thought with a small swelling of pride. She was glad she had thought of her wedding ring, for although the driver had been a good deal kinder than the others, it had been the ring that had got his attention at the outset. Without it he most likely would have turned her down, too. Considering what the others had thought about her, she realized she must cut quite a figure. Bedraggled, muddy, worn out, and looking like almost anything other than a duke's daughter and a viscount's wife.

She had flung the wet shawl onto the seat beside her and used the rough blanket to dry her face and arms. But she was wet to the skin, and damp tendrils of hair hung in her face and down her back. Allowing herself one watery sniff, she hoped Wigan would recognize her and agree to pay the driver without calling Ravenwood.

Late as it was, it was too much to hope that the viscount would not yet have returned from White's, but he would no doubt be in his dressing room with Pavenham in stiff attendance, preparing for the evening ahead. No doubt, if he had even noticed her absence, he had assumed she had stayed overlong at Malmesbury House. Surely she ought to be able to reach her own room and make herself more presentable before having to face him.

She realized she could no longer hope to keep him from discovering where she had been, for she could scarcely give him the address of a chandler in Gray's Inn Lane and hope he would think it had come to her in a dream. However, since she would have to tell him, it would certainly be far better if she could pick the best time and place to do so.

Finally the hackney coach slowed to a stop outside Ravenwood's house. Cicely sat where she was for a moment, loath to go inside. But with a lurch of the hack, followed by the dull splat of feet on the pavement, the door opened to reveal the face of the driver. He was not smiling, but there was amusement in his eyes as he regarded her worried expression.

"This the place?" She nodded. "Best go on in, then. Want I should walk up wi' ye?"

Cicely shook her head. "It will be better if I go alone, I think. I'll send someone back to pay you." She looked at him uncertainly. "Do you want to hold my ring until they come?"

He smiled then and held out a hand to help her alight. "No need fer that as I sees it, ma'am."

She tried to return the smile, but her knees felt weak when she reached the pavement, and it required most of her attention to stand upright. She glanced up at the torchlit door. He was right. Best to get it over, whatever "it" was. One hoped only Wigan or, better yet, Michael would be in the front hall. Since the door was kept locked in the evenings, there was always someone there.

She squared her shoulders, then, with a final glance at the oilskin-bulk beside her, she stepped quickly up to the door and lifted the knocker. Scarcely had the first clank been heard than Wigan himself swung the door wide. He looked vastly relieved to see her, but her gaze went instinctively past him, and what she saw made her stop in her tracks even as she prepared to step into the house.

"Where the devil have you been?" Ravenwood demanded wrathfully.

16

Cicely stood in the doorway, feeling quite small and helpless and bedraggled, overwhelmed by both his size and his anger. This was not her father's sort of explosive fury. This was far, far worse—something well beyond the scope of her experience. Ravenwood stood across the hall, near the stairway, yet he had never looked so large before, never so broad or so muscular, and never had his expression been so black. His dark eyes were unhooded now, and smoldered with fury. She stared back, white-faced, wholly unaware of anyone but him. There was a tension between them so tactile that she felt almost as though she could hold onto it for support, to keep her weakened knees from betraying her altogether.

"I asked you a question, madam," he grated. "Must I repeat it?" He took a step toward her, then, his hands clenched at his sides, he stopped himself. "For God's sake, Cicely, where?"

She swallowed, then a noise of clinking harness below reminded her of the hackney coach. She drew a breath, her gaze still locked with her husband's. "I had no money to pay the driver, my lord. He needn't have brought me home. He was very kind."

Ravenwood gestured impatiently to the butler. "See to it, Wigan. Be generous. Where did he find you, madam?"

"In . . . in G-Gray's Inn Lane." The words were barely audible.

"*Where?*" Clearly he couldn't believe what he'd heard. He took another step toward her. She could have no doubt that he was restraining himself only by great effort. But at least, she thought, he was restraining himself. She drew herself up, facing him more bravely. The sooner this was behind her, the better.

"I followed a man there," she said. "He was the same man I saw in Mama's bedchamber the other night. He—"

"You did *what?*" No longer did he attempt self-restraint. Two long strides brought them face to face, and his hands clamped painfully upon her shoulders. As he shook her his voice thundered in her ears, but she was too frightened to take in the words. Then, suddenly, he scooped her up into his arms and turned purposefully toward the stairs. Terrified, she clutched at him helplessly. What was he going to do? He looked angry enough to kill her.

"G-Gilbert, please," she whispered.

He didn't seem to hear her. Taking the stairs nearly two at a time, however, he seemed to be in a great hurry to do whatever it was he meant to do. Her eyes welled with unshed tears. He meant to beat her. As sure as anything, that was his intent. And it would be far worse than anything her father had ever done to her, for not only was Ravenwood a great deal larger than the duke, but he was younger, stronger, and much, much angrier. She trembled in his arms.

At the top of the stairs he halted, then turned to face the hall below, where Wigan was just shutting the front door. "Her ladyship desires a bath, Wigan," he snapped. "At once, man! Very hot." Without waiting for a response, he turned on his heel again and carried her up to her bedchamber. Once inside, he set her on her feet with enough force to jar her bones, then glowered at her.

"You're a damned idiot, Cicely," he growled.

"Oh, please, my lord, I know it was a foolish thing to do, but I had to see where he went, and I could think of no other means by which to accomplish it! I never dreamed I'd get into such a fix."

"You never thought at all," he snapped, putting his face down close to hers and giving her another shake. "Following a man like that to a place like that with no one to protect you and no money to get yourself home again. Coming back here looking like something dragged out of an Irish bog. A disgrace to yourself. A disgrace to me."

Her head snapped up at that, as her own temper managed to submerge some of her fear of him. "I should have known my appearance would distress you, sir," she said sharply.

"Had I realized you would be waiting on the doorstep, I'd have taken the precaution of stopping elsewhere to put myself to rights, rather than allowing myself to appear before you in all my dirt."

There was a heavy silence, making her wish she had not spoken. She stared stubbornly at the top button of his waistcoat. Despite his uncharacteristically energetic activities, not a thread was out of place, although she could detect several damp spots where he had held her against him. She bit her lip as she realized what she must look like by comparison.

"Where would you have gone, my dear?" His voice was calm, but the very calmness sent shivers up her spine. "Would you have gone to a hotel, announcing yourself as the Viscountess Ravenwood, demanding a bath and a change of dress? That would have required money, you know. Or perhaps you would have asked them to send the bill to me. Assuming, of course, that they believed you when you identified yourself." She shook her head, unable to speak, horrified by the ghastly picture his words conjured up in her vivid imagination. "No? Then perhaps you would have presented yourself to Lynsted and Sally. I don't doubt Sal would have helped, had she been alone, but I fear that Lynsted, despite his flirtations, would have brought you straight home to me. Perhaps, however," he went on, his voice taking on an even deadlier calm, "you would have gone to your cousin. No doubt he would have rendered whatever assistance you required."

"No!" Her fears completely overridden by the suggestion in his words, she clutched at his lapels as though she would shake him. "It was a stupid thing for me to say! You made me angry, and I said the first thing that came into my head, but I would never have gone anywhere else. This is my home, Gilbert! I was frightened—"

"You damned well ought to have been frightened!" he snapped, "for a more cork-brained, idiotic stunt I hope never to imagine. You could have been seriously injured, even killed. That section of London—any section of London—for a gently bred female alone, just doesn't bear thinking of!" He might have gone on, but the door opened just then to admit several footmen with the porcelain tub and buckets of hot water. "You're wrinkling my coat, Cicely," Ravenwood said grimly, watching them fill the tub.

She dropped her hands to her sides but didn't watch the proceedings. Still certain he meant to beat her and had been waiting only until his orders regarding the drawing of her bath had been carried out, she concentrated her efforts upon remaining calm and not disgracing herself by becoming hysterical. The cutpurse and the difficulty of finding someone willing to help her had brought home the foolhardiness of her actions more than anything else could do. She didn't need Ravenwood's fury to tell her she had behaved most unwisely. She knew she well deserved whatever punishment he might decree for her, but that didn't mean she would welcome it. The door closed, leaving her alone with him again. She shivered.

"Get out of those clothes," he ordered. "Here, turn around. I'll get those damned buttons for you."

Miserably she obeyed him, and although she moved slowly, it seemed no time at all before her clothing lay in a wet heap upon the floor. He said nothing for a moment; neither did he move to touch her. Confused, she glanced up at him from beneath damp lashes.

"What are you waiting for?" he demanded. "You'll catch your death standing there like that. Get into the tub."

Her eyes widened, and relief spread through her. "You're not . . . You don't mean to punish me?"

A smile tugged suddenly at the corners of his mouth. "Punish you? Did you think I'd beat you for this, Cilly?" She nodded, still wary, finding it hard to realize he would not. "Well, if I put that fear into you, it can only have done you good," he declared, adding with a thoughtful look, "Not that you don't deserve a good spanking for this day's work, my girl, and if you're not in that tub in five seconds—"

Hastily she turned away and climbed into the steaming tub, but when he picked up the soap and moved toward her, she asserted herself again, holding out her hand to take it from him. "Thank you, sir. I can bathe myself, although I'd appreciate it if you would ring for Betty to help me wash my hair."

"Betty is a chambermaid, not a lady's maid."

"Yes, but she has helped me before, and since Meg is—" Tears welled up again, and she choked off the sentence.

"Meg will be perfectly all right, my dear. You would have heard by now if anything dreadful had happened to her. Rest assured, she is quite safe. However,'' he added before she could debate the matter, ''in her absence, I shall have to take her place. Shall I scrub your back?''

''Ravenwood! You'll ruin your coat,'' she said desperately.

''A very good point,'' he agreed, shrugging it off and tossing it upon the bed.

''But that's a silk waistcoat, and though it's got a spot or two already, I'm sure Pavenham can—''

''Say no more, my dear.'' He tugged off his neckcloth and then the waistcoat. ''No doubt you will notice that my shirt is also silk,'' he added, lifting a quizzical eyebrow. The shirt promptly followed the other clothing onto the bed. ''Anything else?'' he demanded, a wicked gleam in his eye.

She shook her head weakly, trying to slide farther down in the tub, unable to keep her eyes off the muscles of his bare chest and arms as he moved purposefully toward her, armed with French soap.

''Good,'' he said, looking her over speculatively. ''I've never done this before, but I daresay I can do the thing as well as that Betty-wench. We begin with the hair, I expect.'' So saying, he picked up a pitcher that had been left beside the tub and emptied it over her head.

She screeched, gasping for breath, doused with cold water that was meant to be used to adjust the initial bath temperature if necessary. Glaring at him, she shivered, but he had realized his error and dipped the pitcher quickly into the tub, emptying the warmer contents over her head at once.

''Ravenwood!'' she protested, when she could speak. ''You'll drown me!''

''Nonsense,'' he retorted, beginning to enjoy himself as he applied soap to her long hair. ''But don't we need clean water to get the soap out again?''

''Yes, and be careful you don't pour boiling water over me next,'' she answered tartly. He grinned at her, then got to his feet and tugged the bell cord. Meeting Betty at the door, he told her to order up more hot water and to see it was brought just to the door.

He was not nearly so efficient as Meg, and by the time he had finished washing her hair the tub was near to overflowing, and he was nearly as wet as she was. Cicely was not sure whether she was nearer to tears or laughter, but at last he rocked back on his heels and declared the job finished.

"Thank you, my lord," she said with a sigh of deep relief. "Now, if you will very kindly hand me one of those towels, I can wrap my head in it whilst I finish my bath."

Obediently he handed her the towel and helped her twist her hair up inside it, but when she held out her hand for the soap, he shook his head with a teasing little smile. "Oh, no, my lady. I have earned this pleasure as a reward for my hard work. I mean to see you well scrubbed from head to toe."

Though she protested, it did her no good. And if his hands chanced to wander now and again, making her gasp and squirm, he still made good his promise, and when he had finished with her, she glowed rosily clean from tip to toe. The glow was not due merely to the scrubbing, however, and when she saw his eyes gleam again with intent, she tilted her face willingly and gave a little moan of delight as his lips came down upon hers. She felt his hands upon her again, this time gently, caressingly. Her breath caught in her throat, and she leaned toward him, urging him on, letting her own hands explore the contours of his bare chest, then moving them upward, sliding her fingers lightly along the corded muscles of his neck, up behind his ears to toy with the thick, dark curls they encountered there. But despite her rising passions, there were other elements to be considered, and reluctantly she pushed him away.

"This water is cooling rapidly, sir," she said with real regret. "I think it would be unwise for me to become chilled again."

"Unwise indeed," he agreed in a low voice, reaching for one of the larger towels stacked on a low table near the tub.

"Moreover, I wish to tell you what I discovered," she went on.

His jaw tightened. "I think the less said about your adventure this afternoon, the better," he said grimly.

She swallowed, sorry to have aroused his temper again. "But I saw where he went," she protested.

"Much use that will do anyone. He's long gone by now and anyone still there will deny having seen him," Ravenwood growled.

"But he may come back!"

"Very well!" he snapped. "Since you will. Where did he go?"

"Well, I followed him from—"

"Spare me the details," he interrupted harshly. "Just tell me the street and house number."

"It was not a house," she said, wishing he would not look so grim. "Though, to be sure, there is a residence of some sort above it, I think. It is a chandler's shop in Gray's Inn Lane. I saw—"

"That will do. Whereabouts in Gray's Inn Lane?"

But that she couldn't tell him. "It was dark and . . . and raining. I couldn't—"

"Enough!" Practically yanking her from the tub, Ravenwood flung the towel around her and began rubbing briskly enough that she feared he would take the very skin from her bones, but she dared not protest. He stopped suddenly, as though he realized he was being a trifle rough, but when his eyes met hers, he still looked angry enough to send a little chill racing up her spine. "Have you any notion how foolhardy your behavior was?" he demanded.

She licked her lips nervously. "I didn't expect to be—"

"How could you expect anything? You went off without thinking at all. Moreover, you lied to Tom Coachman, told him you meant to walk straight home."

"He told you that?"

"Of course he did. As soon as he discovered you hadn't returned. He was nearly sick with worry, moreover."

"I shall apologize to him, sir. It was only that I could think of no other means—"

"I don't wish to hear another word about what you thought or didn't think!" he grated savagely. "I simply want to ensure that this sort of thing never happens again."

"It won't," she muttered in a small voice, feeling quite wretched again.

"It had better not." Though he was calmer, his anger still showed clearly. "I know you thought to help Meg by this escapade, but your action was foolish beyond permission. Catching thieves is the business of thieftakers, my girl, and you must leave them to tend to it. You can only confuse the issue and put yourself in jeopardy by such addlepated meddling as this, and if you ever do anything like it again," he concluded grimly, "I promise I shall make you regret you were ever born. Is that clear?"

"Y-yes, sir."

"Good. Have you got a warm dressing gown? We've got to get your hair dry."

She stepped to the wardrobe to find the blue woolen gown, then dropped the towel in order to put it on, grateful for its fleecy warmth against skin that had been chilled as much by his threat as by the now-damp towel. She looked at him uncertainly as he stirred the fire and put another log in place. He had slipped his shirt back on, and the shirttail hung loosely about his slender hips.

"It will take some time to dry, sir. We shall be most unconscionably late, I fear."

"I've already sent a message to South Audley Street excusing us from dinner."

"Then we are to meet the Lynsteds at Lady Holland's?"

"No."

"I-I see." She swallowed, wishing once again that she could assuage his anger, but not having the slightest notion how to go about it. Clearly, though, this was not the time to mention her missing pearls. She watched him as he poked at the fire. Then he glanced over his shoulder.

"Don't stand there. Come to the fire. How do you dry your hair?"

"Meg usually makes me sit with my back to the fire whilst she brushes it dry."

He carried the dressing chair over to the hearth. "Are you hungry?"

She hadn't thought about it, but the moment he mentioned it, she realized she was famished. Ravenwood took her expression for an affirmative reply and tugged the bell cord. When Betty entered some moments later, he ordered that their dinner be served in half an hour in the sitting room.

Cicely protested as soon as the maid had gone. "I could have waited an hour, sir, and then we might have sat down to it properly in the dining room."

"There is no point in dressing, my dear. You are going straight to bed once you have had your dinner."

Deciding by the look of him that it was a measure of his extreme generosity that she was being allowed to eat dinner at all, Cicely subsided, sitting meekly in the dressing chair with her back to the cheerfully crackling fire while he brushed her hair. Silence fell between them, but after some moments of the rhythmic brushing, she could sense the angry tension easing from him again. She became aware just then of noises from the next room, where the servants were setting a table for their dinner. Some ten minutes later Betty stepped into the bedchamber to tell them their dinner was served.

Ravenwood put his hand to her head, gently grasping and squeezing first one hank of the fine hair, then another. The long, smooth tresses gleamed almost silvery in the dancing firelight. " 'Tis still a trifle damp," he said quietly, "but not dangerously so, I think."

"I'm quite warm, my lord," she told him, her own voice quite low, "and there is a fire in the other room as well, you know."

Indeed, the table had been placed near the sitting-room hearth. A white cloth covered it, and four candles glowed softly around a low floral centerpiece. Covered dishes sat upon a side table, and Michael stood waiting to serve them.

He stepped quickly to hold Cicely's chair, then turned back to the side table to begin serving. After presenting the last dish, he stood back to await their pleasure. Ravenwood glanced up.

"You may go, Michael. We'll serve ourselves now, and I'll ring when I want you to clear."

"There is another course, my lord," he said deferentially.

"This will do," Ravenwood replied, thus in three words dismissing a day's work by the minions in the kitchen. Michael, however, knew better than to point this fact out to him, and Cicely, though she might have expostulated at any other time, thought it best to hold her tongue. Michael turned toward the door to the corridor. "Ah . . ." The single syllable made him pause and glance back at his master. "You may bring my port when I ring and also a small glass of cognac for her ladyship."

"Very good, my lord." He shut the door softly.

Cicely stared at her husband. "Ravenwood, I don't want brandy."

"It will keep off the chill and help you sleep," he returned briefly.

The tone kept her from arguing with him, and silence reigned until they had finished eating. Ravenwood rang for the servants to clear, and a few moments later the food was gone and the table back in its customary place against the back of the sofa. Their chairs had been turned to face the fire, and Cicely held a brandy glass between her hands, swirling the contents gently and watching the effects of the firelight reflected in the amber liquid. Ravenwood's port decanter and glass rested upon a small table at his right hand. The silence continued, but there was no longer any tension in it. It was a companionable silence now, and Cicely felt no wish to break it, although she did glance obliquely at him from time to time. Ravenwood stared into the fire, seemingly unaware of her glances, but the earlier intensity of that stare had diminished, and it now seemed only sleepy and relaxed.

A feeling of contentment crept over Cicely as she watched him more overtly. He lifted his glass to drink, and she watched the muscles of his throat work as he swallowed. He had tucked in his shirt before sitting down to eat, but he had not bothered with his neckcloth or waistcoat, and the shirt was unlaced at the top, so the collar splayed open in a V almost to the center of his chest.

A sort of melting sensation stirred deep within her, and instinct seemed to draw her to him. Impulsively she stood up and moved to sit upon the carpet beside his chair, her legs curled beneath her. Hesitantly she touched his knee. He looked down at her and she was glad to see tenderness in his expression where there had been anger before.

"Gilbert, I'm sorry I was so foolhardy. I'm sorry if I made you worry."

He placed his left hand gently on her hair, stroking idly. "You frightened me witless, Princess."

The words were simple and brief, but she could not doubt his sincerity. He might not love her, but he certainly had a care for her safety. Again the glowing warmth spread through her. Saying nothing further, for fear she would break the spell, she leaned her head against his knee and sipped her brandy, relaxing and beginning to feel languorously sleepy as a result of its influence. When she had finished it, she glanced up at him and, at his silent gesture, handed him the empty glass. Without taking his eyes from hers, he set it down and got to his feet, extending a hand to help her up. Still without speaking, but feeling closer to him than she had felt before, Cicely let him lead her into the bedchamber, where he gently relieved her of her dressing gown and turned back the quilts for her to climb into bed. A moment later he had shed his own clothing and climbed in beside her.

"You are retiring very early, sir," she murmured.

"Very true," he agreed, speaking softly against her ear, "but I do not intend to sleep yet awhile."

She sighed again and snuggled closer, letting him draw her into his arms. He was true to his word, and it was long before they slept. Before that time came, she remembered that she still had not told him about her stolen pearls. But she wanted to do nothing that would spoil the intimacy they shared. She would tell him in the morning.

When she awoke, however, he had gone, and Betty was opening the curtains to let in brilliant sunshine. The skies were clear, and it was as though there had never been a raincloud over London. Cicely stretched, remembering the evening before. Who would have thought that what had begun so disastrously could end so well?

Once more she remembered the lost pearls. If she told him, his anger would very likely be stirred again. She certainly couldn't blame him if it was. The pearls were especially fine and had no doubt cost him a deal of money. It would certainly be better if she could get them back without his ever knowing they had been gone.

The notion came suddenly, and she sat up a little straighter, absently taking her chocolate tray from Betty. Her pearls had that very distinctive ruby-and-diamond clasp in the shape of her initials. Like Lady Uffington's rubies, they could be described easily to someone who might arrange for their recovery.

She remembered then that she had also neglected to mention her suspicions of George Vaughan to Ravenwood. For a moment she thought perhaps she ought to tell him, but then it occurred to her that, since Vaughan himself had no cause to think she suspected him of anything, he might be the very man to recover her pearls for her. The more she thought about it, the better she liked the idea. But she could not arrange to meet the man by herself; so, much as Ravenwood seemed to dislike the association and much as she wanted to please him at the moment, she would have to speak with Sir Conrad.

That posed another problem. She could not very well warn her cousin about Alfpuddle without bringing Vaughan into the matter, and Sir Conrad would scarcely agree to do business with a man she suspected of being in league with thieves, so she decided to say nothing until she had recovered her pearls. That meant that she must not tell him about seeing the sneak thief either, lest he somehow suspect more than she meant to tell him. She would simply have to concoct some Banbury tale or other to account for being in Gray's Inn Lane that would also account for not wishing Ravenwood to know about the loss of her pearls.

"Is his lordship in the house, Betty?"

"I think he is still dressing, m'lady. 'Tis early still."

"Well, I wish to ride in the park, but I daresay he's not dressed for it, so I shall go alone. Will you order my horse brought round, and fetch out my habit, please?"

"Certainly, ma'am."

Fifteen minutes later she was ready. Hastening to the library, she dashed off a brief note to her cousin, claiming urgency and asking that he contrive to meet her in Rotten Row. Then she waited impatiently until her horse was at the door.

She didn't see anyone to serve her purpose until they were several streets away, when she saw two urchins fighting a mock battle with wooden swords. Hailing the nearer one, and ignoring her groom's muttered comments, she leaned over so that her voice would not carry and asked the boy if he wished to earn two shillings.

"Depends," he said, observing her warily.

"I shall give you one if you will take this note to the big grey house in Mount Street, the one with the double green doors in front. You are to give this note to Sir Conrad Uffington and to no one else. You may then tell him that I said to give you another shilling and he will do so."

" 'N' if 'e don't?" sneered the boy rudely, but with his eye on the sealed missive.

"Well, he will. You may be sure of it," she replied, smiling, "for I have asked him to do so in this note. Will you take it?"

"Aye. Wot if 'e ain't t' 'ome?"

"Then you shall have only one shilling, I'm afraid. But it is still more than you have now, you know."

He digested this information briefly, then held out his hand. She pressed both note and shilling into it. "Thank you."

"Ta," he replied cryptically, before taking himself off.

She saw thankfully that he was actually headed toward

Mount Street and hoped he could be trusted to deliver the note. She had not wanted to send one of the Ravenwood footmen, for fear the viscount would discover what she was about. Now was certainly not the moment for him to suspect her of a clandestine relationship with her cousin.

She had been riding in the park for over half an hour before she saw Sir Conrad riding toward her. "What news, sweet coz?" he asked, drawing up beside her. "Expected to see you at Lady Holland's last night."

"Ravenwood preferred to stay at home," she replied glibly. "Conrad, the most dreadful thing! The pearls he gave me have been stolen, and I dare not tell him. I must get them back!"

"Well, I expect something might be contrived," he answered, smiling, "but why can't you tell the estimable viscount your troubles, luv?"

17

Cicely had thought a good deal about how she would answer that question. She looked at Sir Conrad now, wide-eyed. "He would be angry with me," she said simply. "You see, a cutpurse stole my reticule in Gray's Inn Lane."

"What on earth were you doing there?" he demanded. "That's no place for a gently nurtured female."

"No, I know that now." She lowered her gaze meekly. "I should never have gone there. But one of the maids knew of a fascinating shop there that sells all manner of buttons and dress trims. She has talked of it forever, and I decided to have my coachman take me there when I had nothing else to do yesterday. Of course he objected, and I soon saw why, when I saw what manner of place it was. Not at all genteel, as Meg would say." She glanced up at him from under her lashes, willing him to be amused.

He was. "And when you saw what manner of place it was, minx, why did you not order your coachman to drive you home again?"

"Well, of course, I wouldn't do anything so silly. The shop was right there, and with my coachman just outside, I didn't think anything would happen to me, so I went right in. Only I didn't find anything that I truly wanted, so I came away again. And that's when it happened. A boy—well, a youth, really—just ran up and cut my reticule right off my arm."

"And your pearls were in the reticule?"

She nodded. "The ones that Ravenwood gave me for a bride gift."

"Why were you not wearing them, coz?"

"Well," she said with a wry smile, "it didn't seem to be

198

precisely the sort of place to be puffing off my consequence, you know. Still, I must get them back. Do you think your Mr. Vaughan might be able to help me?"

"Don't see why not." He looked at her speculatively. "You will have to pay him a fee, of course, plus a reward upon the successful conclusion of his efforts. Have you got any money of your own, coz?"

"Yes, of course. Ravenwood makes me a very generous allowance," she said firmly, hoping she would have enough. "How much will be required?"

"For the fee, not very much, since he will not be expected to leave Town. Only his expenses, I think. But for the reward . . ." He named a figure that made her blink.

"But that's outrageous, sir!"

"Nevertheless, my dear, he must be empowered to offer the thief more than a fence will offer him. You would not wish to take the risk of losing all, simply for the lack of a little generosity."

"N-no, of course not," she replied, trying to sound more confident than she felt. "And it will not have to be paid unless he is successful, of course."

"Very true." He looked at her again, searchingly. "Shall I speak to him for you?"

"Yes, please. I would rather not have to deal with him directly."

"Of course. 'Tis not the business of a lady of Quality to deal with such men as that. I shall engage to speak with him and then present you with the reckoning. Fair enough?"

"Indeed, yes," she replied sincerely. "I cannot tell you how much this relieves my mind, sir. It would have been most uncomfortable to have to explain this business to Ravenwood."

"A harsh husband, coz? I shouldn't have thought it."

"No, of course not. But the pearls were expensive, I'm sure, and it was through my own stupidity that they came to be stolen. Confessing the whole would not be pleasant."

"Well, you may still have to confess the whole, dear cousin, if George Vaughan fails to recover the goods. In any case, I hope you have learned a lesson from this and will not go to such a neighborhood again."

"Oh, indeed I have," she answered with a shudder. "If I

had not been so worried about Meg, I doubt any of this would have happened.''

"Must say, 'tis a mystery what became of her," he said. "Don't suppose you've heard a whisper?"

"Not one word, and 'tis that which has me in such a worry, for despite the fact that Ravenwood and the Runners all have men looking for her, no one has seen her, and I'm sure she would communicate with me if only she were able to do so.''

"Well, she may turn up yet with some tale or other." He stopped speaking suddenly, his eyes narrowing as he looked straight ahead. "I believe our tête-à-tête is about to end, coz."

She followed the direction of his gaze and saw her husband approaching in company with two of his friends. He was mounted on a magnificent young black, whose skittish action testified to his lack of company manners. As they drew nearer she recognized Philip Wensley-Drew and Roger Carrisbrooke.

Ravenwood smiled, nodding a greeting to Sir Conrad. "Good morning, my dear," he said to his wife. "I'd no notion you were out and about so early this morning."

" 'Tis the beautiful weather, sir. After the dismal time we had of it yesterday, this brilliant sunshine seemed to suggest exercise. Good morning, Mr. Wensley-Drew, Mr. Carrisbrooke. Do you know my cousin?"

The three men acknowledged an acquaintance, though the acknowledgment did not appear to afford Mr. Wensley-Drew, at least, any particular gratification. He looked as morose as ever. Sir Conrad and Cicely turned to join the others, and somehow Cicely found herself separated from her cousin and riding beside her husband behind the others.

"Betty said you were dressing when I left, sir. I thought you must be going to your club."

"No, this devil here"—he patted the black's muscular, playfully arched neck—"needs to learn some manners. I decided today was as good a day as any to begin. Had I known you wished to ride, I would have asked you to join me, Cilly, but by the look of you when I left this morning, I judged you'd sleep another few hours or so."

"Betty brings my chocolate at nine, sir, unless I give orders to the contrary." Now, why, she thought, had she said that? It was as though she were reproving him, and it would not have suited her purpose at all to have been asked to ride with him this morning.

Was there a touch of mockery in his smile? "We shall ride together tomorrow, my dear. Orcus here will need a deal of training before I can promenade amidst the fashionables with him."

She looked the black over admiringly. He was truly a splendid beast, she thought, realizing how much she had missed working with her horses. "Do you think he might allow me to ride him one day, Ravenwood?"

He smiled but, to her surprise, did not condemn the notion outright. "He has never had a sidesaddle on his back, and though I know you are an excellent horsewoman, with experience training spirited young animals, there is no proper place for it here, and he is not used to you. I couldn't chance his bolting with you into traffic. However," he went on, his tone making her look at him hopefully, "when the Season is ended, perhaps you will like to spend some weeks down at Ravenwood. I've some youngsters there you might try your hand with, with my goodwill."

Her eyes sparkled with delight. "I should like that above all things, sir."

She began to think she would very much like to spend more time with him, but it rapidly became clear that to do so immediately might prove to be a trifle hazardous. That very evening, as they were preparing to leave for dinner at Malmesbury House, Ravenwood laid her cloak gently across her shoulders with his own hands, sending tremors through her as his fingers brushed the sensitive skin at the nape of her neck. But she quickly recollected herself when he spoke to her.

"You look very lovely tonight, my dear, but do you not usually wear your pearls with that gown?"

It was true that she did. The gown was a soft rose silk with a triple, ornately embroidered flounce, and the pearls looked very well with it. And although the words stuck in her throat, she knew she must say something. She fingered her gold necklace.

"I thought I would try for a different effect. Do you not like it?"

"Of course. 'Tis most charming," he said. "I merely wondered. Shall we go?"

He did not ask about the pearls again, but from time to time she caught him gazing at her rather speculatively, and once she thought he had been about to speak to her but had, for reasons known best to himself, thought better of it. She knew he must wonder why she had stopped wearing them, for she had been accustomed to wear them often. Soon he would ask her, and what would happen then didn't bear thinking about.

She twice saw her cousin during the week that followed, but he told her only that Mr. Vaughan had agreed to undertake her commission. He seemed to have heard nothing further.

She was beginning to feel a good deal of agitation, for at Malmesbury House both the duchess and Lady Brittany soon noticed that she no longer wore her pearls. "I thought the clasp was loose," Cicely replied glibly to their questions. "I sent them to Rundell and Bridge to have it looked after." And what, she wondered, will be left to say if Vaughan did not find them? She was sinking deeper and deeper into the briars, it seemed, with every waking moment.

To her vast relief, two mornings after the episode at Malmesbury House, she received word from her cousin that he would call upon her that very afternoon. For a while it seemed that Ravenwood would also be at home and thus prevent any chance for private conversation, but when she asked innocently if he was not bored by his inactivity, he agreed amiably that perhaps a stroll to White's was in order. Even so, he dithered about the house until she was ready to scream, finally departing not ten minutes before Sir Conrad arrived and was shown into the first-floor drawing room.

"Oh, Conrad, how glad I am to see you!" she exclaimed. "Pray do not keep me in suspense! Has Mr. Vaughan recovered my pearls?"

"He has done better than that," Sir Conrad replied with a trace of smugness. "He thinks he has laid the thief by the heels as well."

"How clever of him," Cicely said, not particularly caring whether the thief was caught or not, so long as she got her pearls back. "Where are they? The pearls, I mean."

"Well . . ." He spread his hands apologetically. "There is still the matter of the reward, sweet coz."

"Of course. I have it upstairs." She regarded him curiously. "Since he has caught the thief, he will not have had to pay for their recovery, so I daresay he will not want quite so much from me.''

Sir Conrad lifted an eyebrow. ''The reward must be paid, coz. Anything he might have had to pay for the recovery of the pearls would have been an expense added to his fee.''

She stared at him in dismay. ''Then it is indeed fortunate that he has caught the thief, is it not?'' She was quite certain he had not explained the matter in such terms earlier, but perhaps he had mistaken the way Vaughan did business. Suspecting what she did about the Bow Street man, she could well believe him capable of having changed the terms of his contract capriciously.

''You will want to bring the money now, Cicely.''

''Bring it! Whatever do you mean? You said you would—''

''I know what I said, but Vaughan is not altogether certain this man *is* the thief. He did have your pearls, and he has a reputation for being a nasty piece of work, but the most Vaughan could arrest him for now is possession of stolen goods. That's scarcely worth his effort. But if you can identify him as the thief—''

''Your Mr. Vaughan will have another forty pounds to his credit,'' Cicely finished for him. ''Well, I'm quite sure I cannot help him. It was dark and raining, and I scarcely caught more than a glimpse of the fellow.''

''You must at least see him, Cicely,'' Sir Conrad urged. ''Even if you cannot identify him positively, you might still be able to state definitely that he is *not* the man who robbed you.''

''I tell you, Conrad, I scarcely saw him.''

''Nevertheless, sweet coz,'' he said more firmly, ''there are those who would bear witness against their own mothers for a share of that forty pounds. Vaughan would have little difficulty preparing a case, I'm thinking, and how would you feel if an innocent man were to hang merely because you were too ticklish to have a look at him?''

''I don't think Ravenwood would like it if I went to Bow Street with you,'' she said, unable to repress a shudder at the thought of going to the very police court the viscount had once so graphically described to her.

''Well, he's not there, so the point doesn't arise. I told you, 'tis scarcely worth Vaughan's effort to arrest him on the lesser charge. He is detaining him where they met, and I am to take you there. You can retrieve your pearls, pay Vaughan what's due him, and have a look at this thief of his as well. I'll be right there with you, so there's naught to fear.''

The last three words echoed in her brain. Little did he know. Briefly she debated whether to reveal her suspicions or not. She rather thought she should. But Sir Conrad would be sure to kick up a dust, and that would never do. She must get her pearls back before she confided her suspicions to anyone.

''Very well, sir,'' she said at last. ''Wait here whilst I fetch the money and my cloak.''

Upstairs, as she hastily stuffed the bills into her reticule, she thought wistfully of her pistol back home. It was entirely too large for her to hide on her person, of course, but its presence, under the circumstances, would have augmented her courage a great deal. Suddenly she remembered the little silver-mounted pistol Ravenwood had used to shoot the highwayman. It would be just the thing, and she doubted he carried it with him in Town. If only Pavenham was not in his dressing room or bedchamber!

He was not, and a hasty examination of the tall French armoire in the dressing room soon revealed the little weapon, gleaming brightly in a leather box on the second shelf. She lifted it out carefully and examined it to see if it was loaded. It was one of the new double-barreled percussion pistols, and her father had a similar, though larger model at Malmesbury, so she knew enough about it to ascertain that it was ready for firing and to be fairly certain she would not harm herself with it.

Hastily, for fear Sir Conrad would begin to wonder what was keeping her, she rushed back to her own room, removed the wad of money from her reticule, and stuffed it instead into the inside pocket of a large fur muff. It was a matter of but a few moments more to change her thin satin slippers for walking boots, fling her cloak over her shoulders, and pick up the muff, holding the little pistol carefully inside.

Sir Conrad's coach was waiting in the street, and to her astonishment, she saw Alfpuddle seated on the box next to the driver. ''Why is he here, sir?'' she demanded.

''Alfpuddle? Why, just as a precaution, coz. As you have learned, that section of Town is none too safe.''

''What section?'' she asked suspiciously, remembering belatedly that he had not told her precisely where they were going.

"Why, Gray's Inn Lane, of course. 'Tis only logical that the thief would stay in his own neighborhood, and Vaughan agreed to meet him in a shop there, to collect the pearls. Not going to fight shy now, are you, coz?"

His amusement irritated her, and her chin went up defiantly. "Of course not. There can be nothing to fear with both my cousin and a patrolman present, after all," she said sharply, stroking the little pistol in her muff.

She wished she could think that Ravenwood would applaud her courage if he were to learn of it, but she was only too certain he would recognize it for the bravado it was and roundly condemn her actions. As she settled back against the squabs and glanced sideways at her cousin, she wondered if she was not making another foolish mistake. It was all very well to declare that she would be perfectly safe with him and an officer from Bow Street, but the fact of the matter was that she didn't trust the latter as far as she could kick him. And she didn't trust the man up beside the coachman, either. Again she wondered if she ought to tell her cousin the truth of the matter. But once again she hesitated. The pearls were so near to being back in her own possession, and if she told him what she knew, Sir Conrad would most likely order his coachman to turn right around and convey her back to Charles Street. Of course, the pearls might still be recovered, but there would be a great furor, and she could think of no way then to keep the news from Ravenwood. He would know she had deceived him, and he would be angry again. She had gone too far to turn back. She must go the distance now. Once again she stroked the smooth metal surface of the weapon in her muff. She could take care of herself.

When the coach lurched to a stop at last, she allowed Sir Conrad to help her to the pavement. Carefully adjusting the muff, she glanced around to see what the area looked like on a good day. It was certainly not so gloomy. It looked, in fact, like many streets she had passed through when entering or leaving the city. Certainly it was not so frightening as it had been upon the occasion of her first visit. She realized Sir Conrad was waiting, and she turned to join him, then stopped in her tracks when she realized where they were.

She couldn't be absolutely sure, of course, but it *was* a

chandlery. Sir Conrad exchanged a brief glance with his man on the box. "What is it, Cicely?"

Startled, she looked up at him, then collected herself when she realized she could not explain without making things worse than they were. She was beginning to think, however, that she would have to concentrate her efforts upon getting herself and her unsuspecting cousin out of this mess with whole skins. If there was a counter to the right just inside the door of the shop and a curtained exit at the rear . . . But Sir Conrad was still waiting for an answer.

"Nerves, I expect," she said with an attempt at a smile. "It was pretty harrowing when my reticule was taken, you know, and that shop does not look particularly inviting."

He chuckled. "We'll take Alf with us, then. It will make you feel safer."

It would do nothing of the sort, of course, and she silently castigated herself for not thinking before she spoke of fear. But she gathered her courage and, followed closely by the two men, entered the little shop.

It was as she had expected. The plump grey-haired woman stood behind the counter exactly where Cicely had seen her upon that other occasion. She nodded to them in a familiar way that Cicely assumed must be due to Alfpuddle's presence, until she realized that Sir Conrad might have been there earlier to talk with Vaughan.

They passed through the curtained doorway to a cluttered inner chamber, and the first person she saw there was George Vaughan. But even as he got to his feet from behind a rickety table cluttered with candlesticks and other paraphernalia, another man stepped forward, and Cicely gasped, then tried immediately to cover her dismay when she realized the other three were looking at her rather narrowly. She glanced hastily at Sir Conrad.

"My pearls?" she asked, trying to appear calm and hoping he would merely follow her lead until they were safely out of there.

"On the table there," he said. "Mr. Vaughan, show her ladyship, that she may see them to be her own, if you please."

"Right you are, sir. Here they be, your ladyship, and none the worse for wear, neither."

Cicely saw thankfully that the pearls he held out were

indeed her own. "Oh, thank you!" she exclaimed. Shifting the muff to her right hand, she reached to take them. "I'm so grateful to you, Mr. Vaughan."

"Half a mo', me lady," he said, grasping her wrist. "There be still the small matter of the reward promised for work completed. As it was," he added with a smirk.

"Oh, of course." She reached back into the muff and took out the wad of money. "Please count it, but I'm certain you will find everything in order." Her gaze drifted to the fox-faced man, but she forced herself to look back at the table, wishing she could simply scoop the pearls into her muff and run.

"Well, Cicely?" She looked curiously at Sir Conrad, not understanding him for a moment. He nodded toward the fox-faced man but did not take his penetrating gaze away from her. "Is that the man who stole them from you?"

"No, oh no, it is not," she muttered. "I am quite certain he is not the same man."

"Why so sure, ma'am?" Vaughan asked sharply. "He had them in his possession, after all, 'n' he's known in Bow Street."

" 'Ere now," protested the fox-faced man in shrill tones, "wot 'e pullin' 'ere? I ain't niver seed them beads afore, 'n' well 'e know it. Ye b'ain't weighin' Tom Breck fer forty pound, Georgie Vaughan, 'n' 'at's a fac. Them bits was 'ere afore—"

"Silence!" roared Vaughan. "You've not answered me, ma'am. How are you certain this is not the man?"

"Why, because I saw him—" She broke off suddenly, feeling her cheeks redden as she realized she had been about to say the man couldn't have stolen from her because he had been inside the shop at the time. Drawing herself up, she collected her wits and looked down her nose at Mr. Vaughan. "I saw the thief running away," she said carefully but with icy hauteur. "He was much bigger than that man. And now, Mr. Vaughan, I have said all I am going to say to you. I must get back to Charles Street. My pearls, if you please."

Still regarding her suspiciously, Vaughan nevertheless handed them over, and they quickly disappeared into her muff.

"Cicely," said Sir Conrad gently from behind her, "I received the distinct impression when we first entered this place that you recognized that fellow. Are you quite certain he is not your thief?''

The time had come, she decided, although she would have preferred to postpone it. Sir Conrad would no doubt know she was lying if she tried to fob him off now and would press her for the truth. Calmly she stepped away from the table and took the little pistol from her muff. "Yes, Conrad, I recognized him, but he is not the man who took my pearls. Stay right where you are and do not move, Mr. Vaughan. Nor you," she said sharply to the fox-faced man, who stared at her in astonishment. "Conrad, watch Alfpuddle. He is in league with them. And if you have a pistol by you, I'd as lief you'd let them see it, for there are but two bullets in this one, although I am not particular," she added quickly when Mr. Vaughan took a step toward her, "as to which of them I shoot first.''

"I didn't think a pistol would be necessary, Cicely," Sir Conrad said softly just before his hand clamped her wrist in an iron grip, forcing her to lower the pistol.

"Conrad! Never say you, too, are with them!" she said, staring up at him with more disgust than fear.

"My regrets, coz, but I fear 'tis true. When you said at your mother's ball that you had seen the thief, I feared you might recognize Breck if you saw him again. Then the coincidence of your being in Gray's Inn Lane the same day Vaughan sent Breck here to lie low—despite your clever little tale— was a bit too much for me to swallow. I decided to test matters for myself, and so I brought you here.''

"We'll ha' t' do fer 'er," grated the fox-faced man.

"Conrad!" Cicely protested, understanding the man's meaning well enough. "You professed to care for me. Surely you cannot mean to let them harm me!"

"Care for you, sweetheart? Why should I? When I sought your favors in company with a host of other like fools, I got nothing but icy disdain for my trouble. I'll confess I never meant matters to come to this, but you've only yourself to blame, I'm afraid.''

"Why have you been so attentive, then?" she demanded, shocked by his words.

"Naught but fun and gig to create trouble between you and Ravenwood—a little revenge, if you will. But matters got a trifle out of hand." Cicely did not attempt to struggle with him, but she retained a firm hold on the pistol despite his bruising grip on her wrist.

"What will you do now?" she asked grimly. "You cannot mean to let them kill me."

"She is quite right," Sir Conrad said to the others. "It is known that I collected her from her house, and I doubt Ravenwood would believe for a moment that I simply misplaced her. We cannot release her, of course, but I shall have to leave the country, and I think it would be as well for Breck and Alf to do the same. Nothing is known against you, George, so you may carry on as before."

"She may have told them about this place," Vaughan said.

"Not a chance," Sir Conrad chuckled. "I don't doubt for a moment that she followed Breck here, but I daresay she kept mum, hoping she could get her precious pearls back before Ravenwood discovered what she had been up to. We'll take her with us in case we have need of a hostage. Don't fear she'll escape us, either," he added, grinning. "I'll see she behaves."

"We'll all of us see to it," Alfpuddle murmured, leering. "Might be a bit o' fun in it at that."

"To be sure." Sir Conrad didn't trouble to disguise his amusement at her fury. "Give me the popgun now, sweet coz. You don't want it any longer."

But when he moved to take it from her, Cicely's fury exploded, and she struggled frantically to retain possession of the weapon. But he was far too strong for her. Quickly realizing she could not win, she squeezed the trigger, discharging both barrels. The resulting explosion of sound seemed to reverberate from all four walls.

There was a scream, and to her astonishment, she saw the fox-faced man reel backward into the wall, clutching his shoulder. In the split second after the weapon discharged, Sir Conrad snatched it from her, but in so doing, he released his grip upon her wirst, and Cicely whirled to face him, launching a kick with every ounce of strength she could muster behind it. The toe of her leather boot caught him just under the kneecap, and he howled, grabbing instinctively for the afflicted joint, at which time she doubled up her fist and slammed it against the side of his chin. As he staggered from the blow, both Vaughan and Alfpuddle recovered from their momentary stupefaction and flung themselves at her. Ducking under the latter's arm, she grabbed a large bronze candlestick from the table and swung it in a wide arc, catching his outstretched hand with the force of her blow. It was enough to make him jump back again with a yelp of pain. Breathing heavily now, she hoisted the candlestick again to fling it at him, but at that moment Vaughan closed in from behind, grabbing her upper arms in a viselike grip.

His touch acted upon her senses like a torch to a pile of dry kindling, and she fought him like a madwoman, kicking out at the same time to fend off the approaching Alfpuddle and screaming the while at the top of her lungs.

"Hush that row!" Alfpuddle snapped, attempting without much success to grab her flailing legs. Behind him, Cicely could see her cousin straightening himself and knew it was but a matter of moments before they would render her helpless, but the thought only made her shut her eyes to the sight of him and struggle the harder, blindly using even her finger-nails and teeth whenever the opportunity was afforded her, determined to cause as much grief as possible before they managed to subdue her. There was a sudden flurry of noise, and the patrolman released his grip, but another, stronger one took its place. Thinking it must be Sir Conrad, she tried desperately to reach his hands with her teeth, twisting and turning wildly when she realized Alfpuddle was no longer grabbing for her legs.

"Cicely, stop! Damn it, you little vixen, it's all right. You're safe. Cilly, it's me!"

His voice reached her at last, and she opened her eyes, feeling both relief and dismay. "Ravenwood!"

Eyes narrowed, he held her away, looking her over from head to toe. Her hair was a mess, and her cloak had been ripped away entirely, but he didn't seem to see much amiss with her. "She's little, but she's mighty, my friends," he said. She looked around her then to find the grinning faces of Sir David Lynsted, Sir Reginald Blakeney, Roger Carrisbrooke, Lord Toby, and even Mr. Wensley-Drew. The latter held Sir Conrad by one arm while another plump, familiar figure had him firmly by the other.

"Mr. Townsend! But, Ravenwood, what on earth?"

"Tell you all about it presently. Have you any notion how much damage you've done here?" he demanded with a wry grin. She looked around the room. The fox-faced man lay slumped against the wall, his bloodstained hand pressed against his shoulder. Sir Conrad, glaring at her, had a large bruise forming on his chin and sported a decided limp when they led him from the room; Alfpuddle's hand was bleeding and his face was scratched in several places. Of Vaughan there was no sign. Cicely's mouth dropped open.

"You gave quite an accounting of yourself in this little match, my dear," Ravenwood drawled. "I must introduce you to Gentleman Jackson as a bright young comer. That is," he added, lowering his voice so that only she would hear him, "if you survive the round you've got coming with me."

18

With a tiny gasp she turned to face him. He was still smiling, but the smile did not, for once, reach his eyes, where the expression was a good deal more in keeping with the harsh note she had heard in his voice. She had accepted his display of amusement at first, simply because her head was still spinning and because she had not wanted to question it. But now she realized his laughter had rung false, and his jokes had been a trifle forced. She saw him glance at the silver-mounted pistol lying some feet away on the floor, then to the muff, likewise on the floor, with the string of pearls clearly visible at one end. From there his gaze drifted to the wad of money on the rickety table, where Vaughan, in his initial shock at seeing her with the pistol, had dropped it. Then he looked at her again, and she could have no doubt from his expression that there would be a reckoning between them.

Sir David stepped forward to pick up her cloak and muff from where they lay, and Ravenwood helped her to her feet. Swallowing with difficulty, she shook out her skirts and managed to accept her things from Sir David with a smile. Clearly Ravenwood wished to keep their differences private, and she certainly didn't want to suffer what promised to be a rare trimming in front of the others, so her mood must seem to match his. Though no one, she realized, would blame her if she seemed a trifle distraught over her recent misadventures. Indeed, Sir David regarded her anxiously.

"Are you all right, Lady Cicely? Those villains didn't hurt you, did they?"

"I am perfectly all right, thank you, sir," she responded with a grateful look for his concern. He glanced uncertainly at Ravenwood, and she knew that he at least was not fooled by the viscount's outwardly light manner.

"She seems to have suffered no serious harm, Gil," he said quietly.

"It is to be hoped that her adversaries may say the same," retorted his lordship. "I should dislike any one of them to die before he may be properly hanged."

Lord Toby, who had gone out with the others, now stepped back into the room. "The others have gone with Townsend to lend him a hand. My carriage is at your disposal, Ravenwood."

"Thank you. Take Cicely with you. I've got my horse."

"I'll tend to your mount, Gil. You belong with your wife," Sir David said firmly, his gaze challenging Ravenwood to debate the matter. But the latter merely shrugged.

"Much obliged to you. Come along, Cicely."

"What about my cousin's coach?" she asked Sir David.

"Gil sent it back to Uffington House before we came in. Properly put the wind up that old coachman, too," responded Lynsted, smiling at her.

"How did you come to be here at all?" She wanted to keep talking so as not to think about what was passing through the mind of the big man beside her.

This time it was Lord Toby who answered. "You behold in us, my lady," he said with a confidential air, "special agents of Parliament, if you can believe it." He chuckled, patting his paunch fondly. " 'Tis all due to Henry Grey Bennet's being a cousin of Carrisbrooke's, don't you know."

"Henry Grey Bennet? Is he not the man who organized the select committee everyone has been speaking of?"

"The same." They had reached his coach, and a footman sprang forward to open the door and let down the steps. Only Lord Toby, Cicely thought with genuine amusement, would ride to a criminal raid in a luxurious coach attended by liveried servants. He seemed unaware of her amusement, however, since he was too caught up in his tale.

"There was much opposition to Bennet, of course," he went on, following her into the coach but hospitably taking a forward seat so that Ravenwood might sit next to Cicely. "Fact is, the magistrates insisted the city had never been in a more tranquil state, but everyone knew that was fudge, of course."

"But how did you come into it?" Cicely asked, profoundly

aware of her husband's weight as he took his place next to her. His thigh and arm touched hers, and she resisted an urge to squeeze further into her corner, away from him.

Lord Toby rattled on. "We were bored, don't you know, what with the peace and all, and when his cousin told Carrisbrooke he had little faith in the police being able to investigate the corruption in their ranks, Carrisbrooke suggested that the Inseparables might be able to lend a hand. Bow Street was thought to be above reproach at first, and so Bennet had already spoken to Sir Nathaniel, who recommended Townsend. It was Townsend who suggested we assist him in place of men from his own foot patrols. We thought he was being a bit finicking, but turns out he had the right of it. Fact of this fellow Vaughan being a Bow Street man will surely set the cat among the pigeons."

"It has already become the most elaborate investigation into the London police that Parliament's ever undertaken," said Ravenwood suddenly. "Shouldn't be surprised if it doesn't result in some sweeping reforms at last."

"That Vaughan fellow got away, you know," Lord Toby put in. "Not that it will make much difference. They'll catch him."

"What will happen to Sir Conrad?" Cicely wanted to know.

Ravenwood looked at her, and his expression softened. "Not much, I'm afraid, unless you want me to charge him with abduction."

"He d-didn't abduct me, sir." She wished her voice had been steadier, but she couldn't seem to speak properly. His next words, though spoken matter-of-factly, did not help.

"I thought as much."

"Just conspiracy, then," Lord Toby said quickly. "A fine, no doubt, and he'll probably want to absent himself from Town for a good long while. Hard upon his poor mama, of course."

Cicely did not think there was much love lost between Lady Uffington and her son, but family feeling kept her from expressing these sentiments, so she merely nodded.

"What about the others?"

"Breck will hang, of course, if he don't die from the bullet you put in him. Damned pretty shooting," Lord Toby said approvingly.

"It was unintentional, I assure you," she said, trembling a little at the thought that she might actually have killed a man.

"Well, anyway, it don't matter. And if he implicates that Alfpuddle fellow, he'll hang as well. Good job, too, if you ask me. Nasty piece of work. Seems there's a gang of them operating throughout the city," he said. "Already got evidence against five police officers—six, counting your friend Vaughan. Planning robberies for others to carry out so they can arrest them for the reward money. They've fingers in other pies as well, we're finding."

He rambled on, going into minute detail about both the villains themselves and the efforts of the self-styled Parliamentary agents to gather evidence against them. Most of the work of the latter group, as it transpired, had been of a statistical nature, the gathering of information from various magistrate's courts, which was then interpreted by Mr. Townsend to show clearly that police officers must indeed be involved in a citywide conspiracy. Vaughan had been suspected for some time, simply by virtue of his uncanny knack for recovering stolen property whenever the reward was a lucrative one.

"When you told me about the chandler's shop," Ravenwood put in quietly, "it proved your sneak thief was connected with Vaughan."

"How?"

"The shop belongs to Vaughan's mother-in-law," he explained. "We've had an eye on it for some time."

He lapsed into silence again, and Cicely began to realize at last what sort of business she had stumbled into. No wonder he was angry with her, when her meddling might have jeopardized a parliamentary investigation! Worse than that, she told herself. It might have gotten her killed. She had a notion that Ravenwood knew the whole, too—about her pearls and the fact that she had paid Vaughan to recover them. They were safely tucked in her muff again, but he had surely seen them when Sir David retrieved the muff from the floor. He had also seen her pick up the money from the table, but he had said nothing about it. Nor had anyone else questioned her right to it.

Ravenwood had said he would make her regret she was ever born if she meddled again. The thought came unbidden, and her hands clutched at each other inside the muff. The oblique glance she shot at him did nothing to reassure her, either, for he gazed straight ahead, his expression stern and unyielding. No doubt he was thinking ahead to the accounting that was due him.

She would be lucky if he did not strangle her for this business, she thought. Why, then, did she have the absurd desire to reach out to him, to smooth away the tension in his jaw? No, more than that, she wanted to snuggle in his arms, to hold him and let him hold her. She looked away again, unable to bear watching him, knowing he must be furious and yet unable to comfort him.

One does not comfort rage, she thought, mentally shaking a finger at herself. The very notion showed how addled her thinking had become. One might wish to soothe another's fury for one's own sake, but how silly to think of soothing Ravenwood's for his own sake. It was just that she loved him so very much.

She gave a little sigh as the thought clarified itself in her mind. It was no blinding revelation, of course. She had simply resisted admitting it to herself before. But she could scarcely acknowledge such absurd notions as wishing to kiss away his anger, or wanting to send poor Toby to the devil so that Ravenwood could bellow at her in privacy, without acknowledging as well that she loved him. Above all things, she wished they might have the reckoning over and done, so that they might be comfortable again.

That they *would* be comfortable again she had no doubt, for she would see to it herself, and he was amiable and even-tempered enough, and possessed of sufficient humor that it would not be especially difficult, despite the fact that he had given her no reason to think he returned her love.

Toby nattered away, but he might just as well have been talking to himself for all the heed she paid him. The ride was beginning to seem interminable.

At last, however, the coach turned into Charles Street, and Lord Toby announced unnecessarily that they had arrived. He also informed them that he was expected elsewhere and could not stay to drink a dish of tea with them. The fact that neither pressed him to remain weighed not at all with him, and he bade them a cheery good day, much as if they had been out for a simple turn about the park.

Ravenwood drew Cicely's hand firmly into the crook of his

arm, and she went with him up the steps, thinking that now it would come. The reckoning at last.

Wigan opened the door. "Good afternoon, my lady. Her ladyship is in the first-floor drawing room," he added blandly.

"Whose ladyship?" Cicely asked stupidly.

Ravenwood shot his butler a speaking look and Wigan nodded. " 'Tis Lady Ravenwood, sir," he beamed.

"How do you do, Ravenwood." The fragile, lilting voice wafted down from the gallery, and Cicely looked up to find her mother-in-law peering down at them through her silver lorgnette. "Pray do not look so overjoyed to see me, my dear," she said, speaking directly to her son. "I promise you, there was nothing else I could do. She would come, will you nil you, so what would you? Dear me, I sound like that Shakespeare person."

Cicely hadn't the faintest idea what her ladyship was talking about, so she looked to her husband. But he was regarding his mother and shaking his head a little, a rueful twinkle in his eye.

"It will be all right, ma'am. Where is she?"

"Here." Lady Ravenwood waved her lorgnette, and to Cicely's astonishment, a grinning young woman appeared beside her at the railing.

"Meg!" she squealed, pulling away from Ravenwood without a second thought and racing up the stairs to hug Meg Hardy. "Oh, Meg! Where have you been? Everyone's been looking and looking for you!"

Lady Ravenwood turned the lorgnette toward her daughter-in-law, then lowered it and turned back to peer down at her son, lifting an elegantly arched brow. "I'd not the slightest notion your wife was such a hurly-burly girl, Ravenwood," she said.

"Quite beyond control," he agreed with a little smile.

But Cicely scarcely heard him, for she had flung her arms about Meg and was demanding to be told the whole.

"Have you been with her ladyship?" she asked, astonished.

"Aye, the master took me down and said he would throttle me an I so much as sent a message to you or to anyone else."

"Then you did come here! I knew you would, just as soon as you were free!"

"I never, Miss Cicely. First I was with Mr. Carrisbrooke

until his lordship and Mr. Pavenham fetched me down to Ravenwood. Oh, and 'tis a beautiful place, Miss Cicely.''

"Never mind that! What happened to the men who abducted you, and how did you get to Mr. Carrisbrooke?''

"What men? 'Twas his lordship and the others.''

"What?'' She whirled on Ravenwood, now coming up the stairs at a leisurely pace. "You! You knew she was safe and you never told me! How dare you, sir!''

"I did tell you she was safe, Princess. Any number of times, but you didn't believe me.''

"You never told me that—''

"Never mind that now,'' cut in Meg, who had been looking her mistress up and down with an expression of increasing astonishment. "I should like to know, Miss Cicely, just what in the world you've been about to turn yourself into such a shagrag. 'Tis a disgrace, the way you look. And to be coming into a gentleman's house that way, too. Not but what it isn't your own house, too, of course, for it is, but that's no call to look like something from I don't know where, and no mistake. So just you march straight upstairs, and there you'll bide till we've set you to rights again.''

Cicely would have liked very much to point out to Meg Hardy that it was outside of enough for her to be talking to her mistress in such an impertinent fashion. But she could place no dependence upon Meg's accepting such a snub in the proper spirit. She'd be much more likely to place her hands on her hips and tap her toe while she raked her mistress down in fine style. Cicely glanced at her husband, but there would be no interference from that quarter. His expression, though guarded, showed something perilously akin to unholy amusement. He offered his arm to his mother.

"Come into the drawing room, ma'am, and tell me all about your journey. I trust the roads were passable.''

"Come along, Miss Cicely.''

"Very well. Oh, Meg, I'm glad you're back,'' Cicely exclaimed, hugging her again. "I was so worried about you.''

"Well, I knew you must be, and so I told his lordship, but he said if those villains found out who had snatched me from the Bow Street men, the fat would be in the fire for sure.''

"But he should have told me!'' They had reached her bedchamber, and she strode agitatedly toward the window.

"He couldn't,'' Meg said, opening the wardrobe. "Not

without he told you about Sir Conrad, too, which he'd have
to have done to keep you from spilling the gaff to him, and
you'd never have kept a still tongue over that, Miss Cicely,
and well you know it.''

"He knew about Conrad, then?" That was a depressing
thought, but it explained why he had objected to leaving her
alone with her cousin when he had no qualms about leaving
her with his friends.

"He only suspected," Meg told her. "Get out of that dress
now, m'lady. He couldn't risk letting him get wind of the
facts. They knew I never took nothing what didn't belong to
me. His lordship said he knew full well I'd been made game
of, and he couldn't leave me to be humiliated in Bow Street.
But they didn't have enough evidence against the others yet. I
can tell you, Miss Cicely, I nearly went daft, worrying about
the mess that Betty was likely making of your things whilst I
was away.''

Cicely stood in her shift and held up her arms to let Meg
slip her lavender silk gown over her head. She wouldn't have
to change for dinner later. If she was allowed to have dinner,
she thought ruefully. She remembered the twinkle in his eye
when he had moved away with Lady Ravenwood. Perhaps it
would not be so bad. Still and all, he would have a thing or
two to say to her that she would just as lief not hear, and she
wished they might have a few moments' privacy so he could
get them said. It occurred to her that, had he wished to speak
to her immediately, he was perfectly capable of dismissing
both Meg and his mother in order to do so. Clearly, then, he
meant for her to think about her sins and to anticipate whatever was in store for her.

Well, she thought, sitting down to have her hair restored to
order, thinking about one's sins had never, in her experience,
done anyone much good, and she had learned as a child that
it was better to think of almost anything rather than the
punishment one had coming. So she would simply go down
to the drawing room and renew her acquaintance with the
dowager until it was time for dinner. She was halfway out the
door before she turned back to the bed and took her pearls
from the muff.

"Meg, fasten these for me, will you, please?"

Moments later she entered the drawing room, head high,
and greeted her husband and mother-in-law politely. Decid-

edly the twinkle was back in Ravenwood's eye, but he soon left them, saying he, too, must change or be put to shame by two such beauties at his table.

Her ladyship lifted her lorgnette and peered at Cicely. "A decided improvement, my dear."

"I hope you are well, ma'am."

"Oh, yes. I only look as if I am past praying for. Have done since I was sixteen. 'Tis an asset at times, though, believe me, particularly with menfolk. And by the sound of your recent madcap adventures—oh, yes, Ravenwood has been recounting them to me—'tis a habit you might consider cultivating. Your skin tones would be ideal for it, but you must learn to languish more." She studied Cicely again through the lorgnette. "I was always willowy, you know. Looked as though a stiff wind would blow me to France. The way your chin went up when you walked in just now, you looked more the type to order the wind to cease at once."

Cicely found herself smiling, though by what Lady Ravenwood had said there was little to smile about. The dowager clearly expected her to need a defense of some sort in the near future, which did not speak well for the state of Ravenwood's temper.

Dinner was served an hour later. It was a cheerful enough meal, and afterward they returned to the drawing room for what the dowager called a comfortable coze, but which Cicely quickly discovered meant that Lady Ravenwood intended to catch up on all the latest *on dits*. She was beginning to think she could stand very little more when the dowager suddenly rose from her chair and announced that she was not going to wait up for the tea tray.

"I have had a long day," she said, sounding very frail indeed, "and I intend to seek my bed."

"What a good idea, ma'am!" Cicely agreed with a trifle too much enthusiasm. Then, realizing how she had sounded, she flushed deeply, adding, "I-I mean I, too, am very tired. I daresay I'll go up with you. You will forgive us, will you not, Ravenwood?"

"As you wish, my dear." He got to his feet and bent to kiss his mother. "Good night, Mama. I'm truly glad you came."

She smiled up at him and touched his cheek, then turned to Cicely. "Come along, child."

Meg was waiting for her and had clearly been going through her wardrobe. "Not so bad as I'd feared," she said. "That Betty might make something of herself yet. You're early."

"It has been a long day," Cicely said, listening carefully for sounds from the adjoining room while Meg relieved her of the lavender gown and chemise, and slipped the lacy nightdress over her head. Cicely sat down at the candlelit dressing table then, and Meg pulled the pins from her hair, letting it fall like a silvery veil almost to her waist. She picked up the brush.

" 'Tis glad I am to be home, Miss Cicely," she said after a few strokes. "Just didn't seem right, not putting you to bed each night like I'm used to do."

"You'll have to forgo the pleasure one more night, Meg." He stood on the threshold, having opened the door from the corridor while Cicely watched the door to his bedchamber. She turned toward him, trying to read his expression, but he was smiling at Meg. "I'll finish for you," he said. "You can go on to bed, Meg."

"Yes, my lord." She set the brush down on the dressing table, bade them good night, and a moment later they were alone.

Cicely sat perfectly still, watching him warily while the candles' glow shot dancing highlights through her hair.

Ravenwood loosened his neckcloth and pulled it off, then shrugged out of his jacket and cast both articles onto a nearby chair, all without taking his eyes from her. The expression in them was unreadable. He straightened.

"Come here, Cilly," he said quietly.

Obediently she rose and went to stand before him. He looked down at her gravely, then raised his hands and set them lightly upon her shoulders.

She looked up into his face. "I know you must be dreadfully vexed with me, sir," she said.

He gave a weary smile. " 'Vexed' is a mild word compared with most of the feelings I have had today. I have alternately wanted to shake you, beat you, scold you, kiss you, and hug you. Which do you suggest I attend to first?"

Her eyes stung. "Oh, please, sir, hug me. I have wanted you to do so since I first saw you in that awful place." And when he obligingly opened his arms, she flung herself into them, thinking she had never experienced anything so com-

forting as when they closed around her again. She buried her
face against his chest, attempting to stifle the tears that
suddenly seemed to insist upon plaguing her. Ravenwood
said nothing while he held her tightly for a moment, but then
his hold relaxed.

"What next?" he asked gravely.

She remembered the list he had rattled off and trembled a
little, but then she lifted her chin and looked him in the eye
again. "I should prefer that you kiss me, of course," she
replied, "but I expect it would be wiser to have the scold
first."

"And the other things?"

"Do you truly mean to beat me, sir?" She watched him
from under her lashes, thinking he would not, but unaccountably
relieved nonetheless when he shook his head and smiled at
her.

"After seeing your defense against those four today, I
believe it would be more than my life is worth."

She smiled back. "I would never treat *you* so, my lord."

"Ha!" The crack of laughter surprised her. "How can you
say that when you trounced me before we were even married?"

Chuckling, she nodded. "I had forgotten. But I truly do
not think I would attempt such a thing again."

"Just as well for you if you do not," he said, growing
serious again. A small silence followed, but when she looked
up at him anxiously, he went on. "That was the sop before
the scold, I'm afraid. If my men had not been watching both
your precious cousin and that shop, your tale might well have
been told today. You would have been far wiser to have told
me the whole last week when your pearls were stolen." Her
eyes widened with dismay. "Of course I know. My men in
Gray's Inn Lane told me about the episode, not realizing, of
course, that they were telling me about my own wife. I didn't
realize myself until days later that your pearls must have been
in the reticule. I thought about confronting you then, but I
hoped you would come to me."

"I wanted to," she muttered, "only—"

"You needn't explain, Cilly," he said gently. "I know I
frightened you. The Lord knows I meant to frighten you. But
I meant it to keep you from doing anything foolish, not to
force you to it."

"I thought so long as I was with Conrad, I would be safe."

He nodded. "I should have put a stop to that relationship the moment we suspected him, but I was afraid of setting up your back."

"When did you suspect him?"

"When he made such a point of Vaughan's talents."

"But you were annoyed about him before that," she pointed out.

He nodded with an apologetic grimace. "You and your damned modern marriage!"

"Mine! But I thought that was what you expected!"

"Nonsense. I wanted a wife to love and to love me. I'm afraid I'm an incurable romantic, my dear."

"To love, my lord?" She stared at him, hardly daring to hope he would repeat the magic words.

"Yes, minx, to love. I have loved you since you were fourteen. Until you emptied a bottle of claret over my head, of course. I admit to a second thought or two at that juncture."

Smiling ruefully, she put her hand on his arm. "I have been a fool, my lord, in more ways than one. I thought 'twas for my dowry and to please my father that you married me."

"I didn't need your dowry, love. I'd plenty to keep us comfortable, and even if I hadn't, your father would have made me a suitable allowance as his heir whether I had married you or not."

"Perhaps you *should* have beat me, sir, or at least shake me for being such an idiotish wife," she said, looking woeful.

"No." He pulled her into his arms again, holding her there tightly and kissing the top of her head. "I prefer the kissing part if you don't mind. I think perhaps I shall kiss you till you squirm, my little one. You will discover then what real punishment can be." His eyes twinkled then, and before she realized what he meant to do, he had swept her up into his arms and dumped her unceremoniously onto the bed. " 'Tis time and more to teach you proper respect for your husband," he said firmly. "Take off that nightdress."

Lying back upon the bed, she folded her arms beneath her head and grinned up at him impudently. "Do your worst, my lord. But I fear you'll have to exert yourself. 'Tis certain I'll require a deal of teaching."

COMING IN JUNE 1988

Elizabeth Hewitt
The Ice Maiden

Irene Saunders
The Willful Widow

April Kihlstrom
Miss Redmond's Folly

SIGNET REGENCY ROMANCE